DIG TWO GRAVES

Kim Powers

TYRUS
BOOKS

Published by
TYRUS BOOKS
an imprint of F+W Media, Inc.
10151 Carver Road, Suite 200
Blue Ash, OH 45242. U.S.A.
www.tyrusbooks.com

Hardcover ISBN 10: 1-4405-9191-1
Hardcover ISBN 13: 978-1-4405-9191-4
Paperback ISBN 10: 1-4405-9192-X
Paperback ISBN 13: 978-1-4405-9192-1
eISBN 10: 1-4405-9193-8
eISBN 13: 978-1-4405-9193-8

Printed in the United States of America.

10 9 8 7 6 5 4 3 2 1

Library of Congress Cataloging-in-Publication Data

Powers, Kim.
  Dig two graves / Kim Powers.
    pages cm
  ISBN 978-1-4405-9191-4 (hc) -- ISBN 1-4405-9191-1 (hc) -- ISBN 978-1-4405-9192-1 (pb) --
ISBN 1-4405-9192-X (pb) -- ISBN 978-1-4405-9193-8 (ebook) -- ISBN 1-4405-9193-8 (ebook)
  I. Title.
  PS3616.O8835D54 2015
  813'.6--dc23
                    2015019021

Cover design by Sylvia McArdle.
Cover image of *Pegasus, with Hercules Slaying the Bull*, published 1808–10 (colour litho), French School (19th century)/Private Collection/The Stapleton Collection/Bridgeman Images.

This book is available at quantity discounts for bulk purchases.
For information, please call 1-800-289-0963.

Dedication

For Carrie, Marc, Adelaide, and Casey
And in loving memory of Bob Lange and Ellen Truett

"Before you embark on a journey of revenge, dig two graves."
—CONFUCIUS

I make my living by teaching about the past, the *very* long-ago past. The Classics. Greece. Rome. Latin. *Amo amas amat* and all that. And what I've learned, after years of my own study, and seven years on the job, is this: what happened *then* isn't really so different from what happens *now*, except for the toga and armor part, the laurel leaf crowns, and royal purple robes. Then and now, people want things, and they do whatever they have to do to get them. They take what isn't theirs. They hurt people. They kill people. Dead language, dead people: some things never change.

That's what I teach my freshmen Intro students, just so they can't say I didn't warn them: if you want to learn the classics, if you want to learn Greek and Latin, really learn it, get inside it, you're signing up to learn the language of revenge.

They love that part. Revenge.

I thought I did a pretty good job of teaching it, until I actually lived it. Those books don't have a clue what they're talking about.

I've had offers to tell what happened; calls from the morning shows started coming in the day the very first article hit the local newspaper, and then got picked up by AP. Some publishers have flirted around about a book, but they want it *now*, red-hot. Fresh off the presses and the front pages. One even offered to give me a ghostwriter to hurry it along, but I want to write it all on my own. I let somebody else write *Herc Holt: My Story* thirteen years ago, after winning the gold medal in Sydney, and I spent the

4

next thirteen years regretting my mistake. Starting with letting them using that cursed nickname, "Herc." Herc for Hercules. I was never a Hercules, except in the headlines, and I knew it better than anyone. Maybe by playing around with such a heroic name—taking what wasn't rightfully mine—I offended the gods.

I certainly offended . . . *him.*

I took what wasn't mine. I took his life. At the very start, and . . . at the end.

I'm getting ahead of myself. Running too fast, running toward the future, to keep from being here. Right here. Now. I've always done it, and now it's time to stop.

In the old days, right after the first Olympics, if you offended the gods, they put your name on a statue outside the stadium. It was called a *zane*—a statue of Zeus; it was his face that passersby saw, but with an inscription of your wrongdoing. A god's face, your crime; adding up to a warning to others who might be tempted to do the same.

The worst part, besides the public humiliation? You had to pay for your own fucking statue.

That's *my* punishment, my *zane.* I may not have a statue, but I'm still paying.

But the night it all started, there wasn't any of that. There was no pain, no paying, no blood. There was just birthday cake and melting ice cream, and the smell of wax candles that had just been blown out, and Skip.

My daughter. My life. My everything.

My "I love you more."

CHAPTER ONE

They came to the party with blood on their hands.

That was Skip's idea, my crazy thirteen-year-old's, inviting my friends and fellow professors to wear red paint on their palms. It was her nod to the infamous way I start my first class of every semester—my "blood on the page" speech. I have my Intro to Classics students bring in their favorite book, and it can't be any of the Harry Potters or Twilights. No magic wands or vampires, I say; it has to be real. That's why I *do* allow the Hunger Games. (Pause for laughs then, waiting to see which among them know that ancient civilizations are the *original* Hunger Games.) The kids read from their chosen book, then one by one come up, dip their hands in a tray of water-soluble *Nightmare on Elm Street*–red paint, and mark the passage with their palm prints. All those little creases and lifelines from lives that have barely begun.

I can only imagine the calls back home to their parents after that first day.

He had you do what? *We're spending $40,000 a year to have you mark up a perfectly good book?*

But nobody ever dropped out after that first class; more people usually show up for the next one, to see if there's still room to enroll.

You're the guy with the blood, right?

Yep, I'm the guy with the blood.

And I'm the lucky guy with the daughter who knew how to throw a helluva party on the day I both turned thirty-nine and got tenure. The year 2013; I could never forget how old Skip was because she grew up in tandem with my Olympics; they were both Y2K babies. The year we thought everything might go haywire. But it had been the best year of my life, before now. Standing by the marble island in our kitchen, I looked out at all the people in the den—my fellow professors, staring back at me with their silly red palms—and I thought, "I'm one of you now; I've joined your ranks. I don't ever have to worry about providing for Skip again."

Skip could read my mind, we were that close. My eyes got a little watery; whether it was tears forming, or the vodka tonic I'd already had, I didn't know, but she headed me off at the pass.

"Daddy. Puh-leeeease . . ."

Could anyone but a thirteen-year-old stretch out a single-syllable word so far?

Could anyone but a thirteen-year-old make her old man collapse with pride and happiness?

I knocked a fork against my rocks glass. "All I can say is . . ."

She raised her eyebrows, a Groucho imitation from the Marx Brothers movies I'd taught her to love as much as I do, and I read her mind too: *Please. Don't embarrass me. Don't get sappy on me.*

"All I can say is"—*Don't do it, Daddy, don't do it*—" . . . this looks like a serial killers' convention. Get washed up. And don't use the good towels, which Skip probably put out since she knew company was coming."

Laughter. Fun, drinks, cake, laughter. All of us together.

Skip corrected me, and I knew I'd done okay by her. "I put out *moist towelettes.* By the guest book." More laughter. I swear she'd been practicing that, for days. Maybe the whole party was just an excuse for her to say "moist towelettes" in front of a room full of academics. My string bean. "Please put your palm print on the page, then sign your name and tell my dad how much you love him, just like I do."

So now it was okay for the *kid* to get all schmaltzy.

A round of *ahs* and applause from a roomful of beaming, red-palmed people, for Skip, and I could tell it meant everything to her. She was at that awkward phase, part newborn colt with long legs going every which way, her emotions the same; and part done it all, seen it all, you're embarrassing me. Patti and I had taught her to read at five; she'd had to grow up fast, too fast, at eight, and sometimes, she seemed like she was seventeen. Too smart and clever. Because of her height, people sometimes thought she was about to graduate from high school. Sometimes I was the only one who could still see my little scared girl, deep down inside.

She'd put together this whole party, mostly by herself. For a few weeks before, I'd find her hanging out in the classics department office with Genna, our administrator, whenever I'd come in after class. (The whole campus was her playground; I loved giving her that. Hide-and-seek in the bowels of Sherman Hall. Dress-up in the theater department.)

"Anything wrong? Need me?"

"No," Skip would say, then roll her eyes. Not a *mean* eye-roll, like most thirteen-year-olds; more like a "can't you see we're doing something you're not supposed to see—so please play like you didn't see it?"

When I'd left that day, Genna had tipped me off about the surprise party I was supposed to act surprised at. "Whatever happens, just tell her the cake is delicious. I offered to buy one, but she wanted to make it from scratch. Just ignore the mess in the kitchen; I'll help her clean up."

But I didn't have to lie. The cake *was* delicious. German chocolate, my favorite. We sang "Happy Birthday"—and then "Happy Tenure"—then I blew out the candles, all thirty-nine of them. Winding me. The old Olympic champ, winded at thirty-nine. The scent of match sulfur in the air, Skip picking out the candles and putting them aside, to lick the icing off of later.

"Really? It's okay? You don't taste the burnt part?" That was Skip-as-colt, so insecure. So wanting to do everything perfectly. So thirteen. Squinting through the thick lenses of her glasses. "There are all these ingredients you've got keep track of and like a million different bowls, so the evaporated milk part got a little burned while I was mixing the batter part and . . . "

" . . . and I loved *every* part of it." I grabbed her in a headlock and gave the top of her head a big sloppy smooch. "I'm gonna have seconds. And then I'm gonna have thirds tomorrow morning for breakfast. *That's* how much I love it."

"That's not even the best part. Wait 'til you see your *real* present." Now, she switched to mistress-of-ceremony mode, in her pretty dress. Skip didn't wear dresses; only jeans and hoodies. But tonight, she wore a dress; Genna helped her pick it out. I wasn't very good in that department. "Okay, everybody. Now for your in-flight entertainment . . . "

Skip pressed a button on the remote and the title *This Is Your Life, with Muscles* popped up on our flat-screen TV.

"Jeez, is this what I . . . " I began.

It was.

There I was at twenty-two, racing along the college track. Long dark hair flying behind me. Strong. Able. Untouchable. Muscles powerful enough to get the job done better than—oh, say, anyone else in the world. Four years later, in 2000, twenty-six years old and finally ready, that's what they'd called me: *the best athlete in the world.* That was after I won the decathlon in Sydney—with skills that were of absolutely no use *except* for winning a gold medal: throwing a javelin, a shot put, throwing *myself* over a bar that got raised, literally, higher and higher, until there was no one else left who could jump over it.

"Whoa. I think you missed your calling." That was Randi Tanglen, Junior Faculty, English. The students liked her even more than they liked me, and they liked me a lot; she'd gotten tenure the year before.

"No, it called. I just . . . hung up," I said, knocking back more of my vodka tonic, lime pulp catching on my teeth. It soured the sweetness of the cake icing, for just a second.

They'd all thought it was a joke when I first applied for the teaching job here, my alma mater. Why else would a guy who'd been on a box of Wheaties want to come back to Canaan College, their little Ivy wannabe just south of the Vermont border? It was a school that produced doctors and lawyers, low-level politicians, and other college professors, not world-class athletes. It was strange that I'd even been there in the first place, as a student; even stranger that I'd come back. But I didn't want to use my body anymore. It hurt too much. I wanted to use my head; that's why I'd gone to Canaan in the first place. I'd always wanted something to fall back on: my brain was the real deal; the fact that I had a body that could do things was just a fluke. Besides, I didn't have another Olympics in me. I couldn't do four more years of training. The first four had almost killed me, and I didn't want to end up one of those fat old men, squeezed into Lycra, reliving the past. Doing inspirational speeches or getting paid to make an appearance and open a new gym somewhere. All the loony tunes that came out of the woodwork, to cash in on your fame. Or the fortune they *thought* you had. They all thought they knew you—they'd seen you for two weeks on TV, after all—you just didn't know them.

That's why they called it the past: it was over. When I left Sydney, I'd even left my fiberglass vaulting pole behind in the tunnel that the athletes used to make their entrances. Let it be somebody else's burden. I had different things on my mind now; grown-up things. Teaching. Making a living. Paying off grad school loans. Trying to be both mother and father to Skip, after Patti died. Skip was real; the Olympics weren't. Not anymore.

And now, there it all was again, served up on my giant flat screen with Häagen-Dazs and cake. I wanted to turn the damn thing off, but I couldn't. Maybe it was the booze helping me get there, but I was back in it. I was *living* it. *Re*living it. How much pain I was in. How gaunt and sharp my face was. I'd exercised off every extra gram of fat; I was down to a covering of skin, then muscle and bone, no padding in between. Me, at age twenty-six, in Sydney, arcing over the pole vault bar—5.90 meters, a record— as if there were barely an impediment in my way. Everybody else saw a cocky smile; I knew it was a rictus of pain. It became the most famous Olympic poster of the last decade plus, selling even better than long-limbed Michael Phelps scissoring through the pool: my butt coming down on the winning side of the bar, legs and arms flying, a streak of upper thigh that wasn't as tan as the rest of me. In that split second of free-fall, I turned to the camera and flashed a V for Victory sign.

'Uh oh . . . you can see my underwear!' A thought bubble came up on the screen, as I watched my younger self land in a pile of plastic cushions.

"I know pop-ups are sorta three years ago," Skip broke the spell, almost apologetically, "and that one's kinda lame, but . . . "

"Oh. My. God."

That was Carol Daeley, the English professor who'd been on sabbatical in Cambridge the summer of 2000; not that she would have watched the Olympics anyway. But her "Oh my God" wasn't an *"Oh my God*, how cute"—William Blake scholars didn't say that—it was an *"Oh my God*, look out!"

"YOU'RE DEAD!" someone was screaming at the twenty-six- year-old me on the DVD.

And everyone in my living room was watching me watch it. Now.

For a second, everyone in the stands—and I guess watching at home—had thought that it was a terrorist attacking me. Munich was never far behind in our thoughts. But then they saw the colors, as an arm grabbed me. Red, white, and blue, in spandex. Somebody on our side.

My teammate Mark Casey, strong-arming a cameraman who tried to block him. Greco-Roman wrestling wasn't part of the decathlon, but someone forgot to tell Mark, because that's how he dug into me and pinned me to the track, for everyone to see. Every one of those thousands of people in the arena, everyone watching live on TV, and every one of the forty or so mesmerized academics in my living room, who'd maybe seen blood on the page, but never spurting out of one of their colleagues.

"DEAD!"

The cameraman who'd been knocked to the ground had the perfect vantage point for capturing the moment, and even though the crowd was screaming, the sound on the ground was perfectly clear. So was the look in Casey's eyes, as his massive right arm shot out and landed on my face. My neck whiplashed around and my head smashed into the gravel track. Then Casey ratcheted back, super fast—God, he was good; he should have won *something*—and slugged me again on the nose, and that's when the blood hit the camera lens.

That poster sold like hotcakes, too.

"I'm gonna kill you . . . "

I clicked off the remote; I might as well have clicked off the soundtrack of the party, because, for just a moment, there was complete silence in the room. Not gradual. Immediate.

"You should'a seen the *other* guy," my old coach Sig Nielsen said, trying to fill the void. Still coaching at seventy-six, he was Skip's godfather. He knew what he'd said was the punch line to some joke—and God bless him for trying to save the moment— but he forgot that I *was* the other guy.

"You okay?" He'd raced to my side and asked it then, and he asked me now, the very same thing. Not quite racing anymore, but getting there as fast as he could with his cane.

"That's the last thing I need right now."

That's what I'd said then, too, with two more events left in which to compete—the javelin throw and 1500 meter. But I finished them, and won the gold, with the right side of my face a mottled purple and green.

I felt everyone in the room looking at me, wanting me to do something more than just whisper to Sig. So I did. "Wow. I guess somebody forgot to tell me the decathlon had *eleven* events. Nose breaking. He obviously won that round." They could laugh and talk again, now that I was laughing too. But for me, the party was over, as if I'd just had the fight in real time.

"But wait. We're just getting to the good part." Skip grabbed the remote and punched it back on. "Look. It's me and Mom. When I was just a baby."

Back on screen, my younger self had limped away from Mark Casey, pulling off my tank top to sop up the blood on my face, and staggered to the side of the stands where my wife Patti was holding a one-year-old Skip, barely more than a bundle. Patti looked horrified, but the baby in her arms was smiling and waving a little American flag that Patti had stuck in her chubby little fingers. The cameraman knew his business; that's what was being broadcast to the world. My kid, waving an American flag, no clue what was going on. And my parents, they were there too; my father ready to attack Casey himself.

"Look, that's *me*. With Grandma and Grandpa," Skip said. Almost pleading, "I thought you'd *wanna* see us."

Skip, the *other* prize I'd gotten that year, the same year I got my gold medal. "I do, Skippy, I always do, you know that, but . . . wow. I wasn't expecting that. Seeing that fight all over again."

"But it just shows how jealous everybody was of you. That's why I kept it in. You always say you can't change history, and that's part of history." My daughter had an answer for everything.

"I know, hon, but . . . " How could I explain to her how painful it was? I changed tactics. "And seeing my parents. Seeing your mom. It just makes me sad."

"You just wanna forget about her and be with Wendy."

"Did I just hear my name?"

Talk about wrong time, wrong place. Wendy. Dr. Wendy Borden, my new girlfriend of the last five or six months. It wasn't her fault she was just getting to the party late, but she paid the price. Skip hadn't expected to see Wendy there, because she hadn't invited her. *I* had—to the surprise party that wasn't really a surprise.

"And who the hell invited Dr. Doolittle?" Skip said, storming off to the kitchen, withering Wendy with a glare, as only a displaced thirteen-year-old could.

"C'mon now, Skippy . . . " I said.

"And why did you and Mom have to name me after *peanut* butter?" Her parting shot.

Great; now I was guilty about her nickname, too.

"She's usually the greatest daughter in the world," I said, a weak apology to Wendy, "and then . . . "

"She's a teenager?" asked Wendy. "I was one too, remember? She's afraid I'm going to take you away from her. All teenage girls are in love with their fathers. Or their horses. Why'd you think I became a vet?"

Wendy was a vet in the zoology department, where I'd never ventured before I met her. Some of the other teachers had fixed us up on a blind date—truly blind; they wouldn't tell me anything about her except that they thought I'd like her. On our first date, she made me guess what she did. I could tell she liked the outdoors—she smelled like it, in a good way; she didn't have fancy fingernails—but after a few guesses, I still hadn't figured out that she was a vet and worked at the zoo here. Afterwards, I started calling her the pet whisperer, because she could make any animal better. And me, I'll be honest: the *Prof* whisperer. She made a too-young widower feel better too. She ran laps around the track with me late at night. She signed us up for couple's mud races. She didn't talk down to Skip. She took us around on her little go-cart at the zoo, which Skip liked, until she decided she didn't like anybody who liked her father back.

I was giving Wendy a little kiss—a peck, an innocent little peck, to make up to her—when Skip came back out of the kitchen and saw us. She marched straight to the DVD player and punched the eject button.

Forever after, I'll remember that whooshing sound the DVD tray made as it slid out; it seemed to take forever. And then I'll remember Skip grabbing the shiny silver disk, practically a mirror, which she'd worked so hard on, and breaking it in two.

That seemed to take no time at all.

No, *this is* the last thing I'll remember from that night: Skip— my baby—turning to me and saying, across a room full of people, fighting so hard for those tears to not spill out of her eyes, "I wish it was you who was dead instead of Mom."

Forever after, that's what I'll remember.

CHAPTER TWO

The man with a plan watched from his hiding place in the trees, across the street. Something untoward had happened near the end of the party; he could tell, just from the change in movement behind the living room curtain. Fast, then frozen, then everybody leaving.

He would have enjoyed watching a bit more of the festivities, even if he was the uninvited guest. Actually, could he be both uninvited *and* a guest? Not really. He could be the uninvited *gatecrasher*, but even that indicated he'd actually gone through a gate; that he'd actually *entered* the room in some way. And he hadn't. But what was left? Peeping Tom? Voyeur? *Lookie loo?* Those all sounded so . . . negative, when he was really no more than a little boy with his nose pressed against the frost-covered candy store window, wanting to eat what was inside. Like that German chocolate cake that Skip had made, all by herself.

Now, guests—*invited* guests—were coming out of the house, so he hid even deeper inside the copse of tall conifers. They didn't lose their leaves like other trees in the fall, so there was no telltale crunch to give him away as he backed up, deep inside, the watcher in the woods. And what he watched: on the porch of their Victorian house, in the glow of two sconces that flanked either side of the red front door—red, the classic color of welcome!— Skip and Ethan took their positions and said their goodbyes, a receiving line in reverse. Ethan kissed the women and hugged the men, except for the students; Skip's hair got tousled a lot, and some of the women bent down to hug her. Somebody must have smudged her glasses, because Skip took them off and rubbed the lens with the hem of her pretty little dress.

He'd never seen her wear a dress before.

The night air was clear and chilly, a perfect conduit for sound, with the tall trees of the neighborhood keeping it reined in, so all the goodbyes on the porch carried across the street: *congratulations* and *thank you* and, to Skip, *I want to hire you for MY next party.*

But what the watcher *didn't* hear, when all the guests were gone, and only two people were left, was, *"What a great party, my darling daughter! Thank you so much! It was the bestest party ever! And you're my bestest girl!"*

Isn't that what fathers and daughters left standing on porches said to each other, as they waved goodbye to friends, getting in their cars? The man in the woods had never seen two people work so hard at smiling to their friends but not talking to each other. And when everyone had finally left, except for the old man with the cane, they still didn't talk.

Ethan tried to; he bent down to Skip, he tried to kiss her on top of her head, but she shook him off and helped the old man down the steps instead. They crossed to the watcher's side of the street; he was a mere five feet away from them when she finally started crying, just the tiniest little bit.

"I thought he'd *like* seeing the past. Isn't that what he teaches?"

"Don't worry. He survived it then, he'll survive it now. And I was the asshole who dug up all those tapes for you, so tell him to blame me."

"But it was my idea, so that makes me the original asshole."

"He overreacted. Too many bad memories."

"How bad could they be? He won the medal. I wish *I* could win a medal. At anything. You want me to walk you home?"

"I'll be fine."

"You sure? I don't mind. I don't wanna go back in there."

"I'm sure." He tipped his cane upward, pointing toward the house. "That's the old man who needs some help."

"Love you, Uncle Sig."

"Love you too, Peanut Butter."

Now *that* was a conversation, thought the watcher in the woods. That was how a family was supposed to talk. Give. And take.

Skip stood there until the old man got to the end of the block; he turned around and waved at her with his cane. She waved back, her hand outlined by the street light that shone down through the yellow and gold autumn leaves.

He loved this time of night.

He loved this time of year, late fall in New England.

He loved just being here, watching.

Skip trudged back to the house and began dragging out party trash, big bulging white plastic bags in both hands and more stuff tucked under her elbows, to the curbside garbage can. She pulled the drawstrings tight, then pushed the bags in; some tendrils of crepe paper snaked out. She stuffed them in, then unfurled the roll of paper she'd been clutching to her side: a homemade banner that said "Happy Birthday," decorated with glittery stars.

He might have stored it in the attic until the next birthday party rolled around, but Skip ripped it up and stuffed the bits and pieces inside the trash can.

Such anger, such . . . *disappointment*. Such good decorations, gone to waste.

He thought of the decorations *he* had waiting, back at home. They wouldn't go to waste. He'd use them all to decorate; every inch of every wall would be covered, telling a story.

His story. Well, *their* story.

He could wait to tell it.

After all, he'd been waiting for most of his life.

CHAPTER THREE

Skip hunched down on the cold wood floor outside her father's bedroom, her pajama T-shirt stretched over her knees. She usually did that to pretend she had breasts; now she did it to keep herself from shivering. From the cold *and* anger. She put her ear to the closed door and tried to listen, to see if he was really asleep. To see if she could hear the bed creaking, as he settled in for the night.

Nothing. She tried to imagine if he had the expression on his face, the one she'd seen a million times before, when he knew he'd fucked up; if he was wondering if his daughter was still awake, so he could go apologize to her about inviting Dr. Doolittle to the party, and about making such a fuss over the DVD.

She'd worked so hard on it, and then he'd ruined it.

She'd ruined it. Dr. Doolittle. Outside, on the porch, when they were saying goodbye to everybody, she'd whispered to Skip, like it could make everything better, "I *loved* your present. All I got him was a stupid book about a safari."

That had almost made Skip like her again, until she heard Dr. Doolittle then whisper to her father, "You *did* look cute in your little shorts, even if you *were* getting beat up." She pinched him on the butt, when she thought no one was looking.

Skip was looking, even though she pretended not to.

Nope. Skip hated her all over again. And him. She'd show him.

She went to the attic, where she always went when she couldn't sleep or when she had a new art project to start. This time, it was to paint her fingernails. Paint the *memory* of this night onto them, so she'd never forget. She didn't think she would anyway, but she wanted to show him how much it had hurt. He taught words, so she'd use some of her own to teach him: paint each fingernail black, for the background, then paint in a tiny white letter on top.

Ten separate, carefully chosen letters that would add up to three separate, carefully chosen words that would hurt him the most, just like he'd hurt her.

Her fingernails were so short that it took a lot of patience to finish the job, make sure the letters were clear. She didn't want to turn on the light or he'd know she was up there, so she did it with just the light coming in through the one window. A little streetlamp and some light from the moon—thankfully, it was a full one. Skip's left hand wasn't as steady holding the tiny fingernail brush as her right hand was, and the ether-like smell from the polish made her a little dizzy, but she finally got the effect she wanted, to show her dad in the morning. Orange juice, cereal, maybe a little slice of leftover birthday cake that she'd sneak when he left the room, and then BAM!

She'd ruin his day, just like he'd ruined her night. *Their* night.

All she'd wanted to do was make him proud of her, just like she was proud of him. Winning the Olympics. On TV. Getting tenure. She didn't exactly know what it was, but she knew it was important. She'd saved her allowance to get the decorations and cake ingredients and get all the VHSs from Sig transferred so she could edit them on her computer, and then . . .

He invited *her*.

He told Skip he didn't like her present in front of everybody.

He'd made her embarrass herself by breaking it, in front of everybody.

It wasn't fair.

It wasn't fair that she'd told him she wished he was dead, because she didn't. Not really. Then she wouldn't have anybody.

She never showed her dad anything she made up in the attic; it was her secret place. When they first moved in, she'd found all sorts of junk up there: a concrete lion, the kind an old mansion would have had guarding the front door; an old rocking horse; a trunk; an old doll. For some reason, she started covering everything with tiny little pieces of glass; she liked the way light reflected off them. She'd keep the lights off and light candles, to see if that was enough to see by in the room. And it was. Millions of candles, it seemed like, reflected back to her in little circles. When she ran out of old stuff that was already up there, she started making snowballs, from baseballs that she'd buy new, then cover over with little mirrored, glass beads that she'd buy at the craft store. Even in the dark, she could look in them and see her reflection, dozens of times over, and wonder if she'd look like her mother one day.

Her mother was beautiful. *Had been* beautiful.

Her mother was prettier than Skip thought she'd ever be, much prettier than Dr. Doolittle. She looked like a mother on TV. *That* pretty. Dark hair, blue eyes, and in Skip's memory at least, cheeks that were always flushed. But Skip knew that was just from being out in the cold that last time, not always. Skip had so many freckles she didn't think anybody would ever get to see if she had rosy cheeks or not, and with her glasses, they'd never be able to tell if her eyes were pretty like her mother's. Everything her mother had, Skip didn't. She was too tall, for just thirteen. Her arms hung down too far. Her legs were too long. Her hair wasn't thick enough. And she had braces. That's why she liked going up to the attic in the dark; so she didn't have to see herself in anything except her tiny little mirrors, where she couldn't see all the details of what she really looked like.

They were playing with snowballs, real ones, the day her mother died.

Skip wasn't dumb; she knew that's why she made them, to remind her of that last day. She didn't know why she covered all the other stuff, but she knew why she made the fake snowballs.

"Gotcha!" Skip and her mother bombarded her dad from their hiding place behind the snowman they'd made in the front yard that afternoon. It was the first year they'd moved to the big old house in Mt. Gresh, the first year her father had taught at Canaan.

He'd run to school that morning—he always did, that's how he kept in shape—not knowing how much it would snow during the day; it seemed too early in the season for that. When he got home, he was greeted by a snowman wearing his grad school mortarboard and his decathlon medal. And snowballs that Skip and her mother threw at him, for fun. As soon as the first one hit, he raced at them and grabbed his mortarboard, knocking the snowballs back like ping-pong balls.

"Hey! They expect me to wear this thing at graduation."

"Then you'll have to get you a new one," Skip's mom said, "because I am about to *ruin* this one!"

She scored a direct hit, smack in the middle of its flat top. The powdery snowball disintegrated, its crystals sliding down the gold and maroon tassel, and her father and mother slid down too, attacking each other with snow down their jackets.

"Man down! Man down!" her father barked out; that was Skip's invitation to climb on him too, as he flapped his arms in the snow and made snow angels.

"Help! I give! I give! Uncle!"

They went at him even harder.

"Aunt! Grandmother! Second cousin once removed . . . "

They finally rolled off him, her mom sneaking in an extra hug and kiss. Skip stayed on the ground by herself to make snow angels, like her father had made; she closed her eyes in that first snow of their new lives. Her back was cold and wet, even through the nylon of her jacket, but she didn't mind. She liked feeling the crunch of snow under her head, and her hair crinkling up inside her knit cap.

In Skip's seventh-grade acting class, her teacher Miss Davenport called that a "sense memory." There was one for each of the five senses. Feeling the cold at her back and the pellets of snow against her cap; those were for touch. The way Miss Davenport described it, you just had to remember them, but not do anything about them. You didn't have to pretend to feel anything. If you were doing it right, the feeling just came, whether you wanted it to or not.

Skip thought she must have been doing it right, because she always ended up crying remembering all of that stuff, from the day her mother died.

Outside their house, her father looked at his watch, wet droplets from the melting snow magnifying the hands of the watch, so it took him a second to see what time it was.

"Shit . . . gotta get to FedEx before it closes," he said.

"S-word! S-word!" Skip said. (That was the embarrassing memory, acting so goony about a dirty word; Miss Davenport hadn't said anything about that.)

What her mother said next changed everything about the rest of her life. "I'll go. I gotta pick up some stuff at the store anyway."

"You sure? It's slippery."

"So are you. That's why I like you."

That's where Skip always wanted to stop the memory, because the rest got too sad. But she couldn't stop it, no matter how hard she tried.

The sky was getting dark, but it wasn't all the way dark yet. In the yard, the fir trees had purple-blue berries on them, big fat things with little spikes sticking out; they were the same color as the sky: dark, dusty purple. That became Skip's sense memory for sight: the color of the sky. And a corner of the house was slate blue with bumpy gray trim, from where it kept getting painted over. And the red of her mother's nylon jacket, as she walked away.

The smell of smoke was in the air, from a fireplace somewhere in the neighborhood. Skip could smell her father's breath; he hadn't brushed his teeth since breakfast. She could smell coffee; she could remember the smell of her mother's perfume, too—not anything girly or flowery, but just nice. Skip could even remember her own smell: the smell you get when you play hard, outside.

Sweaty, with heat coming off you. And playing in the snow had a different smell than playing in grass, when the sun was out.

Those were her smell memories.

Her father reached in his pants pocket—he was wearing corduroys. Skip heard a sort of rub the fabric made and the sound of change in his pockets, coins mushed in with dollar bills. He pulled out his car keys and tossed them to her mother.

"Here. Take mine. It drives better in the snow."

That was the sound memory.

Clatter and clunk, as the keys fell short and dropped in the snow, and her mom had to reach down to pick them up.

Soon, there would be another sound, but Skip wanted to delay that one as long as possible. She wanted to remember her mother one last time, laughing and smiling and picking up her father's car keys from the snow.

"For the best athlete in the world, you sure picked a klutz of a wife." Her mother shook the snow off the keys, and Skip imagined she could hear the snowflakes, flinging away.

"Why'd you think I married you? You gotta let me be the best at *something*."

Her mother brushed the keys off on her nylon jacket—a squishy, scratchy sound—and opened the door to her father's SUV.

"We're gonna make s'mores tonight in the fireplace, so it better be lit when I get back."

Her mother moved the driver's seat up a little and put the keys in the ignition. Metal sounds. Levers. The seat stopping when it got to the right place and locked in. The door was still open, so Skip heard a burst of music from the radio: classic rock that her father had left it on. Her mother switched it to NPR. Voices, not music. She closed the door—a creaking sound, like it needed oil—and waved to her family.

That was the last look at her mother that Skip ever had: the *last look* memory.

Actually, there was another one: one Skip didn't really see, but kept imagining. A scene that had *all* the senses in it. She dreamed about it all the time, and she knew it made her cry in her sleep because she'd wake up with her eyelashes glued together. Her father would have to get a warm washcloth to unstick them.

Her mother drove down the road, the SUV settling into grooves in the snow that other cars had made during the day. She veered a bit, but righted herself. She was still fiddling with the radio as she approached a stop sign. She knew to tap the brakes lightly in the snow, but the road was already icing over. She tapped on the brakes a little harder—she still had time, a few dozen yards—but the SUV wouldn't stop.

It was like driving on glass, on her glass mirrors, Skip thought.

Now, there was just her mother, and the ice.

Black ice. That's what the police called it; ice under the snow that you can't see.

Fire and Ice—that's what Skip called it when she got to the part where her mother crashed into the concrete overpass and the car caught on fire. It was from a poem they had to learn at school, by Robert Frost. It was about the world ending. Sometimes Skip thought that was the day it did, even though she and her dad were still living in it.

CHAPTER FOUR

"Just say it. You didn't like it." Skip turned around, running backward in the early morning air so she could face me. And berate me.

"I loved it. I told you that. I loved *it* and I love *you*. You're my best girl. Ever. I loved the party and the cake and everything . . . I just . . . that fight on the DVD . . . I just needed some advance warning. I felt like I was being ambushed."

"It happened. It's not like you've forgotten it. And I felt like *I* was being ambushed by Dr. Doolittle. So there. We're even."

"Not quite. 'I wish it was you that was dead instead of Mom'?" I asked it like a question; she didn't have an answer to that one. At least she knew how much she had hurt me. "Sweetie, ya' gotta give me a break. I'm just making this up as I go along. I'm doing the best I can."

We were a mile into our run, an easy ten-minute-mile pace through the woodsy, secluded part of town we lived in. We could see cows down in the meadows below us, appearing and then disappearing into the cloud of fog that still hung low to the ground at 7:30 A.M. Up where we were in the Berkshires, on the road that went past Victorian gingerbreads into town, the November air was crisp; we were in that last gasp of razor-sharp clarity before the gray winter pall settled in and didn't lift for three months. Right now, we could see our breath; big puffs from me, little wisps from Skip. You'd think, after a lifetime of running, I'd still be good at it. But no, now it hurt. *Because* of that lifetime of doing it. My bones and muscles were worn out. Tendons stretched and frayed. Six feet tall, but not as broad as I used to be. The floaters in my eyes took longer to get rid of in the morning. And when they did disappear, it was all too easy to see the salt that was beginning to mix in with the pepper of my dark hair. When I shaved the stubble on my chin away—the jawline that got me a "hawt" rating on RateYourProfessor.com—I saw the beginning of a double chin.

Still, I endured the run, because I liked the time it gave us together. Skip would tell me about her dreams from the night before or ask for an increase in her allowance for more art supplies or go on about the boy in drama club she has a crush on, then say, "But he's probably gay."

We had some of our best conversations when we ran.

We were best friends when we ran.

Not this morning.

We were still talking, only none of it was good, as Skip picked up mid-stream from some conversation only she was privy to. " . . . and it's not fair to Mom. We were a family. And now *she's* there. Next thing you know, she'll be staying over and making *breakfast.*"

"Skippy, listen, we've talked about this. I treat you like a grownup; you treat me like one. That's the deal. Your mom's been gone five years, and I miss her like anything, but it's not fair to me that . . . "

"You want fair? Then I'll bring my boyfriend over tonight . . . "

" . . . you don't have a boyfriend and you're not *going* to have a boyfriend until . . . "

" . . . then I'll *get* one so you can hear us *fucking* . . . "

"You're just making stuff up now. Enough."

"Hey, any of you wanna be my boyfriend?" Skip yelled out to the track team that Sig was putting through its paces as we rounded the curve of the college track and came onto the outlying reaches of the campus. "I need one so I can show my dad . . . "

"Skip, I mean it . . . "

" . . . what it's like to hear old people *FUCKING* at the top of their lungs . . . "

"Stop it. Now. Nobody was fucking, as you so politely put it." I came to a stop and bent over to stretch my thighs. Skip ran in place, nothing winding her. She was just getting started, in more ways than one.

"Well, you probably *wanted* to. Last night was supposed to be fun, and you *ruined* it. I spent all that time on the DVD . . . "

" . . . which I loved until you smashed it, thank you very much . . . "

" . . . getting all those tapes loaded, getting all that old stuff from Sig at the field house and from up in the attic, but you didn't watch it because you're too busy getting mad about some stupid fight that's ancient history and making kissy faces with Dr. Doolittle and . . . "

"Don't you need to take a breath about now?" I said.

But at least it stopped her. For a second. Just to get enough air for round three. "Do you even *get* what it's like to be a teenager and have all this crap happen to your body and you don't know what it is or if it's good or bad or even if you're dying because there's this *blood* coming out but there's no adult around to ask about it? And then, just when you think you can, there's somebody else taking up all of your dad's time?" That look—just on the verge of tears, but she wouldn't go there. She wouldn't let me see. "Oh. I forgot. My show-and-tell project for today. Finger painting."

She flashed her fingernails at me: "I HATE WENDY" was spelled out on them, one letter per fingernail.

"Jesus Christ, Skip. If you don't wash that crap off your hands right now . . . "

She didn't hear the rest—I didn't get a chance to finish, even though I don't know what my "or else" would have been—because she raced off, leaving me in the dust with another finger pointed in my direction. Her middle one.

◆◆◆

"Can anyone translate 'shit's creek' into Latin? I just realized it this morning. 'Shit's creek.' It could be another name for the Ninth Circle of Hell, where my day started."

I was in my old classroom in Lanham Hall, a creepy old auditorium that looked more like the theater where Lincoln had met his maker than a classroom. There actually was a stage there, with a circular staircase leading up to the catwalk. Maroon velour curtains you could hide behind and long stained-glass windows. Houdini had once performed there, and his wasn't the only ghost you could still feel in the room. It seemed like the right kind of place to learn about the past.

"'Shit's creek.' I'm sure that's what Dante really had in mind. He was kind enough to give us the Italian. Now can any of you give us the Latin?"

"In flumine stercoris?" my best student and teaching assistant TJ Markson said, without missing a beat. He was right, he knew he was right, he was *always* right, but he asked it like a question anyway. If only he knew how good he was, how smart; he was going to have to find out the hard way it took some bravado to go with the brains, to get a teaching job, which is what he was destined for. "It's not really idiomatic, but it's the closest . . . "

"And we have a winner!" I said, cutting him off. "But maybe my TA will let one of the *students* answer next time."

"Then you'd be waiting a long time." That was rare, a sarcastic quip back from TJ. Normally, he'd look back down into his books the minute he said anything, pushing his hair out of his eyes, leaving a greasy streak across his glasses in the process. It was unusual you could even see his eyes, between the flyaway hair and the always looking down, too shy to look up. He wouldn't look half bad if he just washed his hair and got some sleep. And the coffee. Always guzzling from the paper cup of coffee from Wawa's. But now, he was looking right at me, to see if I smiled at his joke.

He reminded me of me, in some weird way. Deep down, the kid I used to be in high school, that I hid by pumping up my body and clamming up about what went on at home: my father always berating me, pushing me, my mother suffering in silence and visiting her orphans for charity. Maybe that's why I'd taken TJ out to Shiner's Pizza at the end of last year, to ask if he wanted to be my TA for this year. The crown of his head bobbed up and down—at least that's all I could see, wolfing down his tuna grinder like it was the first meal he'd had in weeks—because he kept looking down at the laminated placemat that had a map of Italy on it. When we left, he awkwardly hugged me and left a greasy handprint from the garlic knots on the shoulder of my jacket. I took that for his "yes."

On the chalkboard now, I drew a quick visual to go with his "*in flumine stercoris*": a rowboat thrashing in a sea of shit, indicated by rows and rows of things that could be splashing waves, or sea gulls, or floating shit, or sea gulls pecking at waves of floating shit. And I gave Phlegyas, the old ferryman who paddled Dante and Virgil across the River Styx, a thought bubble that read, "I've had enough of this shit."

A thought bubble, stolen from Skip's DVD of the night before.

I began writing a passage from Dante on the portable blackboard, something I'd written hundreds of times before.

And I, who stood intent upon beholding,
saw people mudbesprent in that lagoon,
all of them naked and with angry look.
They smote each other not alone with hands,
But . . .

But what? Squeezing the nub of chalk between my right thumb and forefinger, I stopped. I couldn't remember the rest. I looked at that word "mudbesprent" and all I could think was how strange and wonderful it was, as if I were seeing it for the very first time. I tried to focus, looking at my hand poised to continue, midair, but I couldn't see the next words in my head, just my two fingers holding that piece of chalk.

And then my fingers became Skip's fingers, with "I HATE WENDY" etched in fingernail polish on them.

I knew Dante hadn't written "I HATE WENDY," but I couldn't remember what he *did* write. It was like I had felt last night, a *déjà vu* of a *déjà vu*, watching those old training and Olympic tapes, and disappearing into them.

"Professor Holt?" TJ was the first one to speak. "Uh, the Fifth Circle . . . the Wrathful, the Sullen? Canto Seven?"

Mark Casey and gravel in my face and the broken DVD and Skip telling me I had ruined everything and blood was coming out of her body and she didn't know if she was dying because she didn't have a mother anymore but I had a girlfriend and . . .

"TJ, can you take over for a while? I need to get some water. I'm feeling a little Ninth Circle right now . . . "

At least I remembered that much. The Ninth Circle.

Maybe it was just the vodka tonics from the night before.

"The Ninth Circle . . . for traitors. That's the lowest level of them all," TJ explained to the class, always prepared for an Oprah-esque teachable moment. "Those who have betrayed a special relationship in committing their crimes. Judas, Brutus, and the like . . . "

When TJ looked back from the class to me—eager eyes through thick glasses—he gave me the strangest smile. At least I thought it was a smile. His incisors were prominent, and for just a split second, he looked like a wolf. Snarling.

◆◆◆

I went up to my office on the third floor of Lanham to change back into my running clothes and track shoes. I needed to sweat.

I needed to apologize to Skip. I'd do something special for her tonight; just us, Chinese takeout, no Wendy. I hit the speed dial for the landline in our house; I wasn't sure she'd pick up if she saw "DAD" come up on her cell phone.

One ring, then two, as I looked out my leaded window to three stories below, onto the central quad of the campus. Orange leaves, blue sky, copper bell tower of the campus chapel. A bench made of fieldstone, ringing around the bottom of an ancient silver birch. That's where Titania and Oberon played out one of their squabbles in the school's outdoor production of *A Midsummer Night's Dream*, twinkle lights and all. Skip had been a fairy in it, on loan to the drama department whenever they needed a kid for a play.

"*Peaseblossom? Mustardseed? Cobweb? Which one are you again?*"

"*Dad, I've told you a million times . . .*"

"*Hair dryer? Saxophone player? Rice-A-Roni?*"

"*Daa-aaad.*"

Then a tickle attack.

At our house, a third ring, a fourth, then our outgoing message from Skip clicked on, one made in happier times, before fingernails got painted black and white with initials.

"You've reached the Holts. That's 'Hercules' . . ."

I remembered swatting her then, and her having to turn away from the phone she was laughing so hard, putting her hand over her mouth to keep the microphone from picking up her giggles. My voice took over on the outgoing message, even though I was laughing as much as she was.

"That's Ethan, Ethan Holt . . ."

Skip came back up for air. " . . . and his lovely daughter Skip. Leave a message."

"Now we'll have to re-do . . . " I began, still laughing, but the beep came on, cutting me off.

I started leaving my message. "Hi, honey. I wanted you to hear my voice, first thing when you got home from school. I'm sorry about this morning . . . and last night."

She should've been home now, but she wasn't picking up. She was going to make me work for this. "You're right. I *am* acting like a horny teenager all over again. Truce?"

How many dads said "horny teenager" to their kids? That would make her forgive me, wouldn't it? Make her laugh at how goofy and square—and good?—her old man was?

"Say I bring home Chinese . . . scallion pancakes, spare ribs . . . just us, no Wendy. How's that? Forgive me? Love you, peapod. Love you more."

It's what I always said to her, after she said "I love you" first to me.

I love you more.

◆◆◆

It was an eerie thing for a small college to have, its own cemetery. But it did, and it was one of my favorite places to run, ever since I had been a student here. I loved the old words and carvings on the tombstones; I loved how people were remembered there, and even then—at twenty-one and twenty-two—I knew I wanted to be remembered too. If I won at the Olympics, as my father had always pushed me to do, an only child who had to make his dreams come true, I would be.

Inside, rows of lichen-covered tombstones tilted in every direction, inscribed with the names of the original movers and shakers. On nice days, when the students' minds were a million miles away and I couldn't get them to focus on anything, I took them out here, to do our version of brass rubbings of the tombstones, using ordinary paper instead of brass. I could pretend I was teaching what those dead people had left behind for us.

Mortui vivis docent. The dead teach the living.

As I ran through now, a dig was going on inside the cemetery walls. Not for a burial; except for one Iran War vet who'd been an alumnus, and left a quirky will and lots of money, no new bodies had been laid to rest here since Vietnam. No, this was an old settler's cottage that had recently been detected. It had belonged to Ephraim Gresh, after whom the town had been named. A square of land had already been excavated about eight feet across, down six or so feet, to reveal the bare bones of his cottage basement. In a month or two, when the winter snows came, the pit would be covered over by a tarp, but for now, it was empty, with the outlines of what had once been separate rooms.

Open. Tempting.

Huhn. Could I do it?

Forget it.

At Sydney, I'd done 29 feet, 1 inch in the long jump; not the world record by three inches, but still . . .

I was loose, warmed up, my legs pliable and urging.

C'mon. Old times' sake. If you make it across, everything will be fine with Skip when you get home.

I always made silly bargains like that—with myself, with God, I guess.

If this happens, then that will, too.

I jumped, to prove I still had it.

I didn't.

I landed hard, down on the bottom, and felt as old as Ephraim Gresh.

◆ ◆ ◆

"Hey, Skippy, get your butt down here." Sweating from my run, and my tumble in the dig, T-shirt sticky and glued to my chest, I called upstairs to her and dropped the bags of Chinese takeout on the kitchen counter. There was already another grocery bag there, full of the ingredients for a meatloaf. It was Skip's "I'm sorry" meal, one of her mother's default recipes. Skip must have gotten the stuff before I left my message. Nice to know we were both on the same wavelength, both of us willing to say *I'm sorry.*

I yelled upstairs. "Getting the ingredients is half the battle, sweetheart, but I'm hungry. Now. You know how gummy those scallion pancakes get if they're cold. Let's eat."

On the kitchen counter, the red message light on the answering machine was blinking. I hit the playback button then headed up to her bedroom. I was halfway up the stairs when I heard my message to Skip.

"Hi, honey. I wanted you to hear my voice, first thing when you got home from school. I'm sorry about this morning . . . and last night."

Her bedroom door was closed. That wasn't so unusual; she was always in there on her iPod or computer or cell phone.

I knocked. Nothing. I knocked again.

"Honey, you sorta forgot you have to *make* the meatloaf in order to eat it. I brought home Chinese. I left a message but . . . "

Still nothing.

I cracked open the door; at least she wasn't hiding under a pair of headphones. She was just hiding under the bedcovers. Maybe getting up so early to run in the mornings wasn't such a good idea anymore, if she collapsed when she got home.

"Okay, sleeping beauty, that Chinese food is con*gealing* by now. Like slime. Like that stuff *snails* leave behind on the sidewalk and you know how . . . "

I dived in to tickle her, but all I got was a wad of pillow. Skip wasn't under the covers; her pillows were, scrunched up into the shape of a body.

A body, under the pillows . . .

The *outline* of a body . . .

Her body, spray painted in red onto the bottom sheet, the paint still wet and sticky and bleeding into the fibers of the sheet . . .

She was bleeding . . .

The outline was bleeding . . .

For a split second, I thought, *that's it, no more of those drama kids. They're a bad influence, making you play stupid pranks like this* . . .

And in the next second, I knew it wasn't a joke or anything to do with drama club or anything Skip had done or . . .

A note, handwritten, was jabbed into the middle of the "body" with an open pair of scissors.

"YOU'VE KEPT ME WAITING LONG ENOUGH."

You can't make sound without air, so I didn't make a peep, because at that moment all the air went out of my body.

Gone. Everything gone.

Sound. Air. Everything. Nothing. Skip. Life. Gone.

CHAPTER FIVE

"He should be reading. The note. Just about. Now." He said it for Skip, and for himself.

There was a rattle in his voice, an extra . . . *need* (and a need for oxygen) that he hadn't heard in quite a while. It had been so long since he'd talked in front of anyone; so long since he'd had company that he hadn't had to pay for, that he chalked it up to nerves. And the dust he'd stirred up in his old classroom, where he'd come back to roost.

Four months ago, when he'd first inspected the site, the classroom he remembered best from his old grade school had been empty, except for books. Hundreds of them; textbooks and library books, thin little children's books and big, fat rain-bloated encyclopedias, dumped in a pile in the middle of the floor, as if someone had tossed them there for a pogrom but had forgotten the lighter fluid and matches. All the books he treasured from childhood, dumped in the middle of a buckling floor that was covered with bird shit and mouse droppings, the pages of the books themselves warped and stuck together with black mold. At the front of the room, the wooden chalk rail was still there, now landscaped with stubs of white and colored chalk that had been rained on for years, from a hole in the ceiling. Now, it all looked like anthills of melted calcium, gummy little stalagmites. There weren't any desks to get in his way anymore, as there had once been; the old-fashioned kind with a seat that had a storage for books underneath it, then a heavy metal armature that reached up to a flat surface on top. The only desk in the room now was in the middle, and it was bolted down. It wouldn't move, no matter what.

Skip was seated there now, her arms and legs taped to its sides, her glasses removed and her eyes blindfolded with layers of gauze, a strip of gaffer's tape across her mouth to keep her quiet for a while. That was the toughest part.

For him.

For her.

It took all of his concentration to make his hands do what he was telling them to; they were shaking as much as his voice had been, and he didn't want her to think he was nervous, not up to the task he'd assigned himself. It might give her ideas. He pulled a chair up next to her desk and set to work, as tender as he could be, given the circumstances.

"Tighten your mouth. It won't hurt as much. That way."

She flinched as he put one balled-up hand against the tape on her mouth, to peel off the tape from the opposite side. He hadn't pressed it down that hard to begin with, so it wouldn't hurt when it came time to take it off.

He pulled it off, but Skip didn't make a sound. She breathed a little deeper, and clenched her lips together so tightly that the pink of them almost turned white. He'd thought she would scream; he'd soundproofed the room for that, but still, he was glad it had been unnecessary.

For now.

She moistened her lips with her tongue; they must be dry and burning, from the tape. He'd prepared for that too. He tried to put a straw between her lips, but she tightened them closed, even more.

"I assure you. The water is safe."

She licked her lips again, the tiniest peek of tongue flicking out; some of the color came back. She swallowed, trying to make more saliva. He saw the movement in her throat.

"Please. You're not meant. To go thirsty."

She braced her body, but she didn't clinch her mouth again. He took that as a sign, an *okay*, so he put the straw back between her lips, careful not to touch her flesh with his fingers.

"An old-fashioned straw. From a soda shop. *Shoppe*. With an extra *p-e*. I like old-fashioned things."

He could tell she wanted to resist; she pushed against the curved wooden back of the chair as far as she could, but thirst won out. She sucked at the straw, and when what came through it didn't taste strange—he saw her cheeks moving, swishing the water around inside her mouth, testing it—she took some more. But held it there. He didn't see a swallow.

"We had to . . . a sedative. To calm you down. It happens to all of us, I used to get so . . . " He stopped, remembering something. "Anyway. You're dehydrated. *And* afraid. It's okay. Anyone would be. *I* would be. I *have* been. *Drink.*"

She took in another mouthful of water. She gulped it down, then took some more. The biggest gulp yet. She swished it around, then spit it in his face, level with hers from sitting.

Silence, then he spoke. "Most kidnap victims. Would know. NOT. To do that. Didn't your. *Father* . . . teach you that?"

Whether she was just panicked and could barely talk—or she wanted to get back at him—he didn't know. But the way her first words to him came out, it sounded like she was imitating him. Mimicking him.

"It never. Came up."

That one pause—between *never* and *came*, intentional or not—was what set him off. All his good intentions out the window. The one that was boarded up.

"Then *I'll* play Daddy. Lesson number one. Never *spit*. At your kidnapper."

He slapped her so hard that his handprint formed on her cheek. And then he poured cold water on it, to try and make the hurt go away.

That slap—*that* was the hardest part.

For him.

For her.

For now.

CHAPTER SIX

Detective Aretha Mizell was halfway through her standard speech, walking up the stairs—*"You have a fight? She get mad? She's cooling off somewhere, happens all the time"*—when she saw the outline on the bed, bleeding and red and sticky, and that shut her up.

That's why the policemen had called her in, after receiving the initial report and doing a walk-through of the house and quick intake with me. They'd said the same things, too—*don't worry, it's a fight, a teenage thing, she's run off somewhere to make you sweat it out*—until they saw the bed.

The outline wasn't of just anybody, or *any* body: it was of *Skip's* body. The way she fell asleep. I'd seen it a million times, when I'd tiptoe in to kiss her goodnight: the way she curled up her knees and put a pillow between them, then twisted her torso around to face the other direction. You'd think that would hurt, but she'd be snoring away. My baby girl. Snoring. Dreamland. And now . . . you could see what made this teenager different than all other teenagers. It was like a painting, in brushstrokes of aerosol, of Elizabeth "Skip" Holt. My baby girl. My only girl.

Mizell forgot her 101 speech the minute she saw it.

"Jesus." She thought it was as bad as I did, although she caught herself and tried to mask it. I could see her eyes scrambling, trying to process what she'd just seen, but still come up with something hopeful to say.

"I know this is scary, all this stuff going on in here . . . "

—*The police taking pictures, dusting for fingerprints.* Finger*prints? In* our *house?*

" . . . but it's just to get the ball rolling, for when she comes back and this has all been for nothing."

The look on her face didn't say *nothing*. What they were doing in Skip's room didn't say *nothing*. Bagging up her computer. Looking at the note on the bed every which way. Flashbulbs going off in every inch of the room. That all said *something*—something horrible.

"I called all her friends . . . anybody I could think of . . . and her phone's still here. It was on the kitchen counter when I came in. She can't live without that phone. She'd never go off without it."

"So we'll need to take that too," Mizell said soothingly, almost trying to hypnotize me with her low honey voice to drop Skip's phone into a paper sack before I even know what I'm doing. She was short but hefty; her upper arms were straining against the fabric of her suit jacket. She looked like she should be anything but a detective. HR, maybe; middle management, but with a little bit of power. One of those comforting women, forty-something, who could make any situation better, even firing someone. She was wearing a wig, not a very convincing one. I wondered if she was going through chemo, but the rest of her looked too healthy for that.

Why the fuck was I even thinking about what she was wearing, or how bad her wig was, when my baby was missing?

She hefted the evidence bag Skip's phone was now in. "Plastic. Those cop shows on TV get it so wrong. *Plastic*," she snorted, expecting me to follow. Wanting me to be as outraged as she was—or maybe to know how good she was, that she knew plastic was wrong. Mizell was trying to make this as good for me as it could be, give me something to focus on, a string of conversation, to keep me from howling at the moon.

But I didn't want easy. I didn't want chitchat about plastic. I *wanted* to howl at the moon. I wanted to scratch my eyes out, so I couldn't see any of this: Skip's bedroom, almost alive with fingerprints, brought up by the police with their powders. Like smudgy little dots on a pointillist painting, or pinky swears that Skip and her friends had ground into the room, when it was first painted. Those little swirls—fingerprints or whatever they are: they were all so innocent. I looked down at my giant ham of a fist and was ashamed of it. Ashamed of being grown-up. Ashamed of being a man. That's who had to have taken her. Some man. Some man with a big hand. Somebody strong . . .

"And we'll need to get your fingerprints, too," Mizell said, as if she had just read my mind, "to rule you out against any other adult hits we get." She nodded to one of the techs in the room, who set up a makeshift printing station on top of Skip's bureau. I barely felt his hands on mine, inking them and then guiding them into the correct white boxes on a sheet of paper.

"Some folks are afraid of fingerprints, just like I'm afraid of needles. But no reason to be afraid of anything that can help us do our job. Fingerprints are our friends. That's right, just two more to go," Mizell said, her eyes not just on my hands, but everything in the room.

I yammered on, to keep from dying. "We'll have to move. I could repaint this room a dozen times but I'd never get rid of all that fingerprint powder. I'd always know it's there, whatever color I used. Skip likes pink—it's weird, she's not a girly girl, but she still likes pink—but maybe a dark color. I guess that would cover it up, if I painted it really dark, like a maroon or something . . ."

Mizell, to her credit, didn't look at me like I was losing my mind.

"I'm partial to the green family myself. My bedroom now? Forest green. My bedroom when I was a little girl? Lime green. Go figure. I never was a pink girl myself. Now my daughter, she's a lemon yellow . . ."

Just two crazy people, talking to each other. A big black woman, calmly doing her business and trying to talk me off a ledge.

"Mr. Holt—Mr., that's right? Not Dr.?—maybe it'd be better if we had one of these policemen take you downstairs to wait while we . . ."

I couldn't move. I couldn't stop staring at what the policemen were doing, taking off the bottom sheet that had the outline on it. "I didn't think you could leave fingerprints on sheets. On fabric, I mean. I try to keep it clean, her room, you know . . . she has to pitch in and help, the sheets, the laundry, the cooking, all that stuff. I don't want her growing up thinking that she doesn't have to work . . . or that she's special because of the Olympics, you know, except that she is special, she's the *most* special . . . "

"Mr. Holt. Please." She put her hand on my shoulder, to begin guiding me out of the room, just as one of the techs picked up a jar of Karo syrup on Skip's dressing table, next to a bottle of red food coloring. Underneath it, now ringed with a circle of dried "blood," was the research book that the drama club had put together for their Hell House. Pictures of car wrecks and back-alley abortions and kids on gurneys and teenagers with pimples and syringes stuck in their waxy white skin.

The tech held it up with a gloved hand and a raised eyebrow.

"That was for this Hell House she was in," I said. "At Halloween. You know . . . the drama club. They got extra credit for making their own blood."

The second tech raised his eyebrows too, as they dropped it into a paper sack.

Evidence. Hell House. The damn drama club.

"They needed somebody young. A teenage hitch-hiker. It's the theater department," I said, as if that would explain everything, excuse away what a bad father I was. "She wants to be an actress. Actually she wants to be a little bit of everything. An artist. A singer. Some days she wants to be . . . well, you'll see. We'll find her and you'll meet her and you'll see."

I couldn't stop talking.

I couldn't stop shaking.

"I wanted to be Nancy Drew when I was little," Mizell said. "The black Nancy Drew. We're gonna find her."

She started to take me out, and saw the giant stuffed giraffe that Skip had in the corner of the room, almost hidden away when the door was open. Skip had wanted it—the giraffe—because she said it looked just like her. Too tall. Around its neck was my decathlon medal from the Olympics, just about the only thing in the room that wasn't obliterated with fingerprint powder. The gold on the medal seemed to glow, it was so polished, just like Skip's snowballs in the attic.

Mizell reached out her gloved hands to pull it from over the giraffe's neck, then tossed it to one of her guys. "Don't forget to dust this," she said to them, as she closed the door behind me.

◆ ◆ ◆

They searched the house, even though I already had. Once by myself, and again with the first cops who showed up, before they called in Detective Mizell. In the den, Sig and Wendy tried to keep me busy, while all I could focus on was the sound of their footsteps all over the place; heavy ones, and then the lighter heels of Mizell. I tried to imagine the things in our house the way they'd probably see them.

Would they see clues I missed? Would we pass, as a family? Would *I* pass, as a father?

I did a mental tour that matched their footsteps. Nothing in the basement except for old furniture and workout equipment I didn't use much anymore—a weight bench and treadmill and barbells. A box of tile from a DIY project for the bathroom. A sack of grout. The old smoke alarm that Patti had yanked out of the ceiling in frustration because it kept going off whenever she cooked, and then it still kept going off, even disconnected and down in the basement. We'd thought we had a ticking bomb somewhere until we discovered that the battery was still alive.

What else was down there? A cardboard "wishing well" painted with fake rocks, from when Patti had been drafted to be a class mother and help out with Skip's kindergarten Halloween party, years ago. Patti dressed up like a witch and crouched down inside the well, hooking candy onto a bamboo fishing pole every time one of the kids dropped it in. That cardboard puppet theater, from when Skip went through her puppet phase, now sagging with basement damp. Everything a reminder of the family we used to have, the family we used to be.

The family I couldn't let go of.

When they left the basement and started for the attic, I jumped off the couch to lead the way. "One of the steps is sorta wonky. A board is missing and we've got mouse traps up there . . . maybe it's a raccoon, I don't know, I hear something at night . . . "

Oh. You haven't fixed the step? You let your daughter walk up that? You let her go where mouse traps are set out and animals can get in?

They didn't say it, but I knew they were thinking it: that I was a bad father. They started thinking it the minute Wendy came over, and they saw me hug her. They started thinking it the minute they saw all that stuff from Hell House.

But I didn't *let her be in it,* I wanted to scream at them. *I didn't sign the damn form! She forged my signature and did it without my permission!*

Oh, so you admit *you have a daughter who runs off without permission, who does whatever she wants. That you run a house with no discipline. You let her come home by herself after school, no adult to greet her . . .*

The cops went in the attic first, flashlights aimed in front of them, and got blinded when their beams hit all of Skip's little mirrors. Mizell put up her forearm, covering her eyes.

"She does it to bring back her mother," I said, thinking I was making perfect sense. "The snowballs. The day Patti died, there was snow. We made snowballs. Skip doesn't know I know that's why she makes them, but I know . . . " And then, "She said she wished it was me who was dead instead of her mother. She was right. Her mother would know what to do right now."

"Mr. Holt, *we* know what to do. So just let us do our jobs. Go somewhere else. Please."

◆ ◆ ◆

Mizell found me in my bedroom.

"She gave me the finger. That's the last time I saw her. I yelled at her, and then she gave me the finger. Do kids even *do* that anymore? The *finger*? I've raised her better than that. I promise. She was just mad and . . . this isn't happening. It can't be. This isn't real."

I thought about Skip's finger—telling me to go fuck myself—because it *was* real. The rest of this wasn't.

"I gave my mom the finger for about four years straight, every time somebody made fun of me for having the name Aretha."

"Try living up to Hercules."

"And Skip . . . that's really . . . " she flicked through her notes. "Elizabeth?"

"Yeah, but she's always just been Skip. I don't know why we even bothered with anything else. Her mother said she felt her skipping in the womb, and . . . we wanted more kids, not just one. But we wanted to be settled more, before we had another one. And then Patti died and you can't have kids if you don't have a wife so . . . I was an only child so I know what it's like growing up alone. No fun. Too much pressure to be perfect. I wanted Skip to have a friend. I mean, she has friends. At school. But somebody here. All the time. At home. A brother or sister but . . . "

I was shaking like the Ice Age had come back and I was outside, naked, trying to outrun it.

"Mr. Holt, you have any liquor in the house?" Mizell asked me.

"Yes, but . . . I don't drink it. I mean, not too much. We had a party last night and . . . "

"What I'm saying is I think you should get a drink. You're gonna shake yourself to death. I know it's hard, but you've got to calm down."

I barely heard her; my mind was a million miles away. My mind was down the hall, in Skip's bedroom. My mind was everywhere, and nowhere. I picked up a framed photo of Skip from my night table. "You'll probably need this, I mean, after I make my flyer. Then you can have it. It's last year's, but . . . this is what she looks like."

It was one of those school things they took every year. Skip, with her mother's freckles. The braces she hated, even though they were supposed to be invisible. The little scar on her upper lip, from where she got the clasp of her school ID bracelet caught there in the first grade. Skip had always hated the picture, and to counteract it had tucked a photo booth strip into the edge of the same frame it was in. She called it a "Strip of Skip." Her official school picture on one side, the real girl tucked into the corner. Goofy. Sticking her tongue out. Crossing her eyes. Pulling her mouth wide open. Those were the pictures that should go on a missing person's flyer. That's what she really looked like, who she really was.

"Now we're just taking extra precautions here . . . don't wanna get caught in a scramble, but we're setting up a phone trace downstairs in case there's a ransom call . . . "

"Ransom? A college teacher? Money?"

"Didn't you get a bunch of endorsements after the Olympics?"

"One cereal box. And that mostly paid for grad school."

"Any family money?"

"Are you kidding? I went here on complete scholarship. Academic. I did all the sports on my own."

"Any bad blood with them? Any brothers or sisters?"

"No. Nobody. Just me. Only child."

"Why's that?" Mizell asked. "No other kids? You the apple of their eye?"

"You'd have to ask them. Besides, they had their hands full with just me, grooming me to be . . ." I wasn't sure how to answer. The real answer was 'a machine.' A winner. Whatever it took.

"On the cover of a Wheaties box?" Mizell filled in, when the silence sat too long.

"Yeah, something like that. And they died years ago, right after the Olympics."

"Why'd you quit?"

"What?"

"The Olympics. One win, and . . . you're gone."

"Is this gonna help find Skip?"

"We've gotta look at everything."

"Shit. Why haven't they called? How do I get money? What the fuck do I do if they want money?"

"They're not gonna want money, and let's just slow down for a minute."

"Why won't they want money?"

"They only want money when they know you *have* money, and we already know you don't. So do they, if they've done their homework like us . . . "

I gave her a look.

"We checked. We move fast when a little girl goes missing."

"So you do think . . . "

"I think we want to be prepared for anything. Open your mouth."

She stuck a Q-tip inside before I saw it coming, and had it out just as fast. "What was . . . "

"DNA. Like I said, we need to count you out. There's no problem with that, is there? I mean, we can get a lawyer if . . . "

"Anything. Whatever it takes. I'll do anything. I want to go searching. Now. "

"Um hmm." She was focused on putting the Q-tip into a little vial.

"Have you done kidnappings before? You find the people?"

I meant the victims, but I don't know how she took it. Maybe she thought I meant the kidnappers. She didn't answer either way. I had to keep filling the silence, when she wouldn't.

"I know my daughter. This isn't a prank. She didn't run away. We fight, we make up. We're a team."

That's what I'd said this morning, a million years ago. *We're a team. We've talked about this.*

Mizell put down the framed picture of Skip, then put on rubber gloves to take the note that had been on Skip's bed out of its evidence bag. She was avoiding my question—if she ever got the people back or not.

"'You've kept me waiting long enough.' This . . . it seems so directed at you, so personal. It's about the person finding the note, not the person he took. Otherwise, why leave anything? Is there somebody you, I don't know . . . somebody you . . . stood up or something? Who'd want to get back at you?"

"Maybe I was late grading papers or something. Jesus, I don't know, I'm a teacher. A fucking teacher. All the kids think you've done something to them. You didn't grade 'em high enough. You didn't write their letter of recommendation in time. Jesus, what the fuck do they want? You've gotta get out there, start looking around . . ."

I didn't want this woman to see me fall apart, any more than she already had, but that didn't stop me from grabbing her. And then starting to cry.

A student in one of my classes had written an ode for an assignment, which she then had to translate into Latin: "It is no time to make your fathers cry." That flew back into my head, and made me cry even more. It made me squeeze Aretha Mizell's wrists so hard, I saw her dark skin turn red for just a second.

"Look, I'm begging you. I don't have any family any more. My parents are dead. My wife's dead. I never had any brothers or sisters . . . no aunts or uncles or cousins . . . Skip's it. She's all I've got. You've gotta get her back. I'll do anything. Just tell me. She's all I've got."

Mizell didn't understand. Nobody could understand.

"Janice Miner," Mizell said, gently moving my hand off her wrist, and then using that same hand, now free, to pick up the framed photo of Skip.

"What?" I said, starting to pull myself back together.

"You asked. Janice Miner. Fifteen years old. We got the guy who took her."

"That's good then, right? You have experience . . . you know what to do. In case . . . in case this turns out to be . . . "

She seemed to have drifted away somewhere, not really listening, lost in the memory of that old case. "We got him, but only because we knew all the enemies. The family told us. So start making those lists. We've got to figure out who would want to hurt you. This is about you, not her. She's . . . Skip . . . she's just the messenger."

"What? They took her."

"That note says it all. They took her, to get to you."

CHAPTER SEVEN

Skip could tell it was getting late, even with gauze wrapped around her eyes and her glasses off under that; it felt like it must be near her bedtime, although maybe it was just the shot that was still making her sleepy. Her father would have been home for hours by now. She hoped he saw the bag of groceries she left on the kitchen counter; that would let him know she wasn't mad anymore. She never went shopping. She never cooked. And now, maybe she never would again—but she wanted her father to know that she had tried. Meatloaf, with hamburger and ground-up spicy sausage in it, for extra kick. Really gooey and tomatoey. That's how he liked it. And buttered noodles on the side, sprinkled with the same bread crumbs she used to put on top of the meatloaf for crunch. She wondered if the meat would go bad if he didn't put it in the fridge, after being out for six or seven hours. That's how long she figured she'd been gone. She knew she got hungry every five or so hours, and she'd had lunch at school at noon, then she'd had a snack at home when she got there at three-thirty, and then . . .

Then he took her.

He must have been in the laundry room off the kitchen, after she'd put the groceries down on the counter and turned around to walk upstairs. Her whole body jolted when he grabbed her; something tickled, like when you stick your tongue on a battery. Maybe he used a stun gun on her. That's what they did when they took kids on TV.

She'd been looking at her mother's recipe card for meatloaf and remembering she had to put the smoke vent on after she preheated the oven, because it got all smoky, even with nothing in it, and she felt a sting, a jab, and dropped the recipe card. She thought, for just the second that she was falling, that she saw the index card fall too, under the refrigerator.

She hadn't woken up until she was here, in the chair, so she didn't know how far they had traveled. In town, out of it, into Vermont, she didn't know. All she knew is that she'd cried four times already. The one time she didn't cry was when he slapped her; it hurt, but she wouldn't let him see how much. She only cried when he wasn't there, but it made things worse. It wasn't just the tears falling under the gauze and burning her cheeks, but her nose getting all runny too; the snot got on her face and made her skin feel sticky, and she couldn't use her hands to scratch.

They were tied up, with duct tape. When she tried pulling her wrists apart, behind the desk, that's what she felt. All her girlfriends at school made things out of duct tape; that's how she knew what it felt like. They'd get ziplock bags and cover them with it, to turn into purses. She had one; that's where all the change was, from the money she spent buying the meatloaf ingredients. They'd put duct tape over their book covers too, to make them extra strong, lacing different colors together. They made bracelets with it; one girl even said she was going to make her prom dress out of it. And now, Skip was tied up with it. She opened her mouth and that's when she felt the duct tape there too, sealing her lips together. He'd put it back, after he'd given her the water. After she spit on him. Trying to pull her mouth open to make a sound hurt more than trying to pull at her wrists to get the tape loosened up. She could hear the sticky sound it made, like something coming unpeeled. Thwacking, high-pitched, like when her father pulled off a strip of it to close up a cardboard box.

Her father. She started crying again, knowing how scared he must be. She never stayed out late. Or maybe he was still mad at her from this morning and didn't care if she ever came home again. That's what kidnappers did to kids, to get them not to run away. They told them that their parents didn't want them anymore. That's how they kept the kids quiet and too afraid to scream.

She wasn't going to fall for that. She was going to scream. But if she screamed then he'd slap her again and she didn't know how to keep from crying again, it hurt so much . . .

She didn't know what to do.

He was going to kill her. He was going to rape her. He was going to make her his sex slave even if she didn't have breasts, and then he was going to kill her.

She heard it on the news all the time.

She started crying again, even though she knew how much it was going to make her face itch.

NO.

She snorted the snot back into her nostrils and tried to think. She needed something to focus on, that wasn't about being hurt or being raped or being dead.

Her mother's recipe index card, for the meatloaf. If she could remember that, then it would take her mind off this place and she would stop crying. So she tried to remember everything about the card that she could: pulling it out from where it was stuck in with a bunch of other recipes, between pages of her mom's old *Silver Palate Cookbook*. The grease stains on it, and smears where the blue ink from her mother's pen had run, maybe after she washed her hands. And all the ingredients. Two cans of tomato paste. One can of tomato sauce. One egg. A red pepper, even though the recipe called for green. Onion. That was red too; Skip liked everything red, to go with the tomato paste. Mashing it all together with her hands, the egg yolk exploding and the yellow of it mixing with everything else that was red or meat colored.

He was going to kill her; why else would he take her? That's why they took girls.

No.

Back to the recipe.

Her mother told Skip she got it from one of her roommates in college, in a suite she shared with three other girls. They'd gone to the girl's parents for the weekend and that girl's mother had made this delicious meatloaf and . . .

Skip was never going to college.

She could have gone to Canaan for free—professors' kids could, so she'd save her dad all that money. Canaan was expensive, but she didn't know if they had to let her in if she turned out stupid—but now she wasn't going to go anywhere. She wasn't even going to make it to high school.

Mushrooms. She forgot the mushrooms. They were on the recipe card too. Sliced ones, not pieces and stems. The ones in the glass jars were buttery tasting, better than the ones in cans, better than fresh ones even.

She'd never eat mushrooms again.

She was so hungry, so thirsty.

She wanted some of the birthday cake she'd made for her dad, a big gooey piece of German chocolate with two scoops of coffee Häagen-Dazs on it. That would make her feel better, but then if she had the ice cream she'd want some water to wash it down with, and having water meant he'd have to stick his fingers near her face again. She could try to bite them the next time instead of just spit at him, but then he'd get mad and God knows what he'd do.

He was going to do it anyway, even if he wasn't mad at her.

He was going to stick things in her mouth, and other places.

NO.

At the party Skip had made for her dad, she'd bit into a little piece of pecan shell that got mixed in with the German chocolate icing and it had cut the inside of her cheek. She'd tasted the blood. That's how she knew. She hoped that hadn't happened to anybody else, even though it wasn't her fault. She'd bought the pecans already shelled, so some factory worker let it slip through. Not her. It wasn't her fault. None of this was her fault.

If she could just keep thinking about meatloaf and mushrooms and birthday cake and how this wasn't her fault, then she wouldn't have any room in her brain left over for crying and freaking out, because she wouldn't be thinking about what was happening now, or what was going to happen. If she just kept thinking about how she'd go looking for her mother's recipe card under the refrigerator once she got out of here, then maybe . . .

She was never going to get out. She didn't know where she was; nobody knew where she was and he was going to kill her and nobody would know anything about her ever again. She wasn't going to be an actress or an artist or make meatloaf or go to high school or college, or do anything except keep crying and peeing on herself.

NO. Meatloaf. Cake. Her mother's recipe card.

She was going to get away. She had to.

CHAPTER EIGHT

It was 11 P.M.; it should have been pitch dark outside, November dark, but instead, our street was teeming, alive. The police had set up portable lights outside, cherry red beams were flashing from atop their patrol cars, and it looked like a war zone. But nobody on the block was getting woken up because nobody had gone to sleep. The neighbors were shuffling around on the sidewalk and street like zombies, the walking dead, waiting for information.

But there was none.

Everybody kept asking if they could bring food over. They'd done the same thing when Patti died, but Skip had taken charge then—barely eight years old, stepping up to be the adult in the house while I fell apart—dutifully recording all the names of people who'd brought over covered dishes. We were loved. Patti was mourned. Then, when it was all over, Skip had returned their plates one by one, always with the perfect, tailored remark. *Those cupcakes were delicious, with that green dyed coconut! How did you know I loved macaroni and cheese so much? That turkey was better than the one we had for Thanksgiving.* A little girl with perfect manners, even when she was mourning her mother.

Now, I wanted to tell all those people thanks but no thanks. *You bring food when somebody dies, and nobody's dead here. Nobody's gonna die here. I appreciate the thought but Skip's gonna be back any second now so we won't need any extra food. It'll all be over soon. I'm gonna take her out to Bobby Flay's Burger Palace to celebrate and . . .*

No. Please, everybody just leave. Thanks, but please leave.

Last night, the house had been jam-packed with our friends. Celebrating. Now, twenty-four hours later, it was jam-packed with people I didn't know. People in uniforms. People not in uniforms, but in mismatched suits, a different kind of uniform, detectives with their guns and badges occasionally showing, when a jacket flashed open. Their leader, Detective Mizell, had turned the back of the house into her own personal war room, the dining room table now home base for a search-and-rescue mission. Sig was gridding off maps with his track team, for searching in the morning; Wendy was going through photos from the party, clicking from one frame to the next on Skip's digital camera and telling one of the cops the names of everyone there. The kids guzzled Red Bull and scarfed down pizza that somebody had ordered in; as soon as one box got emptied out, another one got opened and moved to the top of the stack.

Mizell paced back and forth, talking on her cell phone to the FBI, trying to get them involved.

"I know that, I know it's not twenty-four hours yet, but she's thirteen years old and we need . . . "

Mizell was too fucking polite, too official. Too goddamned nice. Not me. I grabbed the phone from her. "Listen, this is her father. Please. Some sick fuck has my daughter and we need help. Please. Send anybody you can. The more people we have . . . "

Mizell grabbed it back from me, with a glare. "I'll take it from here," and back on the phone she went, to whoever was on the other end. I didn't know. I never even gave them a chance to talk. "Sorry about that . . . you can understand . . . yes, I know . . . "

Blah blah blah. It was all blah blah blah. Nice nice nice.

I wanted to fucking do something! Get my hands on somebody! I'd already driven to all the places I could think of, that Skip might go—just in case it *was* a joke. I knew it wasn't, but I couldn't just sit still. I'd already gone to the theater building where Skip hung out with the drama club; searched high and low through all of it, the kids taking a break from one of their rehearsals to help me. I'd gone to the houses of her three best friends, the first three names on her speed dial. Nothing. I'd even gone to Genna's house, to see if she was camped out there. Nada, everywhere I went. Just new people crying, instead of me.

I couldn't cry anymore.

Nobody else was crying in the house either; they were just doing. Maybe they'd been told *not* to cry in front of me. Activity was everywhere, but every time a phone rang, whether it was my cell or somebody else's, it all stopped. Everyone froze and looked at me.

We were all on standby, waiting for a call from the hospital or the morgue to say *it's her.*

Waiting for a call from the kidnapper to say what he wanted.

Waiting to find out who I'd kept waiting long enough.

But who? Who the fuck was it? Who wanted to hurt us so much? Hurt me, not her, if Mizell was right?

It was the only thing that gave me hope: that he, they, whomever it was, wouldn't hurt her.

Please God, not her. The first conversation I'd had with him since her mother died. When I yelled at Him for taking her away.

I'd had the conversation with Mizell ten different ways, but it always ended up the same. "You're the professor, the guy who deals with words, so you tell me. It's all there in the note. '*You've kept me waiting long enough.*'"

"But what did *I* do? I'm a nobody. A teacher."

"But you *used* to be somebody. And you beat people. You won. There's a whole line of people whose places you probably took."

"From fifty different countries! Multiply that by four different guys on every team and you've got . . . it can't be. That's insane. That was thirteen years ago."

"Then some teacher you kept from getting a job here then. Somebody who was pissed off that you got it just because you already had a name . . . some student you didn't pass. Somebody you pissed off at a faculty meeting. Who are those people? That's what we need to know."

But the truth is I didn't have enemies. I wasn't perfect, but I made friends. I served on committees; I took on the junk classes that nobody else wanted to teach, the Heritage of Western Man intro courses you really had to prep for. I led the Marshall's Parade at graduation every May, holding the school flag so ably because I was already used to running with a big stick out in front of me. I hunkered down and did my best as a single father, when that was the last thing I had ever expected to happen. I made mistakes along the way, but I did my best.

No, the only person who ever got mad at me was Skip.

Maybe some stranger? Some crazy person, just fucking with us? For some reason, that idea was even worse. We'd been robbed once, years before, just after we moved in, the TV and coffee maker and a few other things taken. Patti and I both said we felt it, something *off* in the house, the minute we'd walked in. The DNA of the house had somehow changed. At first, the cops thought it was somebody who wanted to see where the big Olympic champ was now living, but none of my sports stuff had been taken. It took Skip to discover the real purpose, showing the cops around.

"They took all the spoons. Look." My gleeful daughter. Fearless. Excited to have her house broken into. She opened the silverware drawer to show that all the spoons were gone except for one that had been left behind in the dishwasher.

"They're freebasing. That's what they use. Spoons. They told us about it in school."

The cops looked impressed; I thought *great, the grade school is teaching my seven-year-old how to do drugs.* Seven going on seventeen. Maybe whoever took her thought she was older than she was; everybody did. I let her watch too much grown-up TV. It was my fault. I should have put one of those parent lock things on the TV and her computer. Nobody really took kids as young as Skip, did they?

Not in Mt. Gresh, Massachusetts, population 38,000. It just didn't happen.

That robbery. It was the only time a policeman had been in the house, until now.

After the break-in, I'd bought a pistol, a .38, even though Patti told me I was being ridiculous. Maybe I was: I didn't even keep the gun and bullets together, for fear that Skip would find them and have an accident. I kept the pistol high up on a shelf, under a pile of sweaters in a rattan basket, and the box of bullets taped upside down to one of the slats, under the bed.

Genius move, Patti had chided me. *Just ask the burglar if he minds waiting while you dig through your sweaters—hey, you want this one? Looks like it might fit, the one with the reindeer on it—actually, why don't you try it on, while I load my gun?*

I knew she was right. I could never pull a trigger. But that was before Skip was gone.

Before. After. Now there was always going to be a before and after, but I didn't know what the after was going to bring.

"We'll get her back. We'll find her. She'll be okay."

Wendy had come up behind me at the window upstairs, without me even hearing her.

I was still hearing Patti laugh at me; I was smiling, remembering how I laughed with her, at how goofy I was. Reindeer sweater indeed, that Patti had bought for me. Wendy put her arms around my waist and I reached for her hands, expecting to smell the Persian lime crème that Patti always put on her hands, after she washed the dishes.

Wrong woman. Wrong everything.

I closed my eyes and held Wendy's hands to my mouth, so she'd feel my breath on them as I prayed. I didn't care who heard me now. I'd scream it from the roof, if that's what it took. "God, take my legs from me, however you want them. In an accident, a disease . . . I don't care. I can take the pain. Take my arms. Take whatever you want, just don't take Skip. Don't let her hurt . . . "

It was another one of my bargains with God: Take anything you want, as long as you bring Skip back. Tit for tat. This for that. I started crying again.

This is no time to make your fathers cry.
Or your mothers.

When I was little, my mother would take me to an orphanage where she did charity work, reading to kids for story hour. Most of them looked ill or disabled in some way, different physical handicaps. "See how fortunate you are," she'd whisper to me, even though the children could hear. "This could have been you." Maybe my father was in on it too, to get me to work out harder, so I *wouldn't* be one of them. My mother would end up crying so much the various staffs started telling her not to come back. She upset the children too much.

She upset *me* too much, seeing her like that.

Now, for some reason, I thought back to that, something I hadn't thought about in years, and it became part of my prayer. *God, I'll do it. I'll be it. Take whatever you want, make me like those kids I used to see, just bring Skip back. How Patti and I had been, when she was first born: every little finger and toe so perfect. Her little mouth, her wet, slicked-back hair. Wanting another child right away, to feel that love again. Never wanting another one, because nothing else could ever be as perfect as Skip was at that first moment, could ever be more than the love we felt just then in the hospital . . . Don't let her get hurt. Oh God please God . . . don't let her come back . . . different.*

And then it was Wendy talking back to me, answering me, not God. "We're gonna find her. Aretha's good, I've been talking to her . . ."

"Aretha?"

"That's what she told me to call her. And Guillory, he's the one who set up the phone trace stuff, he said that . . ."

I had to get away, away from the police, away from a detective named Aretha, back to Skip's room. Back to where her DNA and dust motes still were, where her breath was still trapped, where I knew she was still alive.

"Hey dude, look at this," I heard one of the police say, as I got up the stairs. Maybe they'd found something. I threw open Skip's door to see two policemen, looking at something.

My gold medal.

One of them had put it over his neck, fingerprint powder and all, and was posing and flexing with it in the vanity mirror.

"Yeah, work those muscles, baby . . . you wanna feel my medal? Yeah, come on, touch it, bitch . . . " The cop shifted to a different angle in the mirror, the better to see himself, and saw me instead.

"Oh shit man . . . I'm sorry, I didn't mean—it was just here and . . . oh fuck. Don't tell Mizell."

He gave me the medal and I stuffed it in my pocket.

I didn't feel anger because he'd taken something of mine, but because he'd taken something of *Skip's*. That medal was hers now; she loved it, as much as she loved those snowballs that reminded her of her mother. It said that I was here to her, that I was strong—the fucking strongest man in the world. That I'd always be here, to protect her.

And then today, I wasn't.

I should have just let those cops keep it. It didn't mean anything anymore.

"We've got something." Mizell. Downstairs.

I ran back down, and saw her pointing some kind of blue fluorescent light on the kitchen floor, moving it back and forth from the kitchen island to the back door.

"What?"

"Scuff marks."

"I guess there would be," I said. "Nobody mopped up after the party last night."

"No, *these*. See?" She got down on her knees, using a long wooden spoon from the counter to show me where to look. "'Bout a foot and a half apart, two lines, white rubber. Those long marks, there? Like a car skid? She have anything with white rubber soles? Like erasers?"

"Her running shoes. From this morning."

"Thank God she was still wearing 'em."

"Why?"

"Because *that's* what left these marks, when she got dragged out the back door. Now we know this is real. Now we can really get to work."

CHAPTER NINE

Skip could sense him slowly moving in the room, coming closer to her, but something was off about the way he walked. And she didn't feel a change in temperature either, as he got nearer. More like somebody who was cold most of the time and didn't give off much body heat. She almost wished he did, because that would mean he was scared. That would mean he was hot and out of breath. That would help her, if she knew that this person felt afraid, like she did. Maybe his voice was a sign he was afraid, that weird stopping and starting he did, or catching his breath, or whatever it was that kept breaking up his sentences so much.

"I know you're not. Asleep. Even though it's well past. Your bedtime. So we might as well. Talk. Might as well. Live." He laughed, as he moved the tape off her mouth again. She licked her lips, as little as she could so he wouldn't get any ideas, but he didn't offer her any more water this time. She bit the inside of her cheeks, to try to make saliva.

"Do they teach her. Anymore? Dorothy Parker? 'Guns aren't lawful. Nooses give. Gas smells awful. You might as well. Live.' Perfect for my vocal . . . range. Well, almost perfect. That last. *Live*. Gets me every time."

Should she talk to him? That's what they always said to do on *Criminal Minds* and *Law & Order*—talk to the bad guy to humanize yourself, let him know you were a person. Use your name. But this guy seemed like he would already know all those tricks. He'd figure out what she was doing and get even madder because of it.

"Does my father know I'm here?" Her own voice sound rusty, from how little she'd been talking. She had to clear her throat, to make any words come out.

"That would defeat. The purpose. Let him. *Imagine*."

She tried to listen to him with one ear and then sort of scrunch up her face so she could hear what else was in the room with the other ear, but it didn't work. She couldn't hear anything except him. She couldn't hear anything except her heart, beating fast and heating up her ears.

"What does your. *Father* do? When you're upset?"

Was it a trick question? What should she do? Answer him? Cooperate? Stay quiet? A dozen possibilities, all wrong except for one. But which one? If she could just see his face, she might be able to figure it out, like reading a scene partner in Miss Davenport's class. But she couldn't. All she could do was hear him.

"He . . . he . . . reads to me."

"Ah! Fairy tales? Harry Potter? Percy Jackson and the. *Olympians?*"

The way he said it, did that mean he knew who her dad was?

"Books. *To Kill a Mockingbird. A Wrinkle in Time*. Ray Bradbury. I like him because he's sort of real and not real at the same time . . . "

"That would be. *Sur* . . . real. Real and . . . not real. Like now."

"I read at the tenth-grade level. I know what surreal is. I've been tested."

"Tested. As have I. I knew we had . . . something in common!"

Why did she say that? He'd think she was bragging. He went quiet, but more like he was gathering a breath for his next set of words than getting mad.

"Once upon a time . . . is that how your father's stories. Would start?"

"When I was little, but . . . not anymore."

"Then I'll tell you a grown-up story. About *being* little. About a little boy . . . oh, let's call him. Harry. Harry Potter. He was smart, but he was alone."

"Harry Potter has friends. At school. Hogwarts. Not a lot, but . . . some."

The minute Skip said it, she was terrified he'd think she was making fun of him, of all his starts and stops. She made her face go tight, so it wouldn't hurt as much if he hit her again. But nothing happened.

"He made some. Friends then. The only thing my . . . *little boy* made. Was a volcano. For the science fair."

She heard him take another big breath, closer to her. She pulled her face back; she pushed her whole body as far back into the school desk as she could, to get as far away from him as possible. But without looking like she was; that would make him mad. That would make him hit her again. Or worse.

"A paper-mache volcano. It erupted when you mixed baking soda with . . . what was it? Something acidic. Wet newspaper, chicken wire, flour and salt, and a battery. It was easy to make. So was making it explode. *Boom.*"

He stopped, and she didn't know if he was catching his breath again, or just stopping to think.

"*That's* what he won a prize for. The explosion. The . . . *boom.*"

She heard him take a deep breath, as if he were trying to smell it. The burnt, gassy mixture of an explosion. Skip could smell something in the room—age, decay, mold, neglect—but not that.

The man coughed, then continued. "He was good with his hands, our boy. What were we calling him?"

"Harry," said Skip, afraid because he'd forgotten so quickly.

"Ah, yes. All those hours *Harry* spent, all alone, clicking away on a game box with his thumbs. It was just a short hop, skip, and a jump . . . "—he laughed—" . . . from using his thumbs at video games, to using all ten fingers on the computer. He got into computer hacking and learned things. He walked into the stock market and made money. He walked into real estate records and found things. He walked into doctors' records and took the drugs he needed. He hired helpers and . . . "

What was he talking about? He was going too fast now. He was throwing clues at her and she was trying to keep track but something was different. He'd jumped into being a grownup all of a sudden, talking about grown-up stuff, not about being a little kid, and . . .

He wasn't stopping and starting anymore. He wasn't having trouble breathing. *That* was it. He wasn't telling a made-up story anymore. He wasn't talking about a little boy named Harry. He was talking about himself.

"So by the time I finally came out here, so far from civilization, and I smelled those back country roads again, it was the smell that said, 'I've come home.' I mean . . . *Harry* had."

Now he was moving around. Skip could sense shadows come and go, light and dark, even through the covering over her eyes. And she finally felt body heat, as he stopped in front of her. He was excited. Or scared.

"Vinegar, that was it! The acid in the volcano! That's what made the explosion!"

He leaned even closer, to whisper in her ear.

"*Boom.*"

CHAPTER TEN

The call came at 7:30 A.M.

Somehow, we all knew it was the one. It just felt different, like that time we'd walked into the house after that robbery. The heavy jangle of the landline, against the quiet of the morning. The loudest noise I'd ever heard, jerking me awake from where I'd nodded off for an hour or two in the living room.

Mizell had just come back into the house after leaving at two in the morning, with Starbucks, Krispy Kremes, and a different wig. She was pouring coffee from her giant ten-cup Box of Joe when that phone ringing made a spasm go through her body; she flung a cup of the scalding liquid all over herself. Guillory, the cop who'd set up the phone trace and stayed overnight, stabbed himself with chopsticks, from the container of leftover Chinese food he was eating for breakfast, the same food I'd brought home for Skip more than twelve hours ago. Even hard-of-hearing Sig flew up from the couch, where he'd fallen asleep.

I ran to the old phone, stuck into a recess in the bead-boarded wall underneath the stairwell, but Mizell beat me there, sucking on her burned hand. She slapped it over the top of the phone before I could reach it.

"If it's him, keep him talking, until we can get a trace." She nodded at Guillory, who turned on his recording equipment. Then she nodded at me, a signal I knew in my gut, without ever being told.

Pick up the phone.

But when I did, whatever we'd all been expecting—dreading and praying for both—this wasn't it, as the voice broadcast over the trace equipment into the whole room.

Daniel went to the lions' den;
Do the same with your girlfriend, Wen.
A tussle with the king of the jungle . . .
Becomes a dance of death you don't want to bungle.
For if you do, it's little Skip's life; only question is, bullet or knife?

Whoever was on the other end of the line didn't need to disguise his voice, because it was like nothing any of us had ever heard before: somehow hollowed out in the middle—a center column of air, of nothingness—but with a raspy, grasping shield around it. Like he was having to squeeze out his lungs, to make any sound at all.

"Who the FUCK . . . IF YOU TOUCH HER . . . " I started, forgetting everything Mizell had coached me on.

"And no police. Just you. We have so much . . . to catch up on."

A click, from the other end.

No request for money, no proof he had her, no proof of life, no directions, no address, no *anything* except utter, horrifying, rhyming reality.

Skip's life, bullet or knife . . . Skip's life, bullet or knife bullet or knifebulletorknife . . .

"Oh my God. Oh God. Jesus."

Mizell pushed me down onto the chair next to the phone—as if there was a surge of helium throughout my body and she knew she had to anchor me down to keep me from floating away.

"Focus. Did it sound like anybody you know . . . somebody who writes poetry . . . somebody who . . . you know him. So much to 'catch up on.' That means you've met him before. Just think . . . "

"What the fuck do you think? . . . JESUS CHRIST!" I screamed it, and the helium discharged. Exploded. "OH MY FUCKING GOD."

The call hadn't changed anything, because he hadn't told me anything I could get a handle on, to know where I'd met him before. He hadn't told me where to go or what to do next, except don't bring the police. Don't bring the police *where*? Or *had* he just told me where to go? Something was coming together in my head, as I grabbed a pen and paper that were there for messages and phone numbers, and began scribbling down those insane words I would never forget.

Guillory was listening through his headphones, transcribing the rest of the words. "'Lions' den.' What's that? Is that someplace you . . ."

"Oh my God. Wendy." I'd sent her home late last night, sent her away to him. "The lions' den. That's where she works. Our nickname for it. The zoo. The teaching zoo at the school. King of the jungle. It's the lions there! It has to be."

"Is she there now?"

"First thing every morning." I ran upstairs, two steps at a time, to grab my cell phone, as Mizell raced up behind me, barking out orders to Guillory down below. "Get a car to his girlfriend's house. And the zoo. Now."

In my bedroom, I hit number five on my speed dial. "C'mon, c'mon, pick up . . . " but all I got was Wendy's voicemail. "Hello, you've reached Dr. Wendy Borden. If this is an animal emergency . . ."

"Shit. She's not there." I spun around to face Mizell. "Does he have 'em both? Does that mean he's got 'em both? Oh my God. Oh God." My voice had gone so high-pitched, you could barely hear it. A slice, through the air, then it was gone.

"We'll find out. You stay here while . . ."

"NO. He wants me. He said it. You heard him. No police."

I was throwing on my track shoes and coat, on top of the sweat pants I'd been wearing since yesterday afternoon.

"Let us handle this. We'll get a negotiator . . ."

"*No.* My kid. My way. He wants *me*."

"And what's he gonna do once he gets you there? Take you too? Then I've got two people to worry about. Three if he's got Wendy."

I forced myself to take a breath to slow down, the way I used to before a race. "He didn't say bring money. So what the fuck does he want? Will he have Skip there? I'll switch places. He can take me. He can kill me. I don't care. I just want Skip safe."

I was mumbling to Mizell, to myself, to thin air. To God. I was making my deal with Him: You give me her, then you can do whatever you want.

"You go; we follow. You stay alive. Skips needs you. No horseshit, no heroics. I'll have backup. First sign of trouble, we're there."

Without meaning to, without even knowing I did it, I looked at her legs. She wasn't a runner. She saw my eyes go there. "Don't worry. I passed the physical."

"So did I. Thirteen years ago."

She flashed a smile, the first one since she told me that Skip was probably just playing a joke on me. "'Bout the same time I did. I'll get you a Kevlar vest downstairs."

"A bulletproof vest? You think he's gonna shoot?"

"I don't know." She took the same calming breath I just did. "You don't have to do this, you know."

"Yes I do." I'd never known anything more strongly.

She went downstairs ahead of me, while I began shimmying under the bed to get the box of bullets that was taped to one of the bed slats. *Were six bullets in a gun chamber enough to kill somebody, if I'd never shot a pistol before?*

And I knew one other thing: that I'd never stop pulling the trigger, even when nothing but tiny metallic clicks were coming from the gun.

CHAPTER ELEVEN

"Your father. Sends his. Love."

Skip heard the creak of the floorboards that always announced his entrance. Not like normal walking, but . . . was he bent over? Crooked? Like it was as hard for him to walk as it was for him to breathe. She'd heard it during the night when he'd come in to put a blanket over her shoulders, but she'd pretended to be asleep.

"Truth be told, he said. '*Who the fuck.*' But I'm sure he *meant.* I love you."

"What else did he say? My father?" Then she rattled off more, because that sounded like she was imitating him again, stopping and starting. "I mean—does he know I'm okay? Did you tell him that much? Please. Just let me know he knows I'm okay."

"I can assure you. He is quite worried. And he is beginning. To look. We'll soon see how smart. He is."

His breathing gave her an idea. She could lie and say she had asthma, and that's why he had to let her go, or she'd die if she didn't have her medicine. She had a friend who had asthma, who was always having to breathe in from this little plastic tube. Skip tried it once, when her friend went to the bathroom, and it choked her. A puff of cold air that tasted like metal, or deodorant. Her friend came out of the bathroom and said, "You tried it, didn't you? Everybody does. Getting choked serves you right. Now you know what I have to go through."

"I'll die," Skip said. "You can't leave me here. I have asthma. I need my atomizer."

Thank God she remembered the name of it. Atomizer. Like an atom smasher, her friend always joked.

"Oh, I'd so hoped. You wouldn't resort. To things like. That. Lies."

"But I do. I swear. Especially if I'm scared, it gets worse. And who wouldn't be scared in a situation like this?"

"I've known you since. You were little. Everything about you. You don't have. Asthma."

What, he knew her? How could he know her? How could somebody who knew her do something so bad to her?

"Who are you? How do you know me? Do I know you?" She didn't know anyone who sounded like him, no one she could remember.

"All good things. To those who wait. And now the waiting. Is officially. Over."

He chuckled, to himself.

"Now, in the clear light of day. The house rules. No one can hear you. It would be pointless. To scream. You'll just hurt your throat. And then you'll. Sound like me. And that's no. Day at the park. *The picnic? Day at the . . . picnic?* I'm a little . . . removed from the vernacular."

That one took the longest gulp of air she'd heard him take yet.

"I think it's, uh . . . *no picnic.* Just by itself. Or *no walk in the park.* Those are the ones I know. I'm a little out of it too," Skip said, without meaning to, without thinking. And then she thought—*maybe that* was *smart.* It told him she was like him. Maybe not so popular. Maybe sort of left out. If he thought she was more like him, maybe he wouldn't hurt her.

He was quiet for a moment; she felt him staring at her again. Like he was deciding what to do next. Like he'd been thrown for a beat. That's what they called it in acting: a beat. Like a thought. That's what she was going to do: act.

She was going to survive this whole thing by *acting,* like she was *playing* the character of a teenager who'd been kidnapped. It wasn't really her in the chair; well, it was, but it wasn't. She was just pretending. Nothing would hurt her. It was all make-believe. And her mother's meatloaf recipe card, she was going to think about that too, how it was waiting for her under the refrigerator to pick up, when she finished playing her part and the show was over and she could finally go home.

She heard him go down a hall, and then a door slid open, the same sort of heavy metallic sound she had heard when her mother got in their SUV, that last time.

She heard the outdoors. And then she heard a second voice, a deep, full one which had no trouble getting a lungful of air. "You ready to go, boss? Just tell me when and where and we'll get ya there in no time flat." All of it, said in one fell swoop.

There were two of them.

CHAPTER TWELVE

He thought she would scream, but she didn't. Or if she did, he couldn't hear it. His soundproofing had worked. Nobody would hear it.

Good.

He remembered how easily the windows had opened some thirty years ago, when his volcano explosion had gone off and hung like a mushroom cloud over the teacher's desk, and she had to get the big boys to push open the windows so they could all breathe. But now, if one were to *want* to open the windows, which one *did not*, how hard it would be: paint unsticking from wood; jagged, rubbery splinters of goo; layers of institutional green and gray and beige, painted one on top of the other, pulling loose. It would be very hard indeed to open these windows, even if his helpers *hadn't* already nailed them shut, from the outside.

He stretched his trembling arms out to the sky and, in his head, said a prayer to welcome the morning, a prayer of thankfulness for *quiet*. Most people wouldn't believe him, that he made that prayer, that he made any prayer or that he even believed in God, but he did. They taught them religion at the home. But he kept the prayers in his head, because they sounded better there. He didn't run out of air in his head. Words—sentences—sounded better there. There wasn't the pause, the hesitation that his speaking voice had. Now, whenever he talked, his throat quivered; his lungs couldn't fill up enough to complete a sentence. His breathing had gotten worse these past few months; soon, his lungs would be completely overtaken by his disease, if the rest of his body didn't succumb first. He had to hurry.

The front steps of the old schoolhouse where he was now were where the teachers used to be waiting every morning, when his bus would pull up. Those kind women in their schoolteacher dresses, listening to the morning songs in the woods, the rumble of a bus full of misfit toys . . .

He meant *boys*.

So much life in the overgrown woods around him: deer and snakes, squirrels and chipmunks, little and orange and scurrying away. Life in the woods, which had now grown up and virtually strangled this schoolhouse where children used to learn. Where he had been *allowed* to learn. Even then, he'd known it had been an honor to be selected, to be released from the home to travel there, to learn, to have "lunch" and "recess"—how he reveled in what he thought were such grown-up words, after he had been denied so many other grown-up things. And even in the back of his head, he somehow knew this place would figure into his plan for revenge, years away in the future. Years in the making. Even then, as a child, he knew the what, the why, but not yet *the who*. That would come later.

And now it had.

As an adult, he'd kept his eye on the place. Should he buy it outright, or just squat there, until his project was done? He'd searched the county court records and saw that the school was no longer owned by anyone, one of dozens of properties that had been abandoned over the years, once they'd outlived their usefulness. His project was short-term—two days, forty-eight hours and change—so he wouldn't need to go as far as buying it. That would set off too many alarm bells, but he would need to get running water and electricity. Those could stay off the books as well. No permits for him, except for what he permitted himself. He didn't exactly want a team of inspectors coming in, to see what he'd done with the place. There wouldn't be that much work. He just needed two rooms.

One for him. One for her.

Home away from . . . *the* home.

The original ground plan of the school was long gone, one wing collapsed in on itself, so the roof of shale and slate was on a slant, much of it shattered. There were so many trees and brambles surrounding the place that not much light came through anymore: a little bit here, a little bit there, the forest *deciding* what it would allow.

He was thankful that it had allowed him back in.

He needed beauty and nature, and calm, to get him ready for what he was about to do. He could still let her go; it wasn't too late. Just tell her to count to five hundred after he loosened her bonds, and she could walk out of the forest to the highway and hail down a passing car. She hadn't seen him yet, and with a few years of therapy—and who couldn't use *that*?—Skip would be as good as new. She might be afraid to be alone for a while, but she was scrappy; she'd get over it. He knew. He'd watched her for years. She was a jock in the making, just like her father. And besides, it was her father that he really wanted; she was just collateral damage. What better way to teach an adult a lesson than through a child? After all, that's what he had been when this all started. A child. All those years, he'd spent . . . waiting. And that was the experience he wanted to pass on to her father. The waiting. The not knowing. No—and this was the hardest prayer of all, knowing what was coming at the end—better to stick with the original plan; it had taken so much work to get everything just right, and he wasn't a well man. Not well at all. He didn't want it to go to waste. Eyes on the prize. Ethan Holt had won one, and now he wanted one too.

And with that decision made, he went to the van that was waiting for him, with a long-range rifle waiting inside. And said one last, inaudible prayer to God: *enough air to finish the job. To kill. Amen.*

CHAPTER THIRTEEN

A dance of death you don't want to bungle.
For if you do, it's little Skip's life; only question is, bullet or knife?

Those psychotic words from the kidnapper had burned into my head and would never leave. I didn't need to check them against a piece of paper; they were part of my DNA now. But something else was too: that if I had anything to do with it, it would be a bullet. Shot into him. One of the six I'd loaded in my .38 revolver I'd never shot before, just as I was racing out of the house.

I clicked the chamber around and around, every metallic stop it made a worry bead, a rosary prayer, as I came to a screeching halt at the zoo, jumped out of the car and began running, the pistol stuck into the waist band of my pants.

I was screaming.

So were the animals, in return.

Wendy and Simba both saw me at the same time, racing toward the lion enclosure. Simba was a big cub, already 150 pounds. He snapped his head toward me, disturbed to be taken away from his breakfast bottle. Wendy popped up, the heavy leather belt she always wore when she was "on duty" swinging around, its slots and clips filled with the tools of her trade as a vet.

"Oh my God, have they found . . . " Wendy started.

"No, but . . . your name . . . "

"What?"

"The kidnapper. He called. He said your name. This crazy poem about the lions' den . . . "

"*What?*"

I couldn't tell her the worst part, about the bullet or knife or Skip's life. She came to the edge of the "fence," a glass wall about five or six feet high, with an invisible barrier of mild electric pulses and zaps extending another three or four feet above that. Wendy had told me it was the next wave of zoo enclosures, to see how little could be done to keep animals *and* viewers safe. She'd designed it. It was her pride and joy—well, her *pride* at least, she always joked.

So as much as I wanted to touch Wendy, to yank her out of there, I couldn't.

"I'm supposed to meet him here or do *something* here or maybe he's bringing her here. To the lions' den. I don't know." For all the running I'd done in the past, I couldn't catch my breath. Or maybe my heart had just never raced this fast. "This was all I could figure out, just to get here. We kept calling you but . . . "

"Shit. I left my phone inside."

She was immediately on high alert, both our heads whipping around, looking for . . . anything. Everything. There were so many hiding places. They'd wanted the zoo to look like a forest, and it did. Trees and caves everywhere. Wendy had designed this place; she knew it better than anyone.

"Let me get outta here, get him back inside," she said, trying to move Simba along. He didn't want to go, instead rolling over on his back, for Wendy to scratch his belly.

"Yes, yes, Mommy loves you, but we've gotta go . . . "

He swatted her, lightly, to get her attention back.

"C'mon, Simsy. Inside." She reached toward his neck to pull him up, but all it took was one swipe of his paw to knock her over.

That's when I saw something whizz by, so fast and quiet it was almost invisible. But I could tell that *something* had happened, by Simba's reaction. A yelp that said pain. And with it, a stream of blood started to bubble out of his neck, soaking and matting his fur, but not slowing him down.

"Oh my God . . . he's bleeding . . . " Wendy touched it, and the lion struck at her again, harder. A lot harder.

Then a second something whistled through the air, and this time Wendy was hit. She touched her shoulder, incredulously, and her hand came back covered with blood. Not the lion's, but hers.

"Jesus Christ! Wendy, get outta there." I was looking at her and all around us, trying to find help. Trying to find where Mizell and her team were, who were supposed to be backing me up. Trying to find where the shots were coming from. I reached over the wall towards Wendy, but got zapped by the electrical current I'd forgotten.

"FUCK."

I yanked my arm away and slammed back to the ground, so hard it felt like there was no padding between my lungs and the grass. With my feet, I tried to kick at the glass, but it was too thick. It didn't budge.

"Shit. We've gotta get the current off. Where the fuck is Mizell?" I was screaming it; I didn't care who heard me as I raced up and down along the fence, trying to find a way in, but there was nothing. Just glass, and voltage. Designed to keep them in, and me out. The words from the poem were beginning to make sense, horrible sense. Was it Wendy the kidnapper was after, and not Skip?

A tussle with the king of the jungle . . .
Becomes a dance of death you don't want to bungle.
. . . only question is, bullet or knife?

That question has just been answered. Bullet.

Fuck it. I had bullets of my own. I grabbed my pistol, but what the fuck did I shoot at? The lion or the kidnapper, somewhere I couldn't even see? What if I hit Wendy instead? I couldn't get a clean shot.

Clean shot? Any shot. I'd never shot the fucking thing before.

"NO! Don't shoot him!" Wendy yelled at me. The lion was still trying to get her to fix what hurt, but she was bleeding more than he was now.

"Where the fuck is everybody? How do I get in there?"

The height wasn't the problem—I cleared 7'6" at Sydney—the electricity was. I could grab the top of the glass wall and pull myself over, but my hands would be fried. There wasn't any choice. If whoever it was wanted to shoot at me, at least I was wearing a bulletproof vest. Better he do that, than keep shooting at them.

Maybe I could survive.

Maybe I would be the distraction, long enough to get Wendy out.

I circled back and came running at a curve . . .

. . . braced my body . . . threw my legs over before my torso . . .

Ankles, calves, knees . . .

They got zapped in that order. I couldn't stand up, I could barely *breathe*, but at least I was inside.

"Please, please, don't hurt him . . . don't . . . " Wendy was trying to save herself and the lion, but I didn't know if she could do both. "Cover his eyes. Cover. He'll stop."

I pulled at my coat to get it off, and tried to pull myself along the grass.

The lion weighed forty-five pounds less than I did, but he was all muscle. I wasn't, not anymore. All smelly jowls and fur. And slobber. And blood. And now he was sniffing around, almost on top of me.

"Cave . . . behind you . . . " Wendy said, trying to point with her arm, but she was moaning with pain.

I tried to move toward it, hoping the lion would follow. Herky-jerky, on my elbows, face up. The lion, face down. It was the Colosseum, the dance of death that the kidnapper wanted.

"Come get me, you Goddamn motherfucker . . . "

I was growling at both of them now, the lion and the kidnapper; pushing myself up to my knees and then to my electrocuted legs, flinging my coat over Simba's head.

He thrashed back—blinded, roaring—everything a blur of tawny brown fur and clothes and paws and arms as the lion took me down . . .

. . . just as I saw *another* blur of something out of the corner of my eyes. Some*body*, running toward the enclosure: Mizell, one of her sleeves soaked with blood too, but it didn't get in the way of her perfect aim.

She shot, I yelled, and the bullet shattered the glass fence.

And then her second bullet shattered the lion.

CHAPTER FOURTEEN

"You'll be happy to know. 'Daddy' passed. His first test," the kidnapper said.

"What test?" Skip said. "What are you talking about?"

"All good things. To those who wait. And I am one. Who has *waited*."

He grabbed a nail and hammered it into the wall, as furiously as if he were Ethan, attacking the lion. But this was a different king of the jungle that was being pummeled now, a homemade one being put up on display, made of construction paper and yarn and pipe cleaners and pieces of fur cut off an old jacket. The kind of lion a grade-schooler would make, for show-and-tell up on a bulletin board. But then the hand that put it up there kept stabbing away at it, now with a pair of scissors instead of a hammer. A silly lion, being stabbed to death.

"What are you doing?" Skip screamed.

The hand kept stabbing until it was finished, exhausted.

Then he looked up at his handiwork on the wall, just a few feet below an empty square of institutional green, lighter than the surrounding wall, where the loudspeaker used to be. From that box of golden wood, through a circle of mesh in the center front, the voice of their *principal* used to come out. Their *p-a-l*. The Voice of God, they called it, and probably even thought. Now, there was no box, no God, no stranger's voice, except for the one in his own head, guiding him along.

"What test?" Skip begged again.

He ignored her. A bit of light came into the room, from where his helpers had boarded up the windows. A gap here and there, just enough for him to see to put up his *outsider* art on the four walls. With a few snips and tucks—that old artistry coming back, learned from making his volcano!—he'd already sprinkled gold glitter onto a pair of deer antlers, real ones, four points, that still had skull and bristly hair at the base. He'd smashed a vase into shards for a mosaic. Construction paper and glitter. Elmer's glue and yarn. Paper plates and wax paper and crayons. Old magazines, *Life*s and *Look*s, that he'd collected at flea markets. Using a peeler, he'd sheared the waxy skin of a yellow apple from its flesh, the spiral unfurling in one long unbroken chain. *His* DNA may have had a few breaks in its chain, but his slinky of golden apple skin didn't. And now, the underside of it, bits of pulp left on, had turned brown and decaying.

He hadn't made his artworks in order, but he would start putting them up that way. Everything had already been set down, in the record books; the *new* was what he did with it. And that he had decided long ago; he was going to tell a story. One story, from childhood, from birth even, to death; a master design only he could understand.

"What did Daddy do? *Please.* What test? What are you making him do? *Let me go* . . . I'll be quiet. I won't say anything. I don't *know* anything. I haven't *seen* anything. You'll be safe. They won't be able to find you . . . "

So many words, a torrent, their first real conversation, but he had stopped listening after the first part: *What test? What are you making him do? What did Daddy do?*

"You really want to know?" he asked. "I sometimes find it's better *not* to know. Better to be. Kept in the dark. As it were. And there are *so* many ways. For that to be achieved. Your blindfold, for one."

He touched the back of her head, tightening it up; a few stray hairs of Skip's got caught in the knot; he yanked them out.

"But if you *do* know, and you want to forget . . . because Knowledge. Is. Power. And Power. Is electricity . . . "

"I . . . never mind. Just . . . I'm sorry I said anything. Really." Now she was backtracking. He didn't like that. He wanted a person to say what they meant. He didn't like weakness. Or excuses. Or changing your mind.

"No. Keep talking. I love these little chats. Better to get everything. Out in the open. Better to. Finish things."

He moved into the adjoining room, the old principal's office that he'd turned into his command center. This was where he'd really had to acquit himself. A single school desk was fine for her, but for him . . . he needed things. Things for listening. And talking. Monitors. Computers. Webcams. Remote cameras placed ever so strategically, to see everything that Ethan Holt was doing. A phone, with a voice-filtering screen (as if he needed that!) and enough machinery to scramble any attempt to find him. It was the high-tech payoff to all the work he had done over the last ten years, the money he had made building things. If this gig didn't work out, surely he could get hired on at Radio Shack. Or the Apple Store. At the "Genius Bar."

He kept talking, doing his best to project his faltering voice so Skip could still hear, as he dug through the various pieces of equipment he had already prepared.

"This was one of their favorite ways of keeping us. In the dark. At the home."

A long electrical cord was in one hand; something that looked like an old-fashioned pair of headphones was in the other.

He came back to Skip and put it over her head, moved some hair away so he could adhere the spongy electrodes to either side of her head, just below her ears, just below where the blindfold almost bisected her face.

"What! What are you doing?" She thrashed more than he imagined a skinny girl could.

He should have taped her upper shoulders to the chair too, but he hadn't predicted she'd be so curious about what her father was going through.

"Things have been set in motion that . . . well, you'll see. You'll *feel*. I call this the 'killing two birds. With one stone.' Answer. Share a little bit of myself with you—what I went through at the home. The original 'time out,' you might call it. And share a little bit of what your *father* just went through. To find *you*. Curiosity killed the . . . well, you know."

"But I don't want to anymore! I changed my mind! Whatever I did to make you mad . . . "

"I don't know exactly how many volts your father felt at the zoo, so I'll just have to. *Guess*."

Adjusting for size and age, he *guessed* that 25,000 volts would do the trick for now.

And it did.

CHAPTER FIFTEEN

I tried to make Wendy laugh, since it was my fault she was in a hospital bed, just out of surgery, wrapped up in bandages and butterfly stitches, enough damage to keep her there for a few days. I tried to make her do anything except cry, since it was my fault the lion she had raised from a cub was now dead, and she nearly had joined him.

"Talk about what the cat dragged in . . . " She was too doped up to get the joke, lost in a fog of painkillers and a forest of hanging bags of blood and thick, clear liquids. Good thing, because it was a bad joke. A horrible joke. A horrible . . . everything.

Why the FUCK hasn't he called again? I did what he wanted, didn't I? Is that it then, the end, no more? He called me there, but . . . a wild goose chase. A fucking . . . if he wanted me dead, he could have just shot me. Instead of Wendy. Instead of the lion.

"Go*damn* it." I banged at the wall, setting off a searing pain through my arm. They'd put salves all over me for the electrical burns and shot me full of electrolytes; I'd recover soon enough from that. But from this . . .

That's when Mizell came in. She'd changed, a new jacket now on, covering up her bandaged arm. Oh yeah. He shot her too, but instead of sympathy, all I felt was rage.

"*You.* I told you not to come. He said it. No police. We should have listened. If you hadn't been there, Skip would have . . . "

"If *I* hadn't been there, the Lion King would have ripped you to pieces. I'm sorry it had to go down that way, but . . . he's going after everybody you love. First Skip, now Wendy. You he won't touch; he wants you to see it all."

"*Jesus.* So he just got us there to set us all up. What kind of sick fuck . . . why didn't you get him? You said you were backing me up, and you let this happen to her . . . "

"I think that's when I was mopping up my own blood." Touché, from Mizell; she gave as good as she got. "We found some van tracks, up a few hundred feet away, up on this hill. A perfect vantage point, trees all around; the van could stay hidden. It couldn't have been designed any better. We're making tire molds, see what we can find out. But the position . . . high-powered, long-distance. It fits. This was planned, nothing last minute. Nothing left to chance."

"So he *was* aiming at us?" I asked.

"Hard to tell. Maybe we just got in the way. Because here's the thing: he wasn't using bullets."

"What the fuck . . . of course he was. Look! She's got a bullet wound! You do too!"

"Well, bullets, yes . . . but not with gunpowder in them." Mizell held up something that looked like a smashed vitamin capsule, only metallic, with a cone nose. Looked like a bullet to me. "The powder was scraped out, and instead . . . "

She began digging through her pocket for a piece of paper, which she pulled out. "They ran the lion's blood. Something called . . . 'nandrolone.' That's what it was," she said, reading from a strip of torn legal pad that also held a wad of dried chewing gum. "He wanted to get the lion all . . . hopped up, and just see what happened."

"Nandrolone? Are you sure?" I asked, stunned. In a split second, I'd floated from that hospital room to the track in Sydney, getting my face pummeled.

"What? What does that mean to you?" Mizell stared at me.

"This guy attacked me at the Olympics . . . Mark Casey. They caught him doping. Steroids. That's what he was taking. Nandrolone. You swallow it, you don't inject it. It's not used that much anymore, but in 2000 . . . " I trailed off.

Mizell grabbed the dried gum off the paper and stuck it back in her mouth. "This guy gets all juiced up on nandrolone, and the same thing happens to the lion today? Somebody shoots it full of the *very same steroid*? Isn't that . . . what's that word you college guys have? 'Poetic justice?'"

"Something like that," I said.

"So humor me. You get attacked, and you leave this guy off your enemies list? Maybe I'm just a dumb cop, but . . . "

"That was nearly fifteen years ago."

"'*You've kept me waiting?*' Fifteen years? Seems to be right on target."

"No. It can't be."

"Why not? Pissed off is pissed off, and it just gets worse over time. Sounds like a motive to me. Where's this guy now?"

"You're not gonna find him. Believe me."

"And why the hell not?"

I finally said what I couldn't bring myself to say at the party the other night, what I hadn't wanted to say to Skip, because I didn't want to bring it all back. "Because he's dead. He's not waiting for anything."

CHAPTER SIXTEEN

Ethan's teaching assistant, TJ, got the call from the Dean of
Students that he needed to take over Ethan's afternoon class and
all of his classes until . . . well, just until.

TJ had handed out assignments before, he'd taken over for
short periods when Ethan had to go to faculty meetings, of course
he'd graded papers—harder than Ethan did—but he'd never
actually *taught* before. But teaching was out of the question today,
as was having to be the first one to break the news about Skip.
They already knew. On a small college campus, news traveled fast.
Especially bad news.

"Professor Holt obviously won't be here for a few days, so I'll
be filling in. But since nobody feels like studying, I thought . . .
maybe we could hand out flyers, see if anybody's seen her, do
something to help . . . "

"Do we get extra credit?" asked Matt, the class clown. The
other students were used to him, except for now. Nobody they'd
ever known had been taken, maybe even killed. And then this
asshole kid Matt opened his mouth and made a joke about it.

"Uh, Matthew, isn't it?"

"Matt. True dat."

Nobody laughed, not this time.

TJ knew his name, but he pretended not to. He pushed the
hair out of his eyes. He opened his mouth too, and words he
didn't know he had came from somewhere inside him, words that
made him feel older and more in control than he'd ever felt before.
Words that made him feel worthy of Dante.

"Well then, *Mr. True Dat* . . . I could just fail you now, and you
don't even have to show up for the rest of the semester. Doesn't
look very good on all those grad school applications, or on that

Fulbright I know you're applying for, but . . . it's your choice. That's what we all have. Freedom of choice."

TJ felt like he'd just eaten a steak. He felt like something new and bloody had just gone into him. His stomach grumbled, but for once, he was the only one who heard it.

"Actually, now that I think of it, the choice is mine. *My* freedom of choice," TJ added, yet more words he didn't know he had, words of power. "And I *choose* that you'll be the one to make the flyers for us to pass out tonight. And if you don't show up, you will *definitely* fail. You can paste Skip's picture on a sheet of paper and see all those flyers come pouring out from the Xerox machine, time after time, two hundred times maybe, with these words under the picture: 'Have You Seen This Girl?'"

TJ paused after his monologue. He needed a ta-da.

"Sure beats writing 'I'm an asshole' on the board two hundred times, don't you think?"

The class laughed. For once, with him, not at him.

◆ ◆ ◆

They already called him "Little Ethan" behind his back, although there was nothing Ethan-like about him, except for their shared love of all things ancient. They were Mutt and Jeff, Frick and Frack, Laurel and Hardy, without the funny bits: Ethan filled out his clothes, wore bicep-busting T-shirts to class; TJ always dressed like he was cold, even in the spring and summer, his skinny, pale arms always covered up. Ethan, coming straight into class from a run, looking like he could step into *GQ*; TJ always looking like he got dressed in the dark, pulling on whatever he could find, his hair a mousy brown rat's nest, no matter how many times he had run a comb through it. You'd think he'd be fat from all the sugar he consumed, the cheap slices of cake he lived off of from Claire's Cornucopia, the hippie bakery off campus. Big slabs of cake you could get extra buttercream icing on, for just a quarter. And all those carbs in his containers of Oodles of Noodles. But with all the nervous energy he had, it just melted off him. He'd look okay if he just worked out; maybe he should, to be more like his mentor. Mostly all he lifted were the heavy books in the library, the dusty old tomes that would still be there when the end came, that couldn't talk back to him or reject him.

The sugar kept him going during the day; the library kept him going at night. No one was supposed to sleep there overnight, but since his own apartment was a shithole, he did, no one the wiser. He brought in a throw pillow and a blanket for his study carrel on the fourth floor; whenever the librarian walked by on her nightly pass-through, before she closed up shop at midnight, he'd hunker down below the one tiny window so she wouldn't see him.

Once she was gone, TJ would sneak out with a flashlight and wander through the stacks, where he could disappear into the words and worlds of the past, the world of books and paper and bindings and spines and the stories that were inside them. He especially liked looking for Ethan Holt's name in the back of the books in the 292 section, from the days when students actually had to sign their names to check out a book instead of just swiping an ID card. Ethan's old signatures in faded gray or blue ink, that told what he had read when he was eighteen and nineteen and twenty, when his brain was being formed as much as his body. It was homework for TJ; not just hero worship. Or imitation. TJ wanted to know what had made Ethan the man he had become. Those were the books TJ sought out, late at night, an autobiography of his mentor better than any book; better than even *Herc Holt: My Story,* which TJ had also read.

TJ never told Ethan that. There was so much he hadn't told him, but he would discover it all soon enough.

Like TJ's surprise—and excitement—when he had first written down on some form that Ethan was his mentor, and seeing the word in print, rather than just saying it, came to realize how much it had in common with '*tor*-mentor.'

TJ wondered if he could go back to one of his dead languages and find an explanation for that. He could find so much among the dead.

Mortui vivis docent.

The dead teach the living.

CHAPTER SEVENTEEN

The chapel was deadly quiet; a tomb, inside the middle of a bustling hospital. Stained glass windows, red velvet cushions on the pews, flowers up front, and the carpet freshly vacuumed, but it still smelled like a hospital. Sick odors, chlorine, ammonia; nothing could hide the fact of where I was, shooed out of Wendy's room while the doctors looked her over. But it was a good place to escape to, to *think*, for just a minute; the stained glass reminded me of the finger paintings Skip used to make. To me, they were just squiggles and dots and streaks on paper, but Skip could look at them and tell me whole stories from them: monsters and good guys, in crayon.

It's right there, Daddy. Can't you see?

No baby, I can't, not yet. But you tell me what you see, and then I'll bet I can.

And always signing her name and age to them. Why did kids do that, always put their ages there? Did their kindergarten teachers tell them to, something on *Sesame Street?* Skip said she did it because it helped her to remember.

Remember, at four and five. Six. Seven. Eight. *Remember what?*

Were those scribbles, those mirrored balls up in the attic, all I was going to have to remember Skip by now? That set off another wave of crying; surely not the first person to ever do it in this chapel, wiping off my tears and snot with my bandaged arm.

No. Don't go there. Again.

Who was the monster in this nightmare? I needed Skip to tell me.

I needed everything else to disappear, except for the monster and the good guy, so I could just focus. And think. And find Skip.

It wasn't Mark Casey who'd taken her, that was for sure. He'd been my monster but not Skip's. He was like the stained glass windows in here. *Macula hyalus fenestra,* in Latin. *Fenestra* meant window, like the thing in a wall, but also opportunity, breach, loophole. *Macula* was stained, but not really in a color sense. More like your moral character: pollute, dishonor, taint. Scandal. Fuck up. That was Mark Casey in two words: a fuck up, and he was dead because of it. For years now. That's why I'd never mentioned him to Mizell.

"He's dead, and you didn't think that's . . . " she had snapped at me in Wendy's hospital room, just minutes ago.

"A lot of people I know are dead. That's why I know they're not suspects. So instead of focusing on everybody it can't be, can we please for the love of fucking God focus on who it could be?"

"Janice Miner," she'd said, as she left the hospital to go back to the station. "That's our deal. You tell me the truth, and I tell you. For the love of fucking God."

But if it wasn't Casey then who was it? Who wanted to hurt me so badly that they were taking revenge on me like this? Sig and I had been trying to figure it out—coming up with all those lists of enemies that Mizell wanted—but nobody fit the bill. Guys I beat out, sure, but nobody who was violent, other than Casey.

And my father, but he didn't count either; he was dead too, after nearly killing me in order to turn me into a champ. He hadn't made it in his day, to the winners' platform, so I was his last, best hope. His only child. I was naturally athletic, born with that gift, and my father pushed it as far as he could. Maybe he saw dollar signs in it, if I made it big, after not making much money himself. All I'd ever done was exercise and practice and get pushed by him to win. That was his church, winning, and he taught me to worship there. He'd made me a believer. One Sunday at our house, my father pushing me on—no rest, working out, seven days a week—he wouldn't give me water, until I got through two hundred fifty pushups. I looked up through the sweat and sting in my eyes and said to him, "My Father, why hast thou forsaken me?"

He didn't think it was funny. I didn't either. I meant every word of it.

I started picturing a monster in my head, to make me run faster. A monster that would scare me more than my own father, although he'd be hard to beat. If I could only imagine someone worse than him, chasing me; something I'd have to outrun.

Fire. That was it. Flames, chasing me.

So one drunken night, I went out and got two tattoos: a flame, on each ankle. I thought if I could look back at my legs when I was running and actually see myself *burning*—my legs on fire, starting at my ankles—then I would run even faster, to escape being burned alive.

It hurt like hell getting the tattoos put on, but my father saw them and said they weren't nearly enough.

Why just imagine? he said.

Son of a bitch. Bastard.

He took out his old-fashioned, fake gold cigarette lighter, clicked it on—a spark, that intoxicating smell of butane—and moved it toward my ankles, while he sat on my thighs to hold me down. He said actually *feeling* the fire would truly make me a champion.

If I didn't have the fire in my belly, like he did for me, at least I could have it on my skin.

The tattoo guy had missed so much: he just used orange and red on my ankles, but as my father briefly held the lighter in front of my face, I saw that fire had so many other colors: not just orange and red, but blue and purple and yellow and even green.

My father got closer and closer to the tattoos—I could feel the heat from that one little flame, as I squirmed to get away—then he suddenly changed course and held the lighter to his own ankles. First his left, then his right.

"Look at me," he commanded, his lips going white he was biting down on them so hard, to keep from showing any pain. He never looked at his ankles, just at me, as I literally heard the crisping of hair on his legs, and smelled something like singed rubber.

"Dad, no . . ."

The grimace on his lips turned into a leer as he just as suddenly clicked the lighter closed and stood up, unsteady on his feet. He tossed the lighter to me—maybe *at* me was more his intention—and I missed. The first and only toss of my life that I missed.

"Miss at the Olympics, and I *will* set you on fire."

My Father, why hast thou forsaken me indeed?

My mother told me to pray for him; that was her solution to everything: pray, and do good works. She cowered in their bedroom, a slew of unexplained illnesses and depressions. The only time her eyes came alive is when she'd drag me to church—a real church, not the gym. She'd get her Bible out and look up passages that she thought told her she had to stay subservient. She always found the answer she needed in her Bible, no matter how she had to twist things to see it. And despite being on the fence about my own belief, her Bible is one of the few things I took from their house, after they died. You just can't throw away a Bible, or give it to Goodwill. Skip looked at it sometimes; it was the only Bible in the house, but . . .

Wait. A chapel. A Bible . . .

The story of Daniel and the Lions' Den. What if . . . I'd thought the poem from the kidnapper was just about the rhyme scheme—*Lions' Den rhymes with your girlfriend, Wen*—but what if it was about more than that? What if he had actually meant something about *Daniel? From the Bible?* What if I just hadn't worked out the clue completely? It was like a translation in Latin; everything there had a purpose. Nothing was extraneous, or left out. Everything mattered. What if *Daniel* mattered too? What if the thing I was supposed to finish figuring out—maybe even do next—was actually in this room with me?

Rummaging around, I found a Bible up front behind a speaker's stand and started flipping through to the book of Daniel. I didn't remember the details—I was working out on Sundays, not going to church—but I knew it had some kind of happy ending. Daniel came out alive. The words he said in the cave, or the power of his prayer . . . *something* he did silenced those lions and shut their hungry jaws.

Just like what Mizell had done, to save me.

I flew over the tiny print on the delicate, paper-thin pages— something so old-fashioned, for such a modern version of the Bible—until I got to the part where Daniel was interpreting the dream that the evil King Nebuchadnezzar had.

You looked, and you saw a large image. This big image was in front of you. It was very bright and it frightened people. The image's head was pure gold. Its upper body and arms were silver. Its lower body was bronze. Its legs were iron and its feet were partly iron and partly clay. As you looked, someone cut out a stone. But no human hand did this. The stone hit the image on its iron and clay feet and broke them into pieces. They became like powder. The wind blew them away, until nobody could see them.

There it was, in black and white. In print. The story of my life, same as the dream of Nebuchadnezzar: I'd worshipped an idol made of precious metals, the most precious at the head. Gold. That's what I'd dreamed for, trained for, sacrificed everything for: gold, when my feet were really made of clay.

Somebody knew. Somebody knew what I had done and they were going to punish me for it, through Skip. And if I didn't do what they wanted, they were going to kill her.

For if you do, it's little Skip's life; only question is, bullet or knife?

CHAPTER EIGHTEEN

Skip had tried to come up with a way of keeping track of time, but she had no idea when an hour even ended. Before this, she would have thought she could. Sitting in class, she could feel every minute tick by; she could sense when the bell was about to ring. But in this room, tied up, just waking up from being shocked, everything was off-kilter. The volts were like the Taser sting at her house, when they first took her, but a million times worse; she didn't know how long she had been passed out, only that everything hurt when she came to. Her body still felt like it was buzzing, and her tears were coming out in short spurts, as if the flow of them had been interrupted by the current, but the cutoff switch she had for them in her brain had melted: she couldn't turn them off. She couldn't stop crying. Maybe because it just hurt so much.

Her friend Adelaide had epilepsy, and once she had a seizure in front of the whole class. She kicked and bucked so much one of her shoes went flying off. Afterwards, she was embarrassed; she just lay on the floor of their classroom and cried, and sort of curled in on herself; she told the teacher she didn't want an ambulance, which the teacher had already called; she just wanted to go home. Adelaide said it felt like getting jolts of electricity in her brain, jolts that traveled all the way down to her toes. Skip secretly wanted to have one, a seizure, just to see what it felt like, and now she had. She didn't want to have one again.

She was sorry she ever thought it would be fun to have a seizure. If she ever got out, she'd apologize to Adelaide; confess to her about how she'd wanted one, but now she knew it wasn't any fun, and then she'd . . . she'd what?

She couldn't think anymore. Her head hurt, like the worst headache ever. Maybe the electricity had wiped out her memory. She'd heard it did things like that.

She had to get away, whatever it took. He was going to shock her again, and worse. She didn't want to die, tied up like this, all messy and dirty and terrified and full of electricity.

Maybe if she had a "biological clock"—she'd heard about it but didn't know if she was old enough to have one yet—it would have told her how much time she'd been here, but it didn't. But she could still tell a lot, even with the folds of gauze around her eyes. She could see it was dark, or at least it felt that way, but with it getting dark so early now, even her sense of nightfall was screwed up. But she felt it, somehow—the room cooling off a little bit, like the sun had gone down. She couldn't hear much, but if she got extra quiet, if she tamped down her panic and slowed her breathing as much as she could, she thought maybe she could hear a difference outside. Like things were settling down for the night?

It was the start of her second night. She had figured out that much.

And there was a third person. She'd figured that out too. There was just too much going on, for the main kidnapper and the other man whose voice she'd heard. They'd tried to feed her, but she had resisted, afraid of what might be in the food, so it was surprising she'd still gone to the bathroom three times. That was a number she could keep track of, but it was only the last time that he—or they, it seemed like more than one person—let her go into a regular bathroom, instead of just squatting over a pot. They kept her hands tied behind her back, and her blindfold on, so she had to back into the seat and feel it with her legs. Pulling from the back of her jeans, with her tied-up hands behind her, she got her pants down by herself. She didn't know if anybody was looking at her, but she thought somebody was, and she couldn't go.

"I thought you had to go."

"I can't, not with you looking. Not with anybody looking."

She meant it, but she also said it to get an answer, to see how many people were there. She'd felt hands lift her up, off the desk she'd been tied to, but she was too hungry and dizzy to tell if it was one person or two. One on each side, or just the one big one, the one who didn't have any trouble getting his breath, picking her up from behind?

She knew the man she'd talked to the most wasn't looking at her; she could hear his voice heading away from her, not toward her. Only then could she finally let herself go. But she couldn't wipe, and she didn't want anyone else to do it to her, so she said "I'm done." She felt with her elbows to flush the commode. No one touched her where they weren't supposed to.

The same hands—one pair, two?—moved her back to the school desk, and taped her back in. Not her ankles anymore; her feet were free, she could stretch them out. She'd heard about something called "economy class syndrome" on an airplane, where you got a blood clot if you sat cramped up in your seat and didn't move around and stretch your feet enough, so she lifted them out and flexed them, to get the blood moving. She'd seen it on *Good Morning America* when she got dressed for school one day.

"They die on airplanes, you know," she said out loud, to see if anyone would answer her back. "You come back from flying across the ocean and you've been all cramped up in coach but you don't think anything's wrong and then 'Bam!' You're rolling your suitcase to the taxi stand and you're dead all of a sudden and nobody knows what happened. Not until they give you an autopsy and find out you had a blood clot or something."

She wanted to hear them say something, and they did. *He* did. The main one.

"I've often wondered how they. Sent your father. To the Olympics. Coach? First class? Charter?"

Was he aware of it, that if he broke his thoughts up into questions he could talk easier? Skip thought it would be hard to talk like that, to have to think at the same time you were saying something.

"I've thought a lot. About the Olympics. What they were like. But I've never thought. About that. And how did his. Parents afford to go? They were poor. You know."

"How did you know that? About his parents . . . I mean, my grandparents. I never knew them, I mean, not really. I was just little when they died. But I've seen pictures of them."

It was as if he hadn't heard her, lost in his own thoughts. "No, I think he must have. Traveled . . . " He took a deep breath, filling up his lungs. She could tell he was embarrassed—at least aware—at having to do it. " . . . with the rest. That movie—*Alive*. A soccer team. They crashed. They had to eat. Each other. To survive. In the Andes."

Then he laughed. Or maybe he was just clearing his throat. Skip couldn't tell. When he said something next, he was closer to her. How did he get so close? He was leaning in to her; she instinctively backed up in her school desk, to get as far away from him as she could, afraid he was going to put that headphone thing on her head again. She tried to make herself shrink in the seat; become as small a target as possible. Her bound hands were dangling loose behind the seat; she tried to grab onto the flat surface of the back of the desk, the part where you'd put your schoolbooks, to give her something to steady herself with.

And that's when she felt it. A knob. Some kind of screw. Something that stuck out.

Something she could try to cut the duct tape on her hands with.

"Does he talk? About the Olympics?"

She shrank further down, careful to keep her hands as still as possible, so he couldn't see them moving. She had to play like nothing had changed.

"Will you be. In the Olympics? Is he . . . passing that on?"

Did he really want to know, or was he just testing her somehow? She could tell he was smart. In class, she could tell who was smart by who did their homework and raised their hands, but with him, she just knew, without being able to see any of that stuff. With smart people, there's always a reason they ask stuff. There's a reason they do everything. They already know the answer; they're just waiting to see if you know the same one they do. Skip was afraid if she didn't answer his questions, he'd get mad and hurt her even worse.

First the slap, then the shock. Who knew what he'd do next. Each one was getting worse.

She decided she had to talk, for now. If she talked, maybe she wouldn't cry.

If she talked, and he looked at her mouth moving, then he wouldn't see that she was doing something with her hands behind the desk.

"He doesn't want me to. We run together, but it's not fast. It's just for fun. And I get out of PE if I do it." She stopped, but he didn't say anything. Where was he? She could only tell from his voice. Had he moved behind her? Had he seen the new weapon she'd just discovered, that had been there the whole time? Her way out? She had to keep talking, to distract him.

"He says it was too hard. That's why he quit, he couldn't keep doing it. He says he was already too old, and he was just twenty-six."

"I saw him, you know. On TV. Everybody did. The Olympics. They're not just sports"—a breath—"they're stories. Dramas. Overcoming the odds. Crashing on mountains. Eating your teammates. That's what gets you in the news. This will certainly. Get *him* in the news. *Back* in it."

Good. He was still in front of her. He hadn't moved.

She gripped her thumb and finger tighter around the screw. It had ridges on it, threads, and it stuck out about half an inch from the wood of the desk chair. She was afraid if she shifted to get a better hold of the screw, her knuckles would hit against the chair and he'd hear it.

She talked louder, to hide any noise her hands might make.

"I don't think he wanted to be in the news. I think that's why he quit."

"Quitting is for. Losers. You can't quit. You have to keep going. No matter what. Why, just look at me . . . " He laughed. "Oops. I guess you can't, with your blindfold on."

He was moving away from her now, looking at something else. At least he wasn't moving behind her. She put all her hopes on that little half inch of screw now. As long as it was there, as long as she could hold on to it, she'd be okay. As long as it was there, she had hope.

"I'll take it off soon enough. Your blindfold. Then you'll see my art. All good things to those who wait. Except food. I don't want you to go hungry."

She heard another sound, the clatter of a tray and silverware. The familiar sound she used to hear from her father, when she was little, and he made the oatmeal after her mother died but made it too hot. Rubbing a spoon against the rim of a bowl for just the right amount, then blowing on the food to cool it off.

Skip felt the metal tip of the spoon push against her mouth, trying to pry it open.

"Stew. An old family recipe."

She didn't want to eat, even though she hadn't had anything except water, but she was starving and hunger took over. She didn't want to sit up and move her torso closer to the food, move her hands away from the screw so that she might not be able to find it again, but . . .

She ate. Everything. It tasted almost familiar, like something her father would make her when she was upset, or needed comfort food or stayed home from school. Tomatoey. Thick. Sausage and a dash of balsamic vinegar for an extra kick. She slurped up every offering of it from the kidnapper's spoon, and when some trickled out of her mouth, he wiped up the dribble on her chin. At least she wouldn't die that way, starving to death. And the soup was good.

"Nectar of the gods," he said, giving her the next spoonful.

CHAPTER NINETEEN

Whenever you were hungry but didn't have the money to eat, Cousin Charlie's, a deli on the main drag in town, was the place to go. All the famous people who came through town—as famous as Mt. Gresh ever had—got a sandwich named after them, made up of their favorite ingredients. Ethan even got his own, when he joined the faculty. The "Herc Hero." Beef and horseradish. Swiss cheese and spicy mustard.

"Charlie"—nobody knew if that was his real name or not, that's just what everybody called him—even let you run a tab if you were short. He'd been the first person to put together a sandwich platter with sides of coleslaw and pickles to send to Ethan's house, after he heard the news. And now he offered free food and coffee to the students handing out the flyers about Skip, before they even had to ask.

The middle of November, it was already dark by the time TJ and the class of Ethan's that he'd taken over could meet. Most of the shops on Brockett Street, just a few blocks from campus, were beginning to close, and anybody who was out on the street was in a hurry to get home. Maybe not the best time to hand out flyers for Skip—it was cold, fingers were stiff and dry, you didn't have the friction and oil on your fingertips to peel the flyers apart, one by one—but this was all they had. It would have to do.

TJ could see his own breath, coming out of his mouth. He hugged his jacket around him, hands in the pockets.

Last year, he'd had a boyfriend from the theater department. Rodger, with a *d*. His first boyfriend. His only boyfriend. They weren't together long, just a few months, but TJ went to see all his shows. He was in some original play about George Washington crossing the Delaware—*The Marble Horseman*; Rodger called it

"*Marble Horseshit*"—playing one of the soldiers camped out on shore, in the fog. The soldiers were all dressed in rags and had to look like they were freezing to death; Rodger really did. TJ was convinced he saw the breath coming out of his mouth, up on stage, even with all those hot lights on him. Rodger hugged his arms around his chest above a fake campfire, and took on this hollow look, like he'd never get warm. After the play, when TJ asked him how he did that, when everybody else on stage just looked so fake, Rodger said, "I just studied you. In bed. You always look like there's a bag of ice strapped to your chest. You're always shaking." They broke up after that, and TJ had been too afraid to sleep with anybody since. He didn't want anyone else to see him shaking.

Now, TJ tried to burrow even further into his coat so no one out on the street would see him shaking there, either. But even inside the coat, his arms wrapped around himself, like he'd seen Rodger do on stage, TJ could still feel goose bumps. Still felt freezing, with nerves. He breathed into the fake fleece collar so his breath would come back to him and he could smell how it bad it was. Ripe, that's how bad, after half a tuna grinder and coffee. He'd grab a peppermint off the counter inside Charlie's later; it was time to get started.

"Okay, two or three of you take Old Campus . . . somebody hit the Commons . . . if anybody has a car, take some of these down by The British Maid . . . "

Another breath, and it was time. TJ was as nervous as he'd been teaching that afternoon. He whispered "Passing on the past" to himself—what Professor Holt always said—and with that, stuck a flyer in someone's face. "Have you seen this girl? She's the daughter of a local professor, Herc Holt, from the Olympics . . . "

CHAPTER TWENTY

A full twelve hours since the first call, and nothing. Not unless that Bible verse from the Book of Daniel told me what I was supposed to do next. I kept thinking if I just focused on Skip's room, I'd see something the police had missed, but there was barely anything left in the room. The police had taken away her mattress and box springs, leaving just the big empty metal frame. They'd taken her beanbag chair, too, so that I had to sit on the floor, my back braced against the wall. There was nowhere else to sit in here. Even her giant stuffed giraffe; they'd taken that too. They'd have my gold medal if I hadn't grabbed it away when that cop had it on.

Now, I kept tossing it in my hand, looking from it to the Bible verse that I'd torn out at the hospital. "*The image's head was pure gold. Its upper body and arms were silver. Its lower body was bronze.*" Top to bottom, gold, silver, bronze. First place, second, third. I'd told Mizell about the verse, and the parallel to the Olympics I'd discovered, and she and Sig were downstairs on computers, trying to track down those other two winners. One was from Johannesburg, taller than me, massive thighs; the other from Russia. With even bigger thighs. Yvgeny. He's the one who'd been predicted as the winner, before the Games started. He was actually pretty friendly, for someone who could crush me by just looking at me.

Mizell and Sig were having a hard time finding out anything, even though with that first call from the kidnapper, Mizell had finally been able to get the FBI involved. A team was driving up from the regional office in Boston, and maybe they had some pull with Interpol, to look into those other countries. But the idea that it was one of them . . . it just seemed so preposterous. Why let thirteen years go by, and only now strike? But Olympians were used to that; training for years—waiting—for a goal that would be attained in just a few days. If ever.

If somebody had taken that medal away from me, a medal I had lost blood, sweat, and tears working for, could I get back at them like this?

I was afraid to think of what my honest answer would be.

I didn't have to—not then—because they were suddenly yelling at me to come downstairs.

TJ had just run through the front door, throwing it open so fast they must have all thought it was the kidnapper, ramrodding in to take all of us. I got to the landing as he seemed to take his first breath; his face was red and flushed; even feet away from him, he smelled like sweat, cold sweat, and the outdoors.

"Stop right there," Mizell was saying to him, as he tried to race past her to get to me.

"It's okay, it's my TA. Teaching assistant. TJ Markson," I said, as I came down and he stuck a piece of paper in my hand. "What? What is it?"

"We were handing out flyers, down by Charlie's. It was dark, all these people were going by . . . I charged the flyers to the department account, I hope that's okay, but I didn't have any money and . . . "

"TJ. Short answer. Focus," I snapped, even as I was looking at the photo of Skip and those telltale words underneath her face: HAVE YOU SEEN THIS GIRL?

"I don't know how I got it or who gave it to me, maybe when I dropped all my flyers then bent down to pick them up, but . . . "

"Tell me."

He flipped the sheet over to its backside, where it was covered with a handwritten scrawl. He was poking at it so hard I couldn't focus on the words.

"This. *This.* I went inside Charlie's to get some more coffee, like I needed any more of *that*, and then . . . *this.*"

He stopped as my voice took over, smoothing out the paper and reading aloud what had been written on the back of my daughter's smiling face.

One is done, now two is due.
Whose head grows back if you give it a whack?
Find that reed, or watch her bleed.
Even the score with ten more.
Then post it on Facebook, to get what I took.

Everything that, until now, had just been slow motion and *waiting*, suddenly screeched into place. In my head, I raced past the blood, the head that'd been whacked, *Skip's* head, the Olympics, the gold, that horrible nickname, and saw that everything had been leading to this.

"The *Hydra*," I said, looking straight at TJ, knowing he'd understand. "The Hydra grows its head back 'if you give it a whack.'"

"What the fuck are you talking about?" said Mizell.

"Oh my God," I said, "it all makes sense now. The Hydra. Killing the Hydra. That's the Second Labor of Hercules. 'One is done, now two is due.' One was the lion . . . "

"The Nemean Lion," TJ jumped in, catching on. Two nerds, a little one and a big one, speaking a foreign language together. One only they understood. "It's the First Labor of Hercules. First, second . . . Then 'even the score with ten more.'"

Now I took over. "That's twelve . . . the Twelve Labors . . . that's the ransom. He's making me do the Twelve Labors of Hercules to get my daughter back."

CHAPTER TWENTY-ONE

The kidnapper first learned about the Labors back at the home, to take away the pain.

They tried to get him to walk, but he couldn't. Not without crutches to hold him up and braces on his legs, and even then, his legs turned in on themselves: knees inverted toward each other, his back bent over and his elbows held out to his sides, almost like wings, to balance his legs. A rare type of muscular dystrophy. The doctors had done all they could, but the man who ran the home—Mr. Frank, the boys turned it into Frankenstein; it was really too easy, almost a *gimme*—said his staff hadn't done enough. They hadn't tried hard enough. They needed to know if the boy felt something, anything, in his legs, so that's when the needles began. The pin pricks. First on his calves, then up the back of his thighs, then his butt. He felt them, but he still couldn't walk on his own. Frankenstein said he was just being lazy, he wasn't trying hard enough. His brain clearly worked, he was one of the smartest boys in the home, so why couldn't his brain transmit the signals to his legs?

If they didn't work on his legs, try his spine. If little needles didn't work, use bigger ones.

After the sessions, the youngest nurse at the home put salve on his wounds and blotted up the blood, but she was new and couldn't speak up or she'd lose her job. He couldn't speak up much either because he was usually crying too hard. And words came late to him. He could read them, but he had a hard time saying them. So the young nurse he loved so much, Marie, his Mamarie, because she was more like a mother than a nurse, helped him learn to talk better by making up rhymes for him to say back to her. If he focused on the words and stories she told him, it would give him something else to think about, besides the pain of the needles. Besides the pain of not being able to get two whole lungs full of air. The pain of the words not coming out in person, like he heard them in his head. The pain of his *family*, leaving him there, not coming out in person either.

If he thought in rhymes, which took even more concentration, he'd be even further away from his pain. *Make up poems about Hercules, the strongest man ever*, Mamarie told him. *Be brave and strong like Hercules, and nothing can ever hurt you again. He'll be your friend. Hercules will protect you.*

Then the next session came.

Frankenstein tickled the soles of his feet, getting warmed up.

So was the little boy, who couldn't walk, who could barely talk, except to himself and his Mamarie. He started out by just saying the rhymes in his head. Thinking them, to himself, every time Frankenstein touched him.

Be fi-ne, slay li-on . . .

Frankenstein went to his ankles, to see how the protruding bones reacted.

Wear Lycra, beat Hydra . . .

The little boy tightened his ass, even though Frankenstein was nowhere near it yet. He was still pricking his calves.

Capture hind, won't hurt behind . . .

When Frankenstein got to the crook behind his knees, the little boy started mumbling to himself. The sounds started to come out of his head, onto his lips. He knew the worst was yet to come.

Roar, catch boar . . .

Frankenstein was getting closer, to the back of the little boy's thighs; there was more flesh there, so he stuck the needle in farther.

Not a fable, go to stable . . .

Frankenstein didn't understand what the little boy was saying— the words were audible, but it was the meaning that threw him. He jabbed the needles in even harder. Farther.

The little boy spoke back in kind, his voice gathering strength, and the pain receding even more, as he disappeared into his rhymes. Into his stories of Hercules and his labors.

Love words, not birds . . .

His ass was the target now; Frankenstein would really go to town there.

Have school, hunt bull . . .

"What did you say? *Bullshit?*" Frankenstein slapped him, hard, on the butt.

The boy screamed out a new series of words.

Bring out forces, rein in horses . . .

Then to the small of his back. That was unexplored territory. Frankenstein had never prodded him there before.

In the Labors, in his mind, the boy had just gotten to the belt of the Amazon queen. He imagined Frankenstein's hands were a belt, squeezing him around the waist.

Won't leave a welt, her beautiful belt . . .

"There's something wrong with your spine. If we could only straighten out your spine."

Frankenstein tried to.

It hurt the boy so much, so he said even more words.

Escape I'll tattle, so better count cattle . . .

The rhymes were coming more easily now, but the boy was having to scream them, because the pain was getting so much worse. His spine *could* feel things, even if his legs couldn't. Frankenstein started jabbing in the needles, anywhere he could. The boy screamed out words, any words, just to try to block the pain. Nonsense words, for nonsense cures.

Visit chapels, steal those apples . . .

Frankenstein switched to a different needle now, one with medicine in it, medicine that would make the boy pass out. He jabbed it into a vein in the boy's neck, so he would close his eyes faster. So Frankenstein could do more damage, after the boy was asleep.

That's when the boy let out his very last rhyme, to say he had won, no matter what Frankenstein did to him.

The pain hadn't touched him, and never would, as long as he had his rhymes.

If you want to tame Cerberus, God will preserve us.

It's the last thing the boy remembered saying, as his eyes closed, and his tormentor climbed on top of him.

CHAPTER TWENTY-TWO

"Just think. Concentrate. Close your eyes and . . . you've got to remember *something* about him. You were here and he . . . where was he?"

I was at Cousin Charlie's with TJ, going over the sidewalk outside as if it were a crime scene. Mizell had already been here, hoping to find out that some of the stores had security cameras, but no such luck. She'd gone back to the station with the flyer that the poem was on, for her team to see if they could pick up any fingerprints or trace from it. But I couldn't just sit still, so I'd come downtown with TJ to see for myself. It was my daughter: my eyes would be sharper.

But no, it was still just Brockett Street, still the street I walked down every day near campus. The fancy men's store that was more for the parents who came to visit than for the students. Funny golf pants. Cuff links. IZOD shirts and monogrammed sweatshirts. The art house cinema, its lit marquee just now shutting off for the night, even as the light inside the pizza parlor seemed to get even brighter and more fluorescent, luring late-night studiers with its smells. Every time the door opened, a potent blend of grease, garlic, and oregano filled the street. And then The Purple Pup, one dangling purple light bulb over its door, pulling in students who wanted to pretend-slum, side by side with the real-life drunks and never-left, never-graduated kids who just hung on.

At the crest of the street, where Brockett intersected with the main thruway that went through town, was that triangle of grass with the concrete bench on it. A boy and girl were sitting on it, laughing. A little nervous, nudging close, teasing. How many times had I seen that on campus: first love in bloom? *Who's going to make the first move? Are we going to sleep together?* How many times had I wished I could go back there, and fall in love with Patti all over again? I was half dreading, half looking forward to talking to Skip about something like that, when she was really in love for the first time, and . . .

Normal life, in a small, affluent college town, where girls didn't get snatched out of their homes.

Until they did.

"Are you *sure* you don't remember . . . "

"I'm sorry. I really am. But . . . nothing." TJ's eyes were shining, like he was about to cry. He'd make up an answer if it made me happy, but he had nothing to say. "I didn't notice what was written on the back of the flyer until I went inside, and by then, he was already gone. Whoever it was."

But I couldn't let TJ go. He was the missing link, the only link. Mizell had already grilled him, and now it was my turn. I grabbed him, pleading.

"So now what you're saying is that we just track down a Hydra and cut its fucking head off . . . "

"*I'm* not saying it. *He* is. The *note* is."

We went inside Charlie's with our copy of it. There was nothing more out here for us, but there was something on that note to figure out. I just had to look at it like I had the book of Daniel, in the chapel. I had to work over it, like a Latin translation. It was all there. I knew. He was giving me clues.

I just had to figure it out, where it was pointing us to next.

Charlie kept the place open until two in the morning; it was the campus hangout, for late-night study breaks. Charlie took us to a booth. "I'm praying for Skip. I'm gonna name a sandwich after her. The Skip Special, something strong and spicy. Keep her name out there."

"Thanks, Charlie. Appreciate the food you sent over, too."

"Anything I can do. Anything. You want something to eat? On the house. Just name it. A Herc Hero? Gotta keep up your strength."

"That'd be great, Charlie. Thanks." I said it to give him something to do. I didn't think I could ever eat again.

From where we sat in a booth in the back, I saw one of the Skip flyers that somebody had taped to the front door, only now, through the pane of glass, I saw the big bold words in reverse:

?LRIG SIHT NEES UOY EVAH

It was a foreign language, Kidnapper instead of Latin. Same as the rhyme in front of us.

"So what do we do now?" I asked. "The Hydra's a mythological creature. It doesn't exist."

"He thinks it does," TJ said, in TA mode. "Somehow. Just like the lion. He wouldn't send you on things you couldn't do."

"He's crazy. He'd do anything."

Charlie plopped down a plate and coffees on the table.

"Maybe it's so obvious, we're missing something. Why the Labors? Is it just that damn nickname?" I asked, almost talking to myself, after Charlie left. Maybe I needed to go back to the very beginning. Not just solve the puzzle in front of me, but why the kidnapper was sending the puzzles. Why somebody I'd kept waiting was only now springing into action.

"How'd you get it, anyway?" TJ said, grabbing half my sandwich. He wolfed it down, student-starving fashion. "'Herc' Holt. That's what they called you, wasn't it?"

I gave him a "not you, too" look. "For about fifteen minutes for a bunch of headlines and that stupid book. I wish Casey had never started the damn thing."

"Who?"

"A guy on the team. Mark Casey. It was a joke, but I went along with it. Nobody calls me that anymore."

"But *he* calls you that. *The* guy. He thinks you *are* Hercules. Why else pick the Labors? You've gotta start thinking like him."

Maybe TJ had a point. "So talk it out. Hercules 101."

"Well, he's a god. At least a half god. Father Zeus, the mightiest of the mighty, but a mortal mother. Alcmene."

"That blows the whole thing to smithereens before we even get started. My father was the least godly person ever . . . "

"I can relate," TJ said, for once looking me straight in the eye. Then he grabbed a pen and started taking notes on his placemat, like the face-to-face contact had been too much. "Okay. So family tree. Zeus, Alcmene, a half-brother from her, the Labors, he romances all these women, has tons of children . . . "

"Well, that leaves me out too. I grew up alone. Just me. And I just have one kid. Skip. And he's got her."

"But could it be a woman who's got her? Someone you romanced once and dumped?"

"No. We heard the voice on the phone. It was a man. Besides, I hardly ever dated. And nobody serious after I met Patti."

It was the most I'd ever said about my personal life to TJ. To any student. "Let's get back to the Labors. That's what he's having us do. Hercules has to do the Labors because . . . "

"Punishment," TJ jumped in, adding to his notes. "He's forced by the Oracle to atone for killing his children . . . "

" . . . whom he's killed in a fit of madness . . . "

" . . . so the gods make him purify himself. To atone."

I pointed at our copy of the riddle. "But that's where it all falls apart. *Again.* Maybe this whack job *thinks* I'm Hercules but . . . I never killed anybody . . . I never killed my kids . . . my kid. I've never gone crazy."

"So he blows everything out of proportion . . . he exaggerates, he uses metaphor . . . "

"I guess you could say I *did* go mad, nuts, after Patti died, but . . . I went crazy to win the Olympics, to push my body through that kind of pain. But how could he know that? He'd have to have been there. Or when Patti died . . . I didn't hurt anybody. I wanted to, I wanted to hurt everybody. I wanted to hurt God. Not Skip, though . . . I'd never hurt my child."

"Who *have* you hurt, then?"

"This is ridiculous. I've never hurt anybody," I said to TJ. We were wasting time. "You keep track of all the mistakes you've made? All the . . . the . . . stupid stuff you've done that maybe pissed somebody off? When you don't even know about half of it, it's just in somebody else's head?"

I turned away from facing TJ. In the long rectangular opening into the kitchen, meals were sitting out under orange counter lights to keep them warm. The orange, sulfurous glow of Hell, that's what it looked like to me. And bizarrely, it looked comfortable. Welcoming. I wanted fire, just like I had when I had those dumb tattoos put on my ankles. I wanted to hurt, to feel something greater than this pain.

"What's the worst thing you've ever done?" TJ wouldn't let it go. "To make somebody hurt you this bad . . . "

I didn't like this game anymore. "I wanna get outta here. I'm going to the police station."

"I'm just trying to think the way he does," TJ said, looking down quickly. Embarrassed.

"Then you're in the wrong department. We study old things. Dead things. Things that can't hurt us."

But that wasn't really true. The classics were *all* about people getting hurt, and hurting others in return. Vengeful gods. Wars. Sacrifice. I took a sip from my coffee; it was bottom-of-the-pot stuff, burned, oily streaks floating on top.

"Okay. You wanna play games? Then let's play. The worst thing I've ever done? It was a day ago. Not being there for Skip when she needed me. Doing my stupid run when I could have been there, keeping *him* from getting inside. You want more? Five years ago.

Letting my wife drive the car that day, when it was so icy. More? Thirteen years ago. The Goddamn Olympics. Letting . . . never mind."

"*What*." TJ didn't ask it like a question. "What about them?"

I looked back at that orange glow coming from the kitchen. The hell I'd put myself through. "Winning. It was all I cared about. It's what my father wanted. He'd turned me into this . . . this machine, from the time I was a kid. I couldn't let him down. That's what all that book of Daniel stuff was about. Winning. False idols. Precious metals. Gold. Whatever it took."

Now I was the one looking down at my food, as embarrassed as TJ had just been.

"None of it matters anyway. He's nuts. That's all there is to it. Crazy people do crazy things. No more, no less. Let's get outta here. You should go home and get some sleep. You've gotta take my class in the morning."

"I don't mind staying. I never sleep anyway."

"No, I'm good. And take the other half of the sandwich."

He pounced on it as he stood up, not needing to be asked twice. "Call me on my cell if you find anything. I'll be at the gym after class."

"The gym? That's a first."

He shrugged. "Maybe I'll be like you one day. Strong." He pushed his long fingers through his hair and then stumbled out. "Just remember. It's something you did. Something he *thinks* you did. In his mind, he isn't doing anything wrong."

And with that bizarre bit of armchair psychology, he started heading out as I called out to him one last time.

"Hey, since I spilled the beans . . . Your turn," I dared TJ. He'd pissed me off with that last thing he'd said. "What's the worst thing *you* ever did?"

TJ paused—not even turning back to look at me—and said, "Scies satis." Then left. So fast, I'm not sure I even heard him correctly.

Scies satis. You'll find out soon enough.

For just a few seconds, when he was swinging open the front door, I saw Skip's flyer from in front, like it was supposed to be seen. My daughter's face, and those words, now back in terrifying English: "HAVE YOU SEEN THIS GIRL?"

I whispered a question that was more like a prayer—*Skippy, where are you?*—then went back to the rhyme, the question it was asking no easier to answer. "If I were a Hydra, where would I hide?"

"The Biosphere."

I looked up; a science geek was looking back at me, from way down the aisle. "The Biosphere."

"What? I'm sorry . . . "

"The Biosphere. That new science building. They've got tanks and tanks of 'em."

"I'm sorry . . . my mind is sorta . . . "

"Yeah, mine too. Midterm tomorrow." He opened a science textbook to a diagram and read from the caption underneath. "'Hydra: any of a group of small, soft-bodied, freshwater polyps with a tube-like body and a mouth surrounded by tentacles. Also known as thin reeds.'"

I looked back at the poem, its letters floating around as much as the images in my head:

Whose head grows back if you give it a whack?
Find that reed, or watch her bleed.

CHAPTER TWENTY-THREE

"It's time to. Get you ready. Let you. See. Again."

Hearing the kidnapper say that scared Skip more than the thought of him touching her. Ready for what? *See* what? She didn't want to see anything. If she did, didn't that mean he'd have to kill her, if she could identify him? Her eyes hurt, and her head did too because she'd been in the dark for so long, but still, she was too afraid to pretend she was asleep, or that she didn't hear him.

"No, no, I don't care . . . I don't wanna see . . . I'm used to this now. Please. It's okay. Keep the blindfold on."

But he didn't listen. She felt him behind her, his long thin fingers brushing against the back of her head and the nape of her neck as he fiddled with the knot of gauze at the back of her head.

"Please. No."

With him behind the desk she was tied to, Skip was afraid he'd see how she'd been sawing away at the duct tape that held her hands together. It had been slow going: to get close enough to the little bit of screw that poked out, she had to curve her wrists in such a way that it was agonizing. She couldn't hold them in that position for too long—the ache went all the way up to her shoulders— before she had to take a break, and since she couldn't see what she was doing, she cut into the flesh of her arms more than the weave of the tape. She felt the sticky blood on her wrists, mixing with the adhesive of the tape; the white-blond, almost invisible hairs on her arm got stuck to it, and kept pulling out, every time she got more of the tape cut away. At least now she could flex her wrists out a little more, but she could feel that he'd wrapped three or four layers of tape around them, so it was going to take forever. And who knew if blood from her wrist was dripping onto the floor behind her; he'd see that before he saw what she was doing.

Please God, please, don't let him see don'tlethimseedon'tlethimsee . . .

The first layer of gauze fell on the bridge of her nose, and all she could think was how much it tickled. She scrunched up her face, and he unwrapped the rest of the blindfold. She winced again, feeling some hair come off with it. She thought maybe her scalp was bleeding too, just like her wrists.

Skip had once heard the phrase "the scales fell from his eyes"— maybe it was at church?—and it had terrified her. She got this picture in her head of bits and pieces of eyes falling off somebody's face, or like your eyeballs had fish scales on them or something. That's what she thought of now, as darkness gave way to the light of the room, and her blindfold was suddenly gone. She blinked her eyes to wake them up, as he put her glasses back on her and began talking again.

"Just look forward. Not behind. Not at me. Just at what's in front of you. Don't be like Orpheus in the Underworld. Checking up on Eurydice. Don't look behind. Don't be. Too curious. Not yet."

He was still behind her; his hands were on either the side of her head. Even if she'd wanted to move around, she couldn't. They forced her to look straight ahead, to see.

And what was in the dim light was worse than anything Skip could have imagined.

CHAPTER TWENTY-FOUR

"Wow," Mizell said.

"Jesus fucking Christ." That was me. "No wonder the school's so expensive."

That kid at Cousin Charlie's had been right: a biosphere. There was no other word to describe what we were seeing down in the basement of the new science building, the price tag a reported 38 million *during* a recession. And a lot of it must have gone down here, in the underground hallway a guard was walking us through. For every step you took, a new patch of light came on, and the area you'd just left went dark, each footstep triggering just the light you needed, at least in the middle of the night. Nothing wasted, super-green, super-eerie, as the lights kept fading behind us, like the past literally disappearing into blackness.

And when you couldn't see where you were going, you could hear it. At the end of the hall, something that sounded like water, pooling and bubbling. The whole thing seemed like a cistern or cave, everything a little cooler, damper, as if dark, loamy earth was closing in, like something really was growing, on either side of the cinder block walls. But as the guard kept moving us along, the scent of dirt disappeared, and something clean and fresh took its place.

I'd run all the way all the way here from Charlie's, faster than my best time at the Olympics, yelling at Mizell on my cell phone to meet me here. And then she'd had to do some fast talking to even get us in: waving her detective shield, throwing around some big names. The police chief. The president of the college. The FBI on their way . . .

Michael Dowd, the guard's name tag said. Curly blond hair, a Baby Huey face, a button or two on his uniform straining at his waist. Not exactly the lone guy I'd put in charge of a $38 million treasure, but good for us.

And it was like Fort Knox, whatever the hell they were keeping down here, besides something that might save my daughter.

My daughter. Hydras. That's what. Find that reed, or watch her bleed.

We finally got to a double metal door at the end of the hallway; blue and green and violet light emanated from a small window set into each door; glass embedded with crisscrossing metal mesh. The guard started to punch in a code, but one of the doors swung open by itself, just at his touch.

Like it had been deliberately left unlocked, waiting, just for me.

"That's weird," Dowd said. "These things stay locked all the time. You need clearance . . . "

What if this was a trap, to get me? He'd lured me in here, left the door unlocked. Was he in there now, waiting for me? Waiting with a *gun*?

Mizell must have had the same thought, because she suddenly pulled hers out and went into defense mode, arms held out straight, with the gun in front of her.

Dowd freaked out. "Wait . . . you didn't tell me it was dangerous."

"Just a precaution." I told him, then stepped in front of Mizell, turning to speak to her, almost *sotto voce*. "And you're the one who got shot, remember? He wants me alive. He won't shoot. Not at me at least." I had ten more Labors still to do. He wouldn't take me out, not yet. He was just getting started.

Then so was I.

I pushed the door open—cautiously—and we were inside.

And then we understood.

"Wow." That was Mizell.

"You already said that."

"I know, but . . . wow."

Inside, tanks and water beds and filters, pipes leading from one tank to the next, some glass-enclosed, like aquariums, some open air. Things floated on top of the water and below it, giant masses of phosphorescent tangles and stalks sending out bubbles, as if they were breathing on their own. Life. Biology. An ecosystem, a hi-tech Eden.

A *biosphere*. That was the only word for it, other than Oz.

I asked Dowd the question, even though I already knew the answer. "What are these things?"

"Hydras."

Bingo. Thin reeds. *Hydra*s, in those open-air tanks, floating like seaweed with prickly tentacles that look like faces, branching off a single body.

"But what do they do?" Mizell asked.

"Rumor is they could be a replacement for Botox. That's what the school's hoping. This is their leading candidate."

Thirty-eight million, for the next Botox.

The kidnapper had to have been in here. How else would he have known these were here? Hell, I taught here and I didn't even know this was going on, under my very nose.

Dowd flicked on the lights, and even they came up in the same color as the water. Gentle blues and greens. Growing colors. Nothing too jarring to disrupt the gentle life cycle of the hydras. But enough light to let us see that nobody else was inside. In the strange glow of colored lights from the room, and the wavy patterns that the tanks of water were giving off, we all looked like we were underwater. Swimming.

"Listen, you folks take a look around, but I'm gonna go back and check the log. Call my supervisor. That door shouldn't have been open."

He left, and we were alone, the soothing sound of *burgling*—a Skip word, from *bubbling* and *gurgling* combined—almost making us forget what we were here for. What had been done, to bring us here.

Burgling. Skip. My God. Where was she? What was he doing to her? Even in this place of such wondrous beauty, my brain kept going back there. Why her, when he wanted me?

But now what? The kidnapper hadn't said to get one of the hydras, but that must be what he meant. One giant scavenger hunt, with all of the Canaan campus as my playing field.

I started to plunge my hands into the water.

"What the fuck are you doing?" Mizell hissed at me, the only harsh noise in this place of soothing sounds.

"Don't tell me you care about taking school property?" I said.

"No, just . . . what if it's not water? Some kind of chemical or something. Acid."

There was nothing in here to test the water with, nothing that was loose or extraneous or not attached to something else. All glass and metal and tubes. I ripped off my jacket and dipped a corner of my sleeve into the water, to see if it sizzled or exploded. Nothing happened. It just got wet.

Still, Mizell took out her gun and pointed it at the tank. Just in case.

"What, you're gonna shoot a plant?" I asked her. "You think this could all be just some ploy to get one of these plants? Use us as the stooges to dig one up, so he could walk off with the money?"

"If he somehow got in here, he could dig up his own damn plant. No. It's part of the Labors. It's part of . . . Skip."

My string bean.

That was my cue to plunge my hands inside the water. Now or never. Skip or . . . nothing.

Now we were the culprits, the snakes in the Garden of Eden.

It was cold, but not caustic, that shock of your first jump in the water in June. I reached all the way down to the bottom of the tank, three feet or so, and started trying to pull an entire bunch of the reeds out by the root. For something so delicate looking, they were amazingly sturdy, as if the roots kept going through the layer of mud at the bottom and anchored into the concrete floor. I kept pulling and pulling, but nothing, just the water getting clouded up.

That's when we heard Michael Dowd coming back, his walkie-talkie bleating noises to announce his return.

I was yanking at the plant, now a cyclone of mud stirring up in the tank, but still nothing.

I had to get that fucking plant before he came back in, just in case he decided he was here to protect the school's $38 million investment. I was looking around for a knife. Scissors. Anything. But nothing. I was on my own.

No, *Skip* was with me. An image came to me: her fighting against the kidnapper. Those streak marks Mizell had shown me, in the kitchen. Her getting dragged out. Not going without a fight.

Then I wasn't either.

I closed my eyes and prayed—*Skippy, stay strong, fight back, don't give up, give me strength*—then I grabbed Mizell's gun and shot straight down at one of the stalks, the bullet cutting it in two, inside the aquarium.

Water flew everywhere, as the stalks came flying out of the water, with a maze of tangled white roots that seemed to go on for yards. Ganglia. Water and dirt dripping on the concrete floor, and me.

Just then, Dowd clicked away his last number on the keypad lock, and the door opened.

A change in the air pressure.

I whipped the stalk behind my back, just as Dowd said, "Sorry I kept you so long."

"Oh, no problem." *Don't look, don't look at all the mess I've made*, I prayed. "Well, we'll get out of your way now. Thanks so much. We just needed to make sure the kidnapper wasn't in here."

"I hope you find him. And I hope you find her. Bring Skip back. I'll show her around the place. Kids get a kick out of it."

"I will." I raced ahead of him, switching the hydra in front of me so he wouldn't see it, as he turned out the lights and clicked the door locked behind us.

"Can I throw up yet?" Mizell heaved, as we power-raced out of the building. Both of us heaving.

"Not yet. Not 'til we're away from Michael Dowd and his walkie-talkie."

I collapsed against the side of the building, with *his* words, the words that ended his latest rhyme, still in my head: *Then post it on Facebook, to get what I took.*

We still weren't finished.

In that brilliant, dark November night, I held the hydra up in front of me, like a prized fishing trophy. I turned my cell phone toward me, aimed and clicked the camera button, and the night was electrified by a flash of pure white light. Then the *whoosh* sound that my cell phone made, to tell me the photo had just posted to my Facebook account, for anybody to see.

For *him* to see.

"There's your selfie, motherfucker." I paused, then turned to my partner in crime. "*Now* you can throw up."

CHAPTER TWENTY-FIVE

Dozens and dozens of photos of her father.

That's what Skip saw, everywhere she looked, when her blindfold came off and her vision came back. Blurry, then coming into focus, then . . . *this*.

Before, she'd just been in a room. That's all she knew: a desk, four walls, a madman who came and went. But now, she saw *how* mad, from what was up on the walls.

"Here, let's turn on the lights, to help you . . . understand. Your . . . *art* lesson."

But not even a single bulb, hanging from a cord in the center of room, could help Skip understand what she was looking at. The bulb swung and its light streaked across giant murals on the walls, revealing shadowy glimpses of things she knew her father had once told her about, as he read from mythology books to put her to sleep. Lions and horses, chariots and birds, monsters and men and fire. And Hercules. The real one, and the imagined one: her father.

"It's a diorama. *Panorama?* Something with *rama* at the end . . . *a sweep-orama!* That's it! The Twelve Labors of Hercules . . . with our special guest star."

Everywhere Skip could see—everywhere he *allowed* her to see, as his fingers continued to position her head from behind—were photos of her father. Scattered through the twelve murals, and intermixed with the bizarre iconography of the labors, were old newspaper clippings and photographs of Ethan Holt: his entire athletic career, an obsessed fan's art gallery, a veritable shrine to him. The endorsement carefully cut off the cereal box. The cover of the workout book some publishing house had slapped together two months after the win, along with the cover of *Herc Holt: My*

Story. And in the dead middle, what appeared to be her captor's pride and joy: an autographed picture, signed by her father.

"See! We're more alike. Than you realize, my dear Elizabeth. You and. I. We're both. *Artists*."

How did he know her real name was Elizabeth? Nobody called her Elizabeth. Nobody had ever called her Elizabeth.

"We're not alike at all. I don't take people. I don't hurt people."

"Oh, let's not. *Go there*. Let's not do that at all. We don't want to start comparing. Physical pain. I am a. *Masterpiece*. Of pain. Past. Present. And future."

He stopped. Catching a breath, or changing the topic, she couldn't tell.

"I was happy to see your artwork, by the way. BTW. Isn't that what they say? In the . . . *chat rooms*?"

"What artwork?" She was confused; she'd been looking at his artwork—his horrible, horrible artwork—up on the wall in front of her, and now . . . what was he talking about?

"Your little . . . sculptures. In the attic. You're going to be quite good."

"How did you see what's up there?"

"When I . . . *borrowed* you."

"You went up there?"

"At some point, you're going to have to decide—art, or Art. Capital A. Acting, or . . . *decoupage*."

"How did you know that I . . . that I've been in plays? You know that?"

"I've seen them. I told you. I *know* you. Since you were little. I like what you've done. With the little mirrors. How they . . . *show you* who you are. You can't help but . . . face yourself. See yourself, as others see you. That's hard. That's Art."

The kidnapper held one hand up, gesturing proudly toward the decorated walls, and for just a second, she was free to move her head. Not all the way around; she didn't want to see him, or at least to let him know that she saw him, but just enough to bow her head toward the floor to look behind her, to see if any blood had dripped down off her wrist, from where she'd been sawing away at the duct tape.

No blood. A nice-sized rip in the tape.

Her mother's recipe card, dropped and waiting for her under the refrigerator.

His madness, up on the wall.

She could do this.

She had to do this, or she somehow knew she was going to be up there too.

Pictures of her, after she was dead.

CHAPTER TWENTY-SIX

I'd never been at my office at one in the morning. Mizell and I had gone there to wait it out, because it was closer than going home. Practically the only light in the room was my open laptop; we both felt like we were still in hiding, that Michael Dowd could race in and take back what we'd stolen, any minute now. Mizell had scrounged up a bucket and filled it with water to keep the hydra in, so it wouldn't die, as we waited to see what instructions came back to us, on my Facebook page.

If they came back to us.

If *he* came back to us.

I'd done the insane thing he wanted, posted the photo to my virtually empty Facebook page. For the longest time, I didn't even have a photo of myself there, just that blank gray silhouette that was the default. Skip told me it made me look like a loser, so she put a photo in for me.

Over the years, I've posted a few photos on the page—again, mainly at the insistence of Skip—*Daaa-aaad, it looks like you never do anything.* Thank God she'd taught me how to snap a photo on my cell phone and post it, so that . . .

So that I could get her back.

Selfie with hydra. My face expressionless, dead, like a kidnap victim forced to pose for a proof of life picture, the flash of light against the darkness making me look like someone caught in the act, doing something other people weren't supposed to see. Something so intimate. Life and death stuff, my most sacred private moments. And now they all would. Why would he make me post the photo there? So he could put me on public display, my devastation, like one of the *zanes* at the ancient Olympics?

"We're doing background checks on all of them . . . your friends," Mizell said, almost reading my mind.

"None of my friends would do something like this," I answered.

"Somebody's friend did."

She was walking around the office, taking it all in. A kettle bell on my desk which I used for quick arm crunches. And for a paperweight. A framed photo of me and Skip and Patti. The worn Persian rug that I'd brought in from home years ago; Skip had done her first crawling on it, then her first baby steps, grabbing onto my knees with her chubby fingers then pulling herself up.

I wanted to get down on my hands and knees and sniff it in, grab handfuls of the rug, just to touch something that she had once touched.

"You let Skip have a Facebook page? Don't bother . . . I already know the answer. We've been tracing all her friends too, checking her IM file. Now *my* daughter, she's only eleven . . . she's *begging* me for one, but I think she's too young. I say, 'Why you even need that when all you do is text your friends anyway?' She says . . . well, it doesn't matter what she says. I'm not gonna let her have one and that's that."

"You don't have to do that," I told her.

"What?"

"Talk to me. Make conversation. Keep me company."

"This is who I am. *You're* the one who doesn't have to talk. You're excused. But this is how I roll. I talk. I talk out loud. Helps me think." Mizell was short-circuiting like I was. Her thoughts coming in quick little spurts.

"I didn't mean . . . I don't know what I mean. I'm sorry." Then I said it out loud, for the first time. I allowed it to come into my head: the idea that something bad could actually happen to her, that all of this wouldn't have a good ending. "I'll die if something happens to her."

"I know."

"No you don't. All due respect—nobody could know what this is like."

Mizell didn't say anything back to me, she just kept scratching up under her wig, then straightening it back into place, until she finally yanked the whole thing off. "Starts itching, late at night." Underneath, she was almost bald; her scalp was patchy, flecked with some gray fuzz.

What are you looking at? her expression seemed to say.

"This?" she said, pointing to her head. "See, this is what happens when you go a little crazy. When you think you're gonna die. You lose your hair and have to wear cheap-ass wigs."

She was going as crazy as I was. I didn't know what she was talking about.

"Scoot over," she said, walking toward me and plopping down on the same wooden rolling desk chair I was already in, forcing me to squeeze to the edge. Under the desk, she used the toes of one foot to push one of her shoes off, then repeated the process on the opposite foot. "That feels better."

She pulled the laptop toward her, then started tapping away on the keyboard with her French-tipped fingernails. A new Facebook page popped up: a beautiful little black girl, a little younger looking than Skip. A big wide smile, a swath of long dark hair pomaded and combed to one side of her face, an unfortunate blanket of acne on her forehead. But still, that smile. The photo looked like one of those department store deals: a come-on with purchase, against a mottled blue drop cloth. The girl's hand was resting under her chin; that's how I knew she was younger than Skip. A photographer told her to pose that way. No thirteen-year-old would, not on her own.

"Janice Miner. The one I told you about."

"Who? The one who . . . ?"

"That's right. The little girl who got kidnapped. She's my niece. *Was* my niece. Hell, she *is* my niece. They can't take that away from me. They can take away my hair, but they can't take away her."

"That's your . . . wait. You didn't tell me it was your niece. I thought you said you got the guy."

"We did. We just didn't get *her*. Janice. Not in time, anyway."

Now I saw it, looking beyond the Facebook photo to the rest of the page: RIP's and posts that said "you are our angel now."

"My sister decided to keep her page up, even after she was gone. Said it was a way to remember her. A place for all her little friends to say their goodbyes. I thought it was a bad idea, but my sister and I . . . well, we don't agree on anything. When my niece was born, I told my sister, 'Now what kind of name is *Janice* for a little black girl?' For once, Aretha sounded good. *Janice*."

Mizell shook her head, smiling, a perfect memory. A heartbreaking memory. "I called her Ja-*niece,* just to give it some flavor. It was our little joke, 'cause she *was* my niece. See that little charm bracelet on her wrist?"

With one of her nails, Mizell tapped at the photo, where Janice's chin was resting on her hand. You could see it there, dangling from her skinny wrist: a silver bracelet, laden down with charms.

"That got lost, the bracelet . . . somewhere . . . when he tied her up," Mizell said, forcing herself to tell me the story. "I gave it to her, on her seventh birthday. Every birthday after that, I gave her a new charm. A unicorn, the year she got taken. She was into unicorns that year. Aren't they supposed to bring you good luck? They didn't, not to her. He killed her. That's when my hair fell out. That's *why* my hair fell out."

"Why didn't you tell me?" I asked, so quietly. I didn't want to intrude on the reverence of the moment. I was glad it was so dark, so I couldn't see her eyes. They probably looked like mine.

"They'd have my head, what's left of it, if they knew I told you this. They'd have my head if they even knew you were here with me. I'm supposed to make you think everything's gonna turn out fine. You could even be the kidnapper for all I know. But I know you're not."

I didn't know what to say.

Her finger was scrolling down the page, to a link. She clicked on it and a newspaper obituary popped up. Mizell looked at it and read back to me, with so much pride. And agony. "See? There I am, right there. 'Survived by her mother, Diana Sherwood, and her aunt, Aretha Mizell.' Should'a said, 'who just *had* to be smarter than everybody else and think she could fix everything.' I couldn't. I didn't."

She shook her head again, another memory I couldn't imagine. Or maybe I could.

"That's why I'm gonna find Skip for you. In time. This time."

Then I said the thing I could only say in the dark, to a virtual stranger. The thing I could barely say to myself, as I put my hand over hers. "What if I'm not smart enough? What if I'm not strong enough? To get her back. To figure it all out."

"You have to be. She's counting on you."

A ping on my cell phone told me that something had just been posted on my Facebook page. I grabbed the computer back from Mizell and clicked back to my page.

And there, finally, a "comment," under the photo of the hydra I'd posted:

You've passed the second test, but it's no time to rest.
To get number three, go live on TV.
And if you're going crazy, thinking who I could be . . .
Just think how I felt, waiting for you to come see me.

But it wasn't just the poem that made Mizell gasp, her hand now in a vise around my wrist. It was the name of the person who had *posted* the comment. She saw it before I did, the way the photo attaches to the name, in that rectangle where a new comment appears. That tiny little squared-off photo. That smile, one hand under her chin, that charm bracelet . . .

Mizell said it out loud for the both of us, even though we'd just been saying it, seconds before.

"Janice Miner."

CHAPTER TWENTY-SEVEN

"Don't you just love. Facebook?" He laughed. "So many passwords. So little time."

Skip heard him clacking on the keyboard of a laptop computer, then a computer lid closing, as he spoke again from the other room. "So father *does* know best. Two down, ten to go."

She was glad he was distracted, so he couldn't see the confusion in her eyes, at what was up on the walls. The fear in her eyes too, that he might discover what she doing behind the desk, trying to cut into the duct tape on her wrists. She kept looking from the wall, to behind her, from the wall, to behind her, and then . . .

He came closer. Away from that other room. Near her. And what she saw when she turned her head around was as confusing as the photos up on the wall: the rubber tips, then the two metal cylinders hitting the floor before his actual legs did.

He was on crutches? *She'd been taken by somebody on* crutches? Skip thought to herself. And not the kind you use when you break your leg or something, that support you from underneath your armpits, but the serious kind. Where you have to grip two handles that stick out at about waist height, and there are metal bands for each arm, that your upper arms go into on either side of your body. And even with those, his legs seemed to really scrape the floor behind his body. The crutches *were* his legs; Skip could tell how his weight was planted in them, how the legs of his pants seemed almost empty. Toothpicks inside. The material just hung there; it didn't fill out, like it did on her father. And now that she knew what to listen for, she could hear it: the rubber tips squeaking on the floor, the slightest little creak of the metal of the crutches. Four sounds of things hitting the floor, where two would be normal.

He stopped just short of her, so she could see his legs, but nothing else. Not his face.

She whipped her head forward, so he wouldn't see that she knew.

She could get away from a guy on crutches. She didn't know how, but she knew she could. It was one step easier. One step *she* could make, that he couldn't. She had to celebrate each little thing she figured out, or she would die. She had to go back to cutting the duct tape and wait 'til he was asleep and . . .

"I hope you like my little gallery show. If your father does what he's supposed to, maybe you'll have one someday. With your little . . . snowballs."

"But how did you get up the stairs? I mean, on those?" It just came out, without her meaning to say it. "Shit."

"Shit indeed. You noticed. My 'footprint.' 'Let your . . . crutches do the walking.' I got up the stairs, it just took more . . . strain. More time. Which we don't have."

"I'm sorry. I mean . . . that you . . . can't walk so well. What happened to them? Your legs."

"You'll hear the whole. Story. Soon enough. All good things. To those who wait."

Now she just had to wait too, until he was gone. Night. Asleep.

A man on crutches. Two legs that didn't work. Hers that did, from all those morning runs with her father.

She just had to keep sawing off the duct tape, and wait.

CHAPTER TWENTY-EIGHT

It was six thirty in the morning and the house was still as crowded as it had been the very first night that Skip had been taken. Sig had pretty much moved in, and three or four police were here around the clock, working with all the computers and recording equipment. Wendy was still in the hospital but getting better; I'd called her, waking her up, to let her know I was about to go on TV, as per the kidnapper's latest instructions. He'd gone from wanting no police to wanting the world to know, and I was obliging.

I had to, to get to the next clue.

"But why's he changing now? Why not just keep putting them on my Facebook page? Why not just . . . " I ran out of "why nots."

"Because he can." That was Mizell's only answer. "But now we're upping the ante, with your reward."

"Won't that piss him off? That people are looking?"

"He already knows people are looking. He knows *I'm* looking."

I gave her wig a helpful tug to get it back into place; she kept scratching under it and making it go off kilter. "I'll kill him. I'll fucking kill him." That's what she'd said, back in my office, when she saw the name "Janice Miner" pop up with his latest rhyme. When she saw that, I think she would have pulled out her hair, if she'd had any left.

She'd put her tech people into overdrive, trying to trace who had hacked into her niece's page—to dig at her, as much as he was digging at me. He'd have to have known the password to access it, and to know the password, he'd have to be some kind of hacker. That gave them more info to go on. Now this had become as personal to her as it was to me; it was like he'd kidnapped both girls. "He's fucking with us. So now we're going to fuck with him."

140

Mizell had called the local TV station in Pittsfield for our broadcast, and they'd been here setting up ever since. She wanted it to take place at our house, instead of the police station or TV studio; she didn't want it to look like just another press conference with a cop behind a podium.

"We want him to see how comfy it is here, how homey. Just be real. Be yourself. A wonderful dad. Show what Skip's been ripped away from."

They just needed to look at my haggard face to see what she'd been ripped away from. My face looked as bloody and bruised as it had after Mark Casey slugged me, but this time, no one had touched a thing. It was all me. Not sleeping. Dying inside. Hair wild, hadn't shaved in days, the bags under my eyes almost cadaverous.

My first time back on TV since the Olympics.

"Not that many people catch this early broadcast," said Dana Rossen, the local reporter assigned to the story, as the TV people finished their prep, clipping a little microphone to the collar of the button-down shirt I'd put on. Dana ran her hands under her honey-golden hair and fluffed it out one last time. "If this moves the needle, we'll run it again at noon and five, but your best bet's the ten o'clock tonight."

"I don't have that long. We've gotta get it on now. He's gotta see that I'm following his clues. He's gotta see that . . . "

"If he's looking for it, he will," she said.

Dana switched to her camera face and gave a "Go" nod to the cameraman, who started her countdown. "Five, four, three," he said out loud, then went quiet, switching to just his fingers for "two" and "one." Dana's smile glided on, a perfect segue to air, picking up the relay toss from the guy in the studio who had just introduced her.

"Thanks, Chuck. We're here on Drummond Court at the home of Canaan College professor Ethan Holt, with the developing story of an apparent kidnap . . . "

That's when I blew it. A few seconds in, and I lost it, looking straight into the camera.

You want the real me? This is it.

You want me to be the "face" of the kidnapping? Then just take a look.

"There's nothing *apparent* about it. It happened. It's happening. Right now. My daughter's been kidnapped and . . . "

"Of course. As I said . . . *was* saying, I'm joined by Professor Ethan Holt—Herc Holt, some of you may remember him as—from the 2000 Olympics, before he traded his medal for . . . "

Now I really didn't need her. I didn't need then. I just needed *now.*

"I did it," I said, straight to camera. I knew how sound bites work. I knew what got attention. I'd been doing it in a classroom for years now.

"I figured it out, the thing you wanted, the second thing, the Hydra, the Labors . . . " I grabbed the bucket that the plant was in and practically shook it at the camera, water spilling over and sloshing everywhere. "'One is done, now two is due.' I did two. I posted it. You saw it. You responded. Then you promised three. 'Go on TV, I'll give you three.' So I'm ready. The Third Labor. Just tell me."

Nobody but one person watching would be able to understand *these* sound bites. Only one person watching *needed* to understand them.

"I'll do them, all of them. I don't know what I did, how I kept you waiting, but I'm sorry, I'm sorry. I'm begging you. It's me you want, so just let her go . . . let Skip go so it's just me and you."

I finally took a breath and looked at Dana for the first time, as if I were seeking her permission for what I was about to do. "I'm posting a reward. Twenty thousand dollars. It's all I've got, but take it. Anybody who knows something, it's yours. Just give me back my baby."

I hadn't planned the next thing, but I did it anyway: what else did I have to lose? I grabbed the portable ENG camera from the guy recording us, and everything went haywire, except in my head. I was being real, in the moment, exactly what Mizell told me to be. You couldn't get any more real than this. I was calling the shots now, as I raced through the house with the camera, putting our lives on display, electrical cords straining and pulling down light stands. I didn't care, as long as the camera was still running.

I aimed it at our kitchen, a house tour on crack, the camera weaving everywhere to show my demented POV. "Look. This is where we eat. This is where I fix Skip breakfast. Cereal. Toast. Eggs. I don't let her go to school hungry. I'm a good dad. I am. I swear."

I flung open cabinets to show that they were stacked full to bursting: olive oil and vinegars and pasta and half-full bags of nuts and confectioner's sugar and coconut that were rolled down and clipped with those colorful pins you buy in grocery stores. "Look at this. All this stuff left over from the party she had for me, the night before you took her. She made me a cake. A little girl. No mother. And she's making me a cake, all by herself."

I kept going, no stopping now, still moving the camera with me, yanking the electrical cord into the den. "And this couch. I help her with her homework here. She puts her books in front of her on the coffee table here, and I help. If I can. I'm not that great at math, but she is. She's great at everything."

I stopped, before I started crying.

I started crying anyway.

"I'm sorry, I'm sorry, but . . . take me. Please. Take me for her. Me for Skip."

I put the camera down on the cushion next to me. I looked in the monitor they'd set up and saw that it was pointing at nothing: just a space on a wall. The camera guy snuck up behind me on the couch and grabbed the camera back, trying to hold it steady. You could see it still heaving up and down, as he tried to get his breath under control from chasing me around.

That's when Dana moved back into the frame, her mouth still hanging open in shock, lipstick smearing her teeth. "Uh . . . uh . . . we can all understand your grief . . . heartbreaking, really . . . and as you at home just saw . . . "

Mizell stepped in next to Dana, to try to get this thing back on track. "I'm Detective Aretha Mizell from the Mt. Gresh Police Department. I hadn't planned on speaking . . . "

"Quite a morning here, wouldn't you agree?" Dana said, her tongue sliding across her upper row of teeth to try to wipe away the stray lipstick smears.

"Professor Holt is understandably upset, as any parent would be." Thank God for Mizell, picking up the narrative, as the camera finally settled into something resembling a professional shot. "But as Professor Holt just said, there's a reward for any information that could lead to Skip's safe rescue and return. So if anyone watching has information—any information at all—that could help us, just call the station at 413-732-6675. That stands for 'tip line.' Thank you so much, Dana," Mizell finally said, walking out of camera range.

Dana barely had time to squeak out a wide-eyed "Back to you, Chuck," before the camera went dark. And when it did, it wasn't me that she reamed into—but Mizell.

"Why the hell did you cut him off? That was ratings gold. That was the lead story at noon and five and ten and going national . . . "

Dana was going so full-throttle at Mizell that I was surprised any of us even heard the landline ring. But the minute we did, everything went quiet. A call so fast, right after the TV report, and on the same phone the first call from the kidnapper had come in on. I grabbed the phone, and that voice filled the room, once again.

"What a. Performance. What a. House tour."

"If you touch one hair on her head . . . "

"Well, to *find*. That head. You have to. Find *me*. And to *find* me. You have to do the Labors. *All* of them," he said, in a voice that sounded like it was gasping for air.

"Put Skip on. Now."

"I suggest you. *Take* an order. Instead of. *Give* one. Take a . . . *number*. Number *three*."

Over the recording system, the sound of a piece of paper moving into place, to be read from. We could almost hear the hands that were holding it shake, or maybe that was just the paper itself, wrinkled and creased and worked over so many times to get it just right, his one mad rhyme. Read in a voice that was now bizarrely steady.

> *So far so good, but you're still in the wood.*
> *The Arcadian Deer is next; where is in this text.*
> *Tame the deer, don't hurt the body,*
> *To keep me from getting much more naughty.*
> *You had the body, I had the brains . . .*
> *But you forgot me, so I have her in chains.*

No matter how much I wanted to make contact—and how much Mizell had tried to prepare me for it—nothing could have prepared me for the madness I was hearing. For the terror.

Naughty. Forgot. Have her in chains.

"Please, I'm begging you. Just tell me . . . what did I do? She's a little girl, she's just a little girl. She didn't do anything. She's all I've got. You heard me. *Take* me . . . "

Now, a new sound on the other end of the line. A button being pressed, along with a sort of digitized sound. Numbers falling. A computer clicking away. Click click click. Time, disappearing.

If all's not done in forty-eight hours,
You'll next see Skip pushing up flowers.
If a mere two days seems unduly cold,
It's what you had to win the gold.
Start running numbers, or else she slumbers.

I looked at everyone in the room, as if I had to convince them, instead of the madman.

"I can't. It's . . . it's not enough . . . ten more Labors . . . I can't . . . let me talk to Skip, please. Is she okay? Tell her I . . . "

And then, a sound none of us could mistake. The phone being hung up. The mad poetry at an end, but so was my connection to Skip. I couldn't put the receiver down; I kept holding it like I was holding Skip, like I wouldn't lose her as long as I didn't let go.

The cop at the equipment barely had to say anything for us to know it was a no-go. "He's tapped into router boxes somehow . . . I can't trace it . . . maybe, if he calls again . . . "

"Oh my God . . . who was that? He's insane . . . is that who took her . . . " Dana was going as crazy as I just had.

I put the phone down, and immediately, the landline rang again. I grabbed it, not waiting for Mizell's signal or anything else this time.

"WHAT THE FUCK DO YOU WANT WITH ME?"

"Daddy?"

It was Skip. And then it wasn't.

Click.

CHAPTER TWENTY-NINE

Skip's prayers—one of them—had been answered, because she got to speak to him.

"Daddy?"

The kidnapper had held up the phone to her mouth, touching it to her lips so she could feel it, then yanking the phone away the second she said his name. She kept yelling it even though her father couldn't hear it, even though she knew the kidnapper had cut off the connection.

"Just let me go. Please. I haven't seen you, I can't tell anybody anything. He knows you have me. He's suffered. You've made your point."

He was behind her. "And just what. Do you think. My point. Is?"

She didn't answer.

"That's what I thought. Until *he* knows. The game continues."

From behind, he put the blindfold back on her, then began moving forward on his crutches. Now that Skip knew what it was, the sound made sense. But the next sound that he made didn't: fiddling with something in his lap. A cap coming off something, then another sound, something hollow and plastic. A rattle, and then a sort of *shhhhhhhh*. It wasn't an exhale, or him telling her to be quiet . . .

Skip smelled it first, then she knew.

Spray paint. That was the whoosh, the aerosol coming out of the can. She'd exploded a whole can of it in her face once, when she stuck a screwdriver in the little nozzle to get the spray unclogged. She'd be blind today if the mustard yellow colored spray hadn't gone all over her glasses, instead of in her eyes. She looked like somebody with a bad tan, a real burn, most of her face yellow, except for the perfect squares of her glasses around her eyes. It had been murder getting the paint off her face and her hair. Scrubbing at her skin, having to cut off some of her hair.

Did he know that? He knew everything else about her. Is that why he was using it?

Skip relaxed her face so the blindfold would go just a little bit slack and she could try to see more, from where there was a little gap between her eyes and her nose. If she leaned back slowly, he wouldn't know she was looking at him, and besides, his back was to her. Just a sliver she could see in front of her. His hunched-over shoulders, sort of shrunken looking; a thin, pale neck; tendrils of dark hair that were sweaty and clumped together, causing them to stick out like a bad wig. The only kind they could afford in the drama department at the college. At least from behind, nobody she remembered ever seeing before, despite him saying he'd seen her.

He reached up with the hand holding the can and narrated as he sprayed through two of his murals, his voice at the pressure point, just like the spray paint.

"One down, the Nemean Lion. Two down, the Lernaean Hydra." Four long exhales of the aerosol, the metal ball inside the can rattling away, to keep the paint coming. Doing what, she didn't know. "I hate to ruin my artwork, but you know what they say. You have to 'kill your darlings.' Just as he killed me."

CHAPTER THIRTY

"*'What the fuck do you want with me?'* If that's the last thing she ever hears from me . . . "

I couldn't let it go, as I sat at the dining table with Sig and Mizell, trying to make sense of the latest poem, which one of the cops has transcribed onto paper right after the call came in. This one was too long, too complicated, to keep it all in my head. There were too many moving parts to it, and I couldn't afford to overlook any of them. Especially now that three and a half hours were gone out of the forty-eight he gave us, and we'd made no progress.

Three and a half hours, and I still couldn't get out of my head what I had yelled at Skip. I wasn't moving forward; I was completely stuck back there, more than three hours ago.

"You didn't know it was her. You thought it was him calling back." Sig was trying to make the best of a completely fucked situation.

"It doesn't matter . . . it's still what she'll keep hearing in her ears . . . just like me . . . "

"She's alive. That's all you need to know right now. She's alive," butted in Mizell. "We know that one thing we didn't know before. Plus the FBI's sending us one of their code guys now. Your TV appearance got their attention . . . "

"I didn't do it for that."

"I know, but it worked. Whatever you did it for. But until they get here, you've got to figure out this poem. That's your only job now. Labor number three. We know what it is, but where does he want you to go to do it? You're the professor in the room, so start professing." Mizell was no-nonsense now, barking out her orders to me.

I read it aloud, for the umpteenth time, thinking if I just kept saying it, over and over, I'd hear something different. I'd find the key to translating it.

So far so good, but you're still in the wood.
The Arcadian Deer is next; where is in this text.
Tame the deer, don't hurt the body,
To keep me from getting much more naughty . . .

That's the part that stopped me, every time. My brain seized on that, and wouldn't let go, just like the "What the fuck do you want with me?" that I'd screamed at Skip. "'*Much more naughty . . .*' *More.* Does that mean he's already *been* naughty? Oh my God, what has he done to her?"

"*Here.*" Mizell pointed at a section of the poem. "Focus." Her skin looked ashy now, except for an almost bluish-purple tinge right under her eyes. Even against her dark complexion, I could see it along with a smattering of skin tags I hadn't noticed before. She was as exhausted as the rest of us. She'd seen pictures of how this could turn out; she'd lived through something we hadn't. Not yet. "You're the only one who can do this part. You're the only one smart enough. That's what he's counting on. He *wants* you to get it."

"I can't. I can't stop thinking how I yelled . . . "

"You want me to start yelling? Then yes you can." She pulled her wig straight. "Let's do it together. Play like you're in class, and I'm one of your students. This Arcadian Deer thing. What the hell is that?"

"In the real Labor, Hercules has to capture a hind . . . "

That exasperated look she gave me. "A really dumb student . . . "

"A hind. It's a female deer. But the one in this Labor . . . it's special, with golden horns. The favorite of the goddess of hunting, Diana. But the trick is . . . Hercules can't kill it. For once, the Labor's about *not* killing. He's already proved he could do that, with the lion. This one's about his *skill*. His *control*. Getting so angry he *could* kill, but then stopping short of it. He's got to outrun the deer. Capture it alive. Then bring it back. The kidnapper knows the Labors as well as I do."

"I've got my guys on all your former students. The ones who'd know the Labors as well as you do."

"But there are hundreds of them."

Sig jumped in. "Not the ones who majored. Who went on to grad school. The really serious ones."

"But whatever he wants you to do, it seems like it keeps coming back to the Olympics." Mizell used one of her French tips to stab at a phrase as she spoke. "It's the first time he's specifically referred to it. 'If a mere two days seems unduly cold, it's what you had to win the gold.' Mark Casey. He threatened to kill you."

"But I already told you," I said, sick of going over it. "It can't be him. He's dead."

"Yeah, it checks out. Four years ago," Mizell answered back. "Suicide. But what if somebody killed him and made it *look* like suicide, then that same person took Skip . . . "

"Slow down, Perry Mason. Nobody killed Casey except *himself*." All the noise in the room stopped, even from the cop still working with the recording equipment. I didn't think I'd said it that loud. I didn't think I'd said it with such a sneer.

And Sig couldn't resist adding in, "An asshole to the very end."

"Well, if it can't be Casey, then there are plenty of others you beat," said Mizell, returning to her dead horse theory, which so far, was the only one we had.

"Yeah, but none of 'em threatened to kill me."

Her cell phone rang; she answered. "Mizell here."

As I heard her "uh hunhs" and "yes sirs" on the phone, I went back to the poem. That was my Rosetta stone for now. Translate it, and . . .

"Fuck." With her cell phone in one hand, Mizell was poking around, moving papers on my desk, reading off the number on my fax machine to whoever was on the phone. My desk was piled high with papers to be graded and academic journals, now imprinted with indelible rings from the bottom of coffee cups. Those endless cups of coffee, helping me—and the police—make it through the night. All their heavy surveillance equipment, tape recorders, and call descramblers, plopped on top.

Mizell hung up. "The FBI. They've got their first hit."

"What?" I hopped up to my crowded desk, where she was still standing, waiting for the fax.

"Fuck fuck fuck. Why the fuck didn't I look at him earlier." The muted whine of the printer on the fax started up, spitting out a sheet of paper, line by line; a face in pixels, coming alive.

A face I knew.

CHAPTER THIRTY-ONE

It was another country, the Canaan gym, an ivy-covered building as grand and glorious as the chapel on campus, because they were both built in homage to something bigger: the ability of the body to transcend the mind and what it thought of as pain. They were places of worship and history, these old New England gyms, where boys became men and gloried in the call of brotherhood, the call of sportsmanship, where ghosts were still trapped from their earliest days in the 1850s. The fists that pounded punching bags. The thwack of ropes, interlaced with rhythmic, jumping feet. The smell of resin powder and leather gloves, liniment and sweat that had dripped off bodies and been ground into the floorboards for decades; it was all still there. The sounds from all those years ago trapped there: hits and grunts, falls on sparring mats that had lost their cushioning, water trickling down in old showers.

It was a strange refuge for someone as scrawny and ill-equipped, in every possible way, as TJ Markson. Pumping away on exercise equipment he could barely control, listening to an iPod through earplugs, it was as if TJ were learning another language by even stepping inside, a forgotten language. But it was the place TJ went when he wanted to hurt himself, when he wanted to remind himself of his teacher and what he'd set out to do to him. It was the place TJ went to remind himself of his father, the person he was doing it for. He didn't need the ghosts of all the athletes who had come before to haunt him; the ghost of his father was never far away.

The image of him, hanging from that goal post.

TJ didn't know if his father had meant for him to find his body, when he was just seventeen years old, his senior year in high school. That would remain one of the great mysteries of TJ's life, and Mark Casey's death. That would be the one little thing about his father that TJ was willing to give him a break on, that the discovery just might have been the worst bit of coincidence ever, like his father had always said the worst coincidence in his life was being on the same Olympic team as Ethan "Hercules" Holt.

That was the one great story of Mark Casey's life; he repeated it to his son, every chance he got. He drank and repeated it. He ate hamburgers at the Dairy Queen or the Sonic and repeated it, as little Troy Jefferson Casey tried to hide his *Illustrated Classic Comics* in his lap and read them, while pretending to listen to his father. They had a lot of meals at the Dairy Queen and the Sonic, before his father would have to go off and find another job when he'd lost the one he just had, always thinking he was better than everyone else. Maybe that's the one way father and son were so much alike; Troy couldn't do sports, but he could be a little snob, reading *Illustrated Classics* at the Dairy Queen—eating a hamburger basket and tater tots, his hands gooey with ketchup and grease—and still thinking he was superior to everyone around him, even the adults. He got free parfait sundaes twice a year, when he'd bring in his straight A report cards, and from an early age he knew that living in the past and studying it was his way out of a life of hamburger baskets and a father who drank too much and yelled at him for not being strong enough.

Long after the Olympics, Mark Casey went running every night; he kept trying to relive his high school glory days, his Olympic days, from before he got sent home packing for using steroids. He always looked young—even after he'd been drinking for years, the booze didn't make his face look old and broken; somehow, it kept him young looking. Preserved. Mark Casey liked being mistaken for the high school coach, or better yet, one of the players—although that didn't happen much anymore. To feed his fantasy, Casey went running every night, wearing the same high school T-shirts and sweatshirts he still fit into.

Sometimes, if he was in another mood, an uglier mood, he'd wear his USA Olympic gear.

Little Troy—high school Troy—always knew to brace for the worst, when his father wore that.

So that one night—back when he was just Troy Jefferson Casey, before he became TJ Markson, before death and confusion, anger and vengeance made him take on another identity—Troy went looking for his father at the high school football field, to bring him home. The only time his head ever came out of a book. His mother had given up doing it a long time ago.

At first, he thought it was one of the football players down on the field, at the goal post, maybe trying to do pull-ups on it, but not having much luck. The player seemed to be stuck, hanging on by one arm, like he'd gotten up there on a ladder but the ladder had fallen over and he was afraid to get down by himself.

A football player, afraid? Leave it alone, Troy thought; whenever he went out of his way to help someone, it always blew up in his face. Saying "good game" to one of the players—one of the players he had a crush on—got him knocked into a locker.

For just a second, he thought maybe he'd even caught the guy jerking off, out on the dark, lonely field. He knew how good it felt when he climbed up the metal pole in his backyard, the one his mother hung laundry on. The tingling he'd get in his groin, mixed in with the smell of the fresh laundry drying in the sun. Sheets flapping in the breeze, while Troy climbed the pole and did Kegel exercises. Maybe all boys knew that. Maybe that's what the guy out on the field was doing: he seemed to be banging into the pole, again and again, like he was trying to fuck it.

"Hey, you okay?" Troy finally yelled, walking in the stands, as close to the goal post as he dared. As close as he could get without actually being out on the field itself.

The player banged into the pole some more, and now Troy saw that he was swinging from a rope. He didn't think he had ever seen anything hang as heavily in his life; if ever anything illustrated the phrase "dead weight," that was it.

No, that was his heart, because the hanging face suddenly twisted around and Troy saw that it was his father at the end of the rope, his father who could still look so convincingly like a high school football player, who wore the same workout clothes thirty other kids wore to school every day.

"Daddy . . . Daddy . . . " Troy didn't know if he actually said the words aloud. Nobody else was there to tell him, or help him. None of the other boys ever used the word "Daddy" out loud, either.

He ran over the splintering, weather-beaten boards to the end of the football stand, then ran down the access ramp to the chain link fence that surrounded the field. He was up and over it like he hadn't climbed since he was little. Over the slippery grass of the field that hadn't been cut in weeks since the team wasn't in season, that already had a thin coating of late night dew on it, enough to make Troy slide down on one knee before he could get there and . . .

And what? He didn't know what to do.

He touched his father's pant leg, and the body swirled around. Troy grabbed a ladder that had been knocked over and righted it and tried to tug at the rope, to loosen it around his father's neck, but it was too tight. He couldn't get a single finger wedged under it, to take off the pressure on his father's neck; he wasn't strong enough.

Hercules could have gotten him down. Ethan Holt could have done it. He was strong. Troy's father had always told him that. Troy began researching and found out that his father's greatest rival taught college just sixty miles away, while his father went from job to job, selling appliances or selling ads in the *Penny Saver*—working on commission and only getting paid for the ads he sold, and then working as a security guard, and then not working at all, except working out, and planning his big return to the Olympics, for justice, that would never happen.

Or maybe it would.

That's when Troy started planning; that's when he changed his name from Troy Jefferson Casey to TJ Markson.

Mark's son.

Now TJ would find justice for his father, and he would build his body up to do it, in the very same place that Ethan Holt had once built up his very own body. He'd go to the gym and find if some sort of rage got set off there in the body, enough to propel him to take revenge, and hurt people. He didn't care how long he took. He just knew that one day he'd find the right chance, and he wouldn't be afraid to take it.

CHAPTER THIRTY-TWO

I knew this gym so well—I had spent four years of my life in it, after all—that I could find the exact place to stand, to cast a shadow over TJ, without him even knowing it.

I wanted to have the element of surprise.

I wanted to scare him.

I wanted to kill him, this boy whom I had just found out was Mark Casey's son. Markson. Mark's son.

TJ didn't even see me, his eyes closed, lost to the music on his iPod.

The first thing he knew, I was directly over him, yanking the ear buds out of his ears so fast they flew back and smacked him in the face.

"SHIT! Fuck . . . you scared the piss outta me."

Sweat was running off his forehead, into his eyes. Mine too. Maybe it was a Pavlovian response to coming back to my old stomping grounds. Maybe it was just my pulse already racing, at this bizarre trick being played on me.

"Any word?" he said, trying to catch his breath.

"No." I wanted him confused, off his game.

I could mean *No word . . .*

I could mean *No, she's dead . . .*

I could mean *No, how could you?*

"Uh . . . we're going out with more flyers this afternoon," he said, struggling to sit up. His core was all dough. Soft. It didn't have any power on its own. "Over by the mall. I thought if we could . . . "

"Your form is shit. Here. I'll spot you."

I pushed him back down on the bench. So many ways this could go.

"Are . . . are you okay? Did they hear anything? Did you hear something? Tell me . . . "

I went back to the rack, behind TJ's head, and added more weight to the bar. I sized things up—not heavy enough, not *punishing* enough—and added some more.

"Uh . . . I'm just a beginner. I don't think . . . " He tried to get up. Again.

I pushed him back down. Again.

"Try it. It's just weight. You must be used to carrying that around."

He couldn't tell if I was joking or not, although there wasn't any smile on my face. So he started joking out of nervousness. "Yeah, those books get heavy. Especially the old ones. They sure didn't care about wasting paper back then. All that tiny print . . . "

His words echoed in this cavernous room, all the way up to the vaulted ceiling and back down, but they didn't sound big. They sounded tiny, as tiny and pathetic as he was, in this shrine.

"Really. It's gonna be too heavy. I know I can't do it."

"Just DO IT. You know—like the Nike ad?" I flashed him one of those sick smiles he was always giving me, then kicked at his feet. Sneakers, with black socks. I grabbed his hands and squeezed them against the metal weight bar, my own hands clamping over them so they couldn't move. Idiot. He wasn't wearing gloves. When his hands came off, they'd have the imprint of the metal crosshatches, cutting into his palms.

Good. Every boy needs a tattoo, to remind him of Daddy.

TJ tried to bench press the weight—he looked too afraid not to—but his arms quivered. I gave him a little assist. "You should'a seen me in the old days . . . the stuff I could do in here. I really *was* Hercules."

I started to hoist the bar back into the holding rack, but all of a sudden I pushed it back down on TJ, pinning him across the chest. "So much better than your *father* ever was."

I had to hand it to him. He didn't pretend to not know what I was talking about. He'd been caught, which is what he wanted all along. He pushed right back—with words, the only weapon he had, even though he could barely breathe. "Only *he* never got a chance to prove it."

I pressed the bar harder into his chest. I didn't care if he couldn't breathe. "Where's my daughter? Who the fuck are you?"

He could barely get his breath, but it didn't matter. He'd planned these words for years. He didn't need oxygen to say them. "What kind of person . . . could make a man. Kill himself?"

"Where. The fuck. IS SHE?"

With two clean jerks, I threw the bar onto the floor with one hand and yanked TJ up with the other, then slammed him into the wall behind him. Mats hanging there, throwing up dust when TJ hit them.

That's when Mizell came running in—door banging open, her shoes echoing on the wooden floor. That was our bargain, to let me at him first. Get a confession. I got it, at least the first half. He was Mark Casey's son.

"That's enough," she yelled.

No, it wasn't. My palm went smashing into his face. His cheek turned white, then red, then it stayed that way, tattooed with my hand.

Good. Another tattoo. Two of them. Just like mine.

Now he was alive. Now he hurt, just like me.

Now he spit out these words, to the man he'd blamed for killing his father, all these years. "You tell me what happened at the Olympics . . . and I tell you . . . what I know. About Skip."

CHAPTER THIRTY-THREE

The two shadowy figures that Skip had sensed in the background before, the men who must have strong-armed her because the man on the crutches couldn't have, came into the room. With three people guarding her, there was no way she could escape on her own. And she'd been making good progress on cutting through the tape, even though he must have used three or four layers of it. She just had to keep sawing away at the duct tape, and remember to keep her hands tight together, behind her, so they couldn't tell that there was some slack there now.

But maybe they were letting their guard down, even with the two extra helpers. Maybe she still had a chance. They'd taken off her blindfold and put her glasses back on; they kept it so dark in the main room that she couldn't see anything, except for the glow that the two giant *X*s through the first two murals gave off. And that wasn't enough to see anybody's face, not really.

That's when she thought of another trick, to help catch them when she got out.

She shook her glasses off. She was terrified and already shaking, so they pretty much fell off on their own anyway, to the floor. But she gave her head an extra jerk, and they went flying.

One of the "helpers" bent down to get them, then put them back on her face, leaving a big smudge on one of the lenses. Dirty glasses normally drove her crazy; she was always cleaning them with dishwashing liquid at the sink at home or asking to go to the bathroom at school, just to wash them.

But now she *wanted* them dirty.

With a *fingerprint*. Somebody's fingerprint. A clue she could give the police, when she got out of here. That would push her on. Another small victory. She twitched her head again so her hair would fall down over her forehead, so they wouldn't see the smudge and take her glasses away to wash it off.

She noticed the one helper smiling at her. She'd have missed it without having her glasses on: him mouthing "I'm sorry," then looking around to see if the main man had seen him. The helper wore glasses too, and they were just as smudgy as hers, but he seemed to not even notice it. She had to get somebody on her side, somebody who could untie her. He was the one, if it was going to be anyone; a man with smudgy glasses needed friends. Wanted friends.

She smiled at him, so he'd know she didn't blame him.

He looked normal, or almost normal. Small, with a suit and dark red hair. A lot of it. Too much, actually, for such a little head. He needed a haircut. Big bushy eyebrows topping those glasses, like caterpillars crawling across his brow. His tie had a stain on it, but at least he'd tried to look nice.

He whispered it again: "I'm sorry."

"Help me!" Skip whispered back. "Untie me!"

And then his face went blank. The other helper was coming close to them, carrying a TV tray covered by a napkin. This guy was the opposite: big. She couldn't tell if he was strong, or just burly. Fit-fat, her father called it. His sleeves were rolled up, exposing his biceps, but they weren't really defined like her father's. They were more like they used to have muscles on them, but then the fat took over. A shaved head, sort of Hispanic looking, a belly sticking out over the belt of a gray work uniform. A uniform like the janitors wore, at Canaan College.

He wouldn't look at her, like the other one did. She wasn't going to get any help from him. She had to get the first guy alone somehow, but not now. The main guy was coming in, only now she heard a rolling sound behind her, not the usual tip-tap tip-tap his crutches made on the floor. No, now there was more of a metal sound, and rubber.

Wheels. He was in a wheelchair now. She saw just the front of it as he bent down and adjusted some levers to lock the wheels into place. His feet resting on the two separate footrests near the bottom of the chair; his legs sort of leaning over to the left, falling on themselves, like you did when somebody fat had to squeeze past you in your row at the movies.

"Thought I would make. *Tire tracks* today. Instead of being on my feet. Nice to have an option, when I'm just too worn out. A *seat* to come home to. Now, it's time for us. To all get acquainted. Some of my old classmates. From the home! A class reunion! We've been through. So much together! Haven't we boys? Since I'm obviously . . . unsuited to . . . heavy lifting, I depend on my 'helpers.' And all they ask in return is a little . . . pick-me-up. They've had theirs, now it's time for mine."

Skip thought he must have already had some, because his breathing was easier now. He could say more, for longer periods of time.

"I go to a lot of doctors, as you can well imagine; well, you *probably* imagine. *Not nearly enough*, and you wouldn't be wrong. But enough to take what I need, a prescription pad here, a prescription pad there. The doctors are so busy eating their free lunches the drug reps bring that they never even notice. Now. To my partners in crime. I've given them ancient names. Like something your. Father would do. My trusty 'charioteer,' Iolaus, who drives me . . . "

The big one bobbed his head—she saw the bristles on his scalp shake in her direction—but he still wouldn't look her in the eye.

" . . . and Hippocrates, who *shoots* me. Up, that is."

As if on cue, he lifted the napkin off the TV tray to reveal several syringes underneath it, next to a vial of clear liquid.

"What are those for?" Skip asked. "I don't like shots. Please."

With a determined set to his face—not daring to look at Skip again, in view of the others—the small man began drawing the liquid into the first syringe, then thumped it, to make sure there were no air bubbles.

"Not exactly the ring of fine crystal, but . . . it'll do in a pinch," the man in the wheelchair said. "Now, if you'll pardon us while he gives me my medicine . . . he's got to keep *me* alive long enough for me to keep *you* alive."

On TV, they always said juries wouldn't look at you, when they were about to say you were guilty. When they were about to announce your death sentence.

Is that why they took her blindfold off? Like they didn't care what she saw anymore, because they knew they were going to kill her anyway?

Oh my God. Skip began squirming, trying to pull away, even though she knew it was useless.

"No. No! What's in that! Please. Don't."

"I like to do. This part myself. Stay in the game." Still behind her, the kidnapper took a cotton ball saturated in alcohol; the sharp smell of the alcohol cut through the odor of decay in the room, the unwashed smell that was now on Skip.

"Please. I'm begging you. I hate shots. They hurt."

"Oh, you'd be quite surprised. What you can. Adapt to. Just look at me. Well, *not all of me,* not just yet."

He pulled his wheelchair closer to her, then plunged the syringe directly into the flesh of his leg, right through the material of his pants.

Skip jerked back in her chair, as if she'd been the one who got stabbed. She was relieved she hadn't, but almost horrified at what he'd done to himself.

"I'll stay behind you, just like a psychiatrist. An analyst, listening to your dreams. Those *doctors* I've seen a lot, to deal with my . . . anger issues."

Then a sound came out of the slit for his mouth: a deep breath, a sort of *ahhh* that was part pain, part pleasure.

"Now, I'm ready. For a story. Aren't you? I've actually been ready to tell this story—*waiting* to tell it—for quite a number of years now." His voice was relaxed and easy now; the shot must have worked immediately. "Boys, leave us alone. You've heard it before. My . . . broken record. My . . . broken self."

Skip made one last, plaintive look toward her only help—the man who had prepared the syringe—and found that he was looking back at her, trying to say a million things with only his eyes. Was one of them that he would come back and save her? She was torn between yelling for him to stay, and at last, hearing the story that the man in the chair had saved up, just for her.

"Let's see. How shall I start? How about 'Once upon a time.' Don't all great stories begin that way? 'Once upon a time'?"

And he took a deep breath, gathering strength.

CHAPTER THIRTY-FOUR

TJ wasn't in handcuffs because Mizell didn't know what to charge him with. Not yet. But there was no fear of him escaping, even without handcuffs, because *I* was the one dragging him in, as we entered the Mt. Gresh police station. Dragging him, that is, until I stopped short at the sight of what was in front of me, the minute I rounded the entry hallway.

My life, and Skip's, on three dry-erase boards that had been pushed together like a bay window. All the crime scene photos they took at my house, squiggly black arrows pointing every which way, blown-up versions of all the rhymes so far. Six photos of men, all under the heading "Registered Sex Offenders." And Skip. Ten or eleven photos of Skip. I only gave them one; I don't know where they got all the others, but now a wall of them confronted me.

"Jesus Christ."

"I forgot about this," Mizell said to me. "Holt, you're gonna have to leave . . . "

"Not until we find out what this *shithead* knows about." I turned on TJ again, ready for another round.

"I didn't *do* anything to Skip. I wasn't anywhere near your house. I wouldn't hurt her! But . . . but . . . "

My hands went around his neck, pushing him down to the ground. "WHERE THE FUCK IS MY DAUGHTER?"

Two men in suits ran in to split us apart, introductions even with their hands all over us. "You must be the father. I'm Special Agent Michaelson." Tall, with an even taller forehead, until his shock of brown hair met it. A hint of something Southern in the way he sounded, a good 'ol boy. The good cop.

His buddy, the bad one, his suit at tight, sharp angles, an American flag pin on his lapel. "And I'm Special Agent Zaccaro. From the FBI's CARD team."

Mizell spelled it out for me. "Child Abduction Rapid Deployment."

"You fucked up on the 'rapid' part. Why the hell did it take . . . "

In no time flat, I was as furious at them as I was at TJ. They were Frick and Frack as far as I was concerned. Interchangeable. But they weren't here to make apologies. "We'll need to interview you as soon as possible."

"'As soon as possible' was two days ago, and *he's* the one you need to interview." I practically threw TJ at them. "His father tried to do me in years ago, and now he's repeating the process. Like father, like son. Ask him what he knows about my daughter!"

"We've got a protocol in cases like this and . . . "

"'Cases like this?' Have you ever had a 'case like this' where the kidnapper puts your daughter on the phone and all she gets to do is squeak out your name before . . . " I was losing it again.

TJ broke in, talking for the first time since we'd taken him from the gym. He shut us all up. "I wanted to blame somebody for so long, for my dad . . . for what happened at the Olympics . . . for you beating him . . . for him dying . . . "

"*I* didn't put the goddamn noose around his neck. And what the fuck were you planning on doing, anyway? Your big revenge? Spill coffee on my laptop? Jump me in a dark alley?"

"Remind you he was dead. And why."

"How the fuck could you remind me if I didn't even know who the FUCK YOU WERE?"

Silence. Everybody was watching, waiting. Even Frick and Frack. TJ couldn't look at us anymore, couldn't look at anything except his shoes.

"And why wait 'til now?" I kept going at TJ. "You've been here four fucking years."

"I started liking school too much. I was good at it. Finally. Something I was good at. I started liking you."

TJ was still in his workout clothes, and they stank; he was sweating more than anybody I'd ever seen in my life. Not from what he'd done in the gym, but from fear. I remembered it. Afraid of Daddy. Afraid of getting in trouble. Afraid of not winning. That was the one thing TJ and I must have had in common. We'd both been terrified of our fathers.

Fathers. That's what I had to work with. That's how I could get TJ. Switch tactics, now that I'd roughed him up. "Please, TJ. I'm begging you. Just like I begged him. The kidnapper. Just think about Skip. I don't care what you think about me, or what your dad did. Do this for Skip. You came to our house . . . she came to the office . . . she baked cookies and brought them to the office and . . . you knew her."

That's when I nearly lost it again, changing tenses. Making everything past instead of present. "You *know* her. Tell me. Tell me what you know."

TJ sat down and started pulling at his socks. Those pathetic, nylon black socks. Up and down, up and down. He couldn't look at us. He couldn't look at me. "We're handing out the flyers, and this guy comes up, and I think . . . this is how I can do it. This is how I can get back at you. I don't tell you what he looks like."

"You've been sitting on a description this whole time?" Now Mizell was the one who wanted to pummel him.

TJ whipped off his glasses and started rubbing at his eyes. Surreptitiously, so as not to scare him off, I saw Mizell quietly nod to one of the women in the station, who brought over an Etch A Sketch sort of gizmo to start pulling together pieces of a sketch.

"Maybe 45, late 40s," TJ started. "He doesn't look like a weirdo. More like . . . half the profs at Canaan. A nerd in a bad suit." On his own face, TJ pointed to his nose. "He needed to clip his nose hairs. I was that close. I could see. Pale skin. Ginger hair, but it's gray at the sideburns, like a bad dye job. And glasses. He wore glasses. And he . . ."

The sketch woman pulled in a portal of different eyeglass shapes and waited for TJ to point to one, but he was lost, somewhere else, with that short stop he'd made.

"What?" Mizell knew when a stop, when silence was just like another word. I recognized it too, from class.

Zaccaro prompted him. "You're looking at withholding evidence, so if you know something else . . ."

"We should take this into an interview room." That was the other one. Michaelson.

"No. I wanna hear. I deserve to. He did this to me."

TJ picked back up, lost in his memory. "Most people were avoiding me, the way people do . . ."

"Tell me about it," I sneered at him.

"Holt. You're here on good behavior," Mizell said. "So shut it."

" . . . I mean, the way *anybody* does, when a stranger sticks something in their face. But this guy . . . he seemed like he was actually coming up *to* me, like he *wanted* what I had. Like he wanted to *say* something. And his eyes . . . you know how your eyes get when it's cold outside? They sort of sting? His eyes were like that. I thought maybe he was drunk, or high, so I move out of the way. But then he pushes *two* things in my hand and keeps walking. The rhyme on the back of one of the flyers and . . . something else."

What the fuck?

"He gave you something *else* and you didn't give it to us? You have another clue and . . . " I wasn't even yelling anymore. I could barely talk. "You have to arrest him. You have to put him in jail and . . . I can't take this. I can't take this anymore."

"Let's see what it is first," Mizell said, holding her hand out like a teacher confiscating a cell phone in class.

TJ dug in the pocket of his sweatpants and pulled out a folded piece of paper, damp around the edges with sweat from his body. He handed it to me. "I swear, I was gonna give it to you, just make you . . . wait a little bit."

I opened it up, and before I could actually take in what it said, I saw who wrote it.

Skip. Her handwriting. Shaky. Uncertain. Scared.

My baby. My "I love you more." Scared.

He *made* her write it.

"*Fui quod es, eris quod sum*," I read out loud, in Latin. "I once was what you are, you will be what I am."

The words were there, but not what they really meant. Not what a real classics scholar would pick up. This was even worse than it sounded. I looked at TJ. He understood. We both did.

"What does that mean?" said Mizell. "Sounds like gobbledy-gook. Is that a common phrase or . . . "

"It's advanced. Not just the translation, but . . . what they used it for. They used to put it on the tombs of Roman soldiers. An epitaph about death, like . . . we all die. We all end up in a grave. Nobody's immune. But there's more to it, almost like . . . a Roman would understand it like, 'We used to be the same. We *knew* each other. And *now* we're going to trade places.'"

"Wait. That's wrong," TJ said.

"Since I'm the one who taught *you* how to translate, I think . . . "

"Not that. Up there." TJ went up to the evidence board, pointing a finger at the blow-up of the last rhyme. "'*So far so good, but you're still in the wood. The Arcadian Deer is next; where is in this text.*' That's a mistake."

"What?" Michaelson jumped up after him.

"Right there." TJ pointed to the word *Arcadian*. "It's not the Arcadian Deer, it's the *Ceryneian* Deer."

It was staring me right in the face and . . . oh my God. I ran up to join them; now all of us were clustered around the evidence board. It was just words to them, but not to me. Not to TJ.

"He's right. I completely missed it. The Third Labor is to capture the *Ceryneian* Deer. Not Arcadia. Ceryneia was in Greece. Why would he . . . "

Mizell got to it first. "Wow. He's playing hardball. This is no mistake. He's telling you, 'Think you're so fucking smart? Then catch my mistake, which is no mistake at all. Which is deliberate.'" Now she was picking at other phrases in the poem. "*'You had the body, I had the brains.'* He's daring you again. 'I'm smarter than you. Figure it out.'"

"So where are you supposed to go now?" That was Michaelson. "Greece? Everything's been local so far. The lion, the hydra . . . "

Fuck. I had it. "*Arcadia.* That's what they called that old ski resort on the way to Pittsfield. I used to go there with Patti."

Mizell started taking command. "Get me a map. That's Route 248."

It was all making horrible, sick sense. I forced myself to keep reading aloud. "*'Start running numbers, or else she slumbers.'* Run the numbers *together.*" The kidnapper hadn't missed anything; the riddle kept on going. Nothing wasted, nothing just for show. "Two forty-eight. Route 248. Two days. Forty-eight hours. *That's* where I'm supposed to capture the deer. That old ski resort. Arcadia."

Mizell looked at me, desperate. I could smell it on her, just like I could smell TJ. She thought I didn't see her look up at the clock on the wall, but I did. The countdown. I did the math too. Nine and a half hours gone, since the kidnapper gave me his ultimatum.

"What about me?" TJ said, as we got ready to leave. The sniveling, the tears, the snot. Rubbing it in his hair as he took off his glasses and wiped his face. "I'll die if anything happens to Skip."

"It already has," I said, pushing my way past him, the last to leave. I never wanted to see him again.

I never wanted to hear another rhyme or read Latin again either, but I had to, if I wanted to find Skip. And now, this was the last thing I had to go on, the only thing in my head anymore:

If all's not done in forty-eight hours,
You'll next see Skip pushing up flowers.
If a mere two days seems unduly cold,
It's what you had to win the gold.

CHAPTER THIRTY-FIVE

"Once upon a time, my dear Skip, I came to see my birth. *After* my birth. My . . . afterbirth."

"What do you mean?" Skip asked, too caught up in how bizarre his story was to stop herself. She didn't want to know, but she had to. "How can you see your own birth? You mean, like a home movie?"

"No, not with a camera. With my . . . imagination. Or memory. Take your pick. It's quite a riveting story, actually," her kidnapper continued, his voice warmed up now and relaxed, from whatever was in the syringe.

Skip had teachers like him, teachers she didn't like, who liked to hear themselves talk, and didn't like to be interrupted. They talked at you, but you could tell, from where they were looking, that they didn't even see you anymore; they were telling stories they'd already told a thousand times before. But with her kidnapper, it sounded like he was starving to get the words out.

"Roberta DeGuilio was her name. A professional 'rebirther,' to guide you through remembering how you came into the world. Rebirthing. Quite the fashionable thing to do, back in the day, in some circles . . . my circles.

"You could say I was on a . . . journey, a spiritual path. To find out . . . what had gone wrong. Whose fault it was. I don't want you to get the wrong idea. That makes me sound so . . . *angry*. And I don't think I was. Not all the time. Angry. That only came later. Well, it actually came that day, at Roberta's apartment."

◆ ◆ ◆

Just twenty-five minutes away from the Canaan campus, it was a different world, I thought, desperate and derelict. Forty thousand bucks a year to go to Canaan, with its Gothic stone buildings and perfect lawns, and this is what you saw, on your way out of town: a racetrack, for greyhounds. Strip bars, already full by mid-afternoon. Gun shops. Rows of "For Rent" or "For Sale" signs, scrawled across windows in whitewash paint. Houses that were almost leaning, that had seen their last good coats of paint years ago. New England winters up in the mountains ate up paint, turning everything gray and chapped. No wonder the Arcadia ski lodge had closed up. The snow was too erratic to attract tourists who wanted to ski, and they sure as hell didn't want to drive through Hoovervilles on their way to do it, in their fancy North Face parkas. A road trip I'd made dozens of times before, but somehow, seeing it from the back of a cop car—thinking my daughter might be *out there* somewhere—it felt like I'd never seen it before.

It felt like it had never been this ugly or foreboding. This scary.

Mizell drove in the front seat, with one of the FBI guys next to her; I was in the back, with the other one. A mesh grill was in front of us; doors with no indoor handles on either side. I felt like the criminal.

On our way out, we'd made a pit stop at the hospital, to check in on Wendy. In the chaos of the last few days, she'd had to make do with just phone calls from me. But even that stop I felt guilty about: it wasn't just to see her, to find out when she was getting home, but to have her call the zoo so I could pick up something there. A weapon I was going to need, in Arcadia.

That had been our second pit stop.

"Take a right here." I remembered it from when I had come a few times with Patti; the turn off Route 248 up into the mountains, marked with a homemade cross, two boards nailed together and hammered into the ground as a makeshift memorial, where a car had gone off the side of the road and crashed into a tree. Someone's name was written on the cross in Magic Marker, a fraying ribbon wrapped around the tree trunk, but the ribbon was so faded it was impossible to tell whose name, or what color the ribbon had originally been. Yellow, pink?

It had been fresh, the last time I'd come with Patti.

The ribbon was almost white now, the same as the sad plastic flowers that were stuck in the ground around the cross.

We came to another turnoff, onto an even smaller dirt road. A barrier gate guarded the way, but a fallen-down, splintering sign told us we were at the right place: "Arcadia Ski Resort: Where Winter Is Fun."

◆ ◆ ◆

"I was twenty-one, twenty-two, and I walked. Better than now. Canes, instead of crutches. I still had some balance. I was never *whole*—don't get me wrong—but at least I just needed two canes to . . . amble along. At a gait. Wait, is that something . . . *fast*?"

Skip had gone through her horse period. She knew. "It's slow, like a canter. Sort of . . . loping."

"Then what do you call it when a horse tries to walk on broken legs? When you need to . . . put it down? Maybe *that's* a more accurate description. I moved like a . . . *Slinky*. Do you play with those anymore? That thing you can . . . *push* down stairs? And it still survives?"

"I had one. When I was little."

"Good. Then I've painted a . . . portrait. Something you can visualize." He took a deep breath.

"So. Roberta. Middle-aged, graying at the temples, she greeted me in her slippers and housecoat. A rose pattern, if memory serves. She navigated me down her tiny hallway into her apartment: a narrow little passageway, much like a birth canal. She had set the scene well, whether she knew it or not. Either side crowded with shelves and books and coats hanging on the wall. But I did it. I made my way through, without knocking anything over. I was so proud of myself!"

His hands working the wheels, he moved his chair closer to Skip.

"Roberta got in her Barcalounger, then instructed me to lie on the floor . . . and breathe. That's all. Just breathe. The lying down part was easy. I was used to being on the ground, from falling so much, or being pushed. But the breathing . . . all I had to do was breathe! In. Out. Fast. Slow. However she directed me. And I thought, if ever there's a job I could do, that was it. Just breathe! Who needs a college degree for that?"

Even if Skip couldn't see him, she could almost *hear* the expression on his face. For once, he wasn't being sarcastic. Or ironic—Skip thought that was the word, that she'd heard adults use a lot. He sounded . . . in awe.

"Roberta must have been very skilled, because I did begin to . . . just breathe. And even more, I began to *see* my birth. My . . . pre-birth. In the womb. That place where I hid from the world, before it was time to make my . . . grand appearance."

A quarter of a mile into the woods, and for some reason, I was thinking about seeing *Bambi* as a kid—that line somebody in it says, "Man is in the forest, man is in the forest."

I said it now, to try and break the spell of gloom, to send out a warning. "Man is in the forest." But which one? Him, or me?

"You say something?" Michaelson asked.

"Nothing important."

The trees were mostly bare up here. Peeling silver birches, and maples, but after that brilliant burst of color is gone, and all that's left is brown. The color was leeched out of everything; a sort of gray fog hung in the air. The whole mountain seemed like a cemetery—not just of trees, but machinery. I was following the path Patti and I used to take to the ski lift, and everything I saw was a reminder of what used to be, when "Arcadia" was in full swing: giant rusted poles and ski lift cable wheels littered the ground. Gondolas teetered in the air, covered with graffiti from some kids who risked climbing up there somehow, to tag them.

Mizell dropped back, alongside the FBI guys: near enough to get to me if something happened, far enough to stay somewhat hidden. It was me the kidnapper wanted, me who was supposed to complete the task. I heard the *crunch crunch crunch* all three of them made in unison, stomping through the leaves.

And then—something else. I held my arm up to halt them . . .

. . . a skittering sound. Something that didn't belong in the woods. Not nature, and not natural. Like high-heels clacking on a concrete floor, but fast. The sound seemed to echo around us, and then a different sound joined it: *thwacking*. Something strong but hollow—tubes, maybe?—hitting each other. It went on for a while, then stopped. Then the other sound started again— somebody running across a slick floor?

It was coming from the old chair lift platform ahead of us, thirty, forty yards up the hill. It was a narrow enclosure, like a faux-Swiss railway station picked up on lifts. I remembered Patti and me riding up the chair lift to it, our skis dangling in mid-air. Even from this distance, I could see that the big double wooden doors in front were padlocked, through holes where their doorknobs used to be; the heavy metal chain picked up the little bit of sun that was peeking through the gloom.

Now everything was silent. Was I wrong? Maybe the sound was coming from somewhere else, and the echo just made it seem like . . .

No.

Something ferocious—something *terrified*—was banging against those doors now, a battering ram pushing them out a few inches, as far as the straining chain would allow.

Something was attacking, from inside.

And it could only be one thing: the hind I was supposed to find. Labor number three.

◆ ◆ ◆

"It was like a ballet; an amniotic ballet, but something else. A *battle,* in Mother's belly. I moved in that warm bath of blood and fluid that had been my home, and thought, *don't make me go, don't make me leave, something's not right!*

'I was squeezed out anyway, through that narrow birth canal. And . . . well, what ya see is what ya get. Or you will, soon enough. A perfect storm of birth defects, caused by an umbilical cord being wrapped around my neck. The oxygen cut off, for a few vital seconds. A brain that worked, but a body that . . . didn't. And I relived it all.

"I looked into Roberta's eyes, and she looked into mine. I had seen my birth. I knew my truth. Even she was a bit misty-eyed. Our work together was finished. Roberta, God bless her soul— and I do mean that—asked what I had seen—*this is the important part, Skip, so listen carefully*—and told me that what I 'saw' might not represent my real birth. It might just be a metaphor. Have you studied 'metaphor' at school?"

"We haven't, but . . . I know . . . I read a lot on my own . . . "

"Well, this was no metaphor. I knew what I saw. Pushed out, too early. A cord around my neck, like a noose. I gave Roberta my hard-earned one hundred dollars. As my hand touched hers, transferring the money, she said, and I'll remember these words until the day I die, she said, 'I hope this brings you peace.'"

"I assured her that it would, as I tried to stand on my own, pulling myself up onto my canes. But I was wrong about one thing. Our work together *wasn't* yet finished."

◆ ◆ ◆

Up on the ski lodge platform, all of the windows were boarded up. Shutters with Alps-like cut-outs on them were shut tight, hammered closed against plywood on the inside. I walked around the perimeter of the platform, wood creaking with every step. Up at the top of the hill like this, I felt the wind in a way I hadn't down below; the upside-down metal *T*s that used to hold the chair lifts were like a wind chime, writ large. Still attached to the sagging cable and clanging in to each other, thudding.

Even with a wall between us, I could hear the thing inside keeping in step with me, as I made my way around to the back of the building. One window there was still open, almost waiting. Inviting me in, just like the basement door in the science building, which led to the hydras.

And that's where I saw it. A four-point buck, its antlers literally shining gold with glitter, banging its head against the walls, pawing at the floor. The poor creature had been trapped inside that long lonely room, droppings of excrement all over the floor.

The first thing I thought—how did the kidnapper get the poor thing up here? It would have been kicking with everything it had, unless he had doped it first. Put it to sleep, to awaken later. Left for me.

Just then, that majestic beast swiveled its head and saw me.

It looked in my eyes, and *knew*.

Man is in the forest.

I pulled myself through the window, to get a better look at what I couldn't believe, at what couldn't be, but there it was.

My mind scrambling, to take it all in—getting the thing up here, in this enclosure, the poem guiding me to it, and then . . .

That's what it was. A hind—the hind in Hercules's labor—was female. A hind *is* female. This wasn't. This bloody beast I was looking at was male. It had antlers. The female of the species didn't. Either the kidnapper had fucked up—and from the poem guiding me here, we knew he didn't, he didn't make casual mistakes—or there was something extra I was supposed to read into all this.

And looking more closely, I saw it.

Sick. As sick as the poems the kidnapper was sending me.

Somehow a set of antlers had been attached to the deer's head—turning it from female to male. Making it something it wasn't. Antlers had somehow been *mounted* on it, just like my father used to mount his hunting trophies to our walls. Blood was running down the deer's head from where strands of wire wrapped around and attached the antlers. God knows how long the deer had been trapped inside, waiting for me, in agony: the antlers were tilting, where the weight had been too much, and the deer had been blindly knocking them against every solid surface to try to get them off.

What did that mean? What did that sadist want me to figure out from this? Something turned into something else. A female turned into a male. Forced to wear a disguise, a crown of antlers. A female being hurt, someone getting back at a woman?

And something else: speared through one of the points of bone and moss was a piece of white paper, now streaked red with blood.

My next clue, delivered without mercy.

Was that it? Being forced to wear the antlers, just to have something to stick the next sick clue onto?

I tried to get close to it to unhook the antlers, but it took a run at me every time I got close, sideswiping me with blood.

The poor animal reared back, but it was already on its last legs, as if it had never recovered from being doped up and somehow transported here. I saw its belly, dipped low like a barrel, hair matted. A pitiful sound like nothing I'd ever heard before—a cross between a moan and a bleat—came from the deer as it fell back on its rear haunches, too spent to even attack. It couldn't stand anymore, but kept trying, its legs splaying out from under it in all the blood that was already on the floor, that I kept slipping and sliding in as I tried to figure out what to do.

But there was nothing to do. Except one thing.

"What the hell?" Mizell and the FBI were at the window now, their weapons drawn.

"No! Don't shoot! Don't shoot!" I yelled back at them.

Tame the deer, don't hurt the body,
To keep me from getting much more naughty.

The deer had already been tamed, past the point of no return. But I couldn't leave it here like this. In agony. Not even a genius like Wendy could fix it. I had the tranquilizer gun she'd helped me get from the zoo, that I had thought in advance I was going to need to capture it. But the time for that was long gone.

He had seen to that.

Mizell took out her own gun and aimed, but I took it from her. "No. This is mine. Damn the Labors. I can't leave it like this." I pulled the trigger, and the bang echoed through the hills.

◆ ◆ ◆

"I raised one of my canes and started to bring it down on Roberta's head."

"Oh my God," Skip let out, shaking her captor into remembering that he had an audience.

"Funny. People never expect that from a gimp," he continued on, seeing the scene in his head once more. "I guess that explains the look of . . . *shock* on her face. And *started*, I said, but didn't follow through. I couldn't. I ran . . . well, I stumbled my way out. Horrified at what I'd almost done. She had simply reported the truth—or caused *me* to; she hadn't caused it.

"Tame the dear, my dear Roberta, don't hurt the body," he started keening, over and over, "tame the deer, don't hurt the body, tame the deer . . . she was tamed alright . . . "

"What? What are you saying? What do you mean?"

And ever so quickly—for someone who couldn't move anything except his arms—he bent down in his wheelchair behind her and started tying her wrists back together. "Tame *Skip*. Thought I didn't. *See*. What you were doing. Your. Escape plan. I wanted you to. Hope. We all need hope. *I* had hope. Back then."

The duct tape from a roll in his lap sounded like it was screaming as he ripped off giant strips of it and began binding her wrists again. "Now you know. What *I've* gone through. Hope. It doesn't exist. Not anymore. For either of us."

"I'm sorry! Please . . . I won't move. I promise. I didn't mean to . . . you'd be scared too. You'd try to get away . . . "

He ferociously snatched off another length of tape. It sang. It shrieked.

And so did Skip, as he tied her hands back up.

Hope. Gone.

For her.

For him.

CHAPTER THIRTY-SIX

"Be careful. There's blood."

I heard Mizell say it downstairs to Wendy, finally released from the hospital. This woman I loved, finally out, and all I could do was cower upstairs in my bathroom, hiding from her after what I'd done.

The sound of that hind, rearing up, snorting, trying to buck, collapsing. We taught children all the barnyard sounds—the moos and cluck cluck clucks and oinks—but we never thought to teach them the *real* sounds of nature. The important ones. A deer, fighting for its life. I'd never heard it before, and now I would never forget it.

The sound of clicking my cell phone made, when I forced down my revulsion and snapped a photo of the dead animal, another trophy for the kidnapper to post on my Facebook page.

Skip on the phone: "*Daddy?*"

I wanted the spray from the shower to seep into my ears and clog them up for the rest of time, but it wasn't working.

I could still hear those horrific sounds from the last few hours, even though they were just in my head.

Downstairs, Mizell continued to prepare Wendy. Warn her. "He didn't want to do it, but . . . he had to. Be careful. Go easy on him. There's blood. A lot of it."

Mizell was wrong about that. There *had been* a lot of blood, but now I was watching it all disappear down the drain, as I bent over and let the hot spray rain down on my spine, my arms dropped all the way down to the shower floor like some hulking beast.

"Ethan? It's me . . . I'm coming up, okay?" she said.

Wendy could follow my trail of breadcrumbs, my trail of bloody clothes to lead the way. Bloody boots, bloody shirt, bloody pants, all leading to the bedroom, like the droppings of animals she could track in the wild.

Wendy jerked open the shower curtain. "What's wrong? Is it Skip . . . have they . . . "

"Twelve hours. Twelve hours gone. He made me kill. Like Hercules. The real one."

On the sink in the bathroom, my laptop computer, its top opened and set to my Facebook page. After nothing for months—except birthday greetings from a few days ago—I was going crazy with posting what he demanded.

Me, in a flash of bare white light, holding the stolen hydra.

Me, next to a dead deer in a pool of blood, its eyes still open. A macabre trophy. I was holding the piece of paper with the next Labor in my hands, dead eyes myself.

Wendy stopped and looked at it, a recap in two photos.

"I did that. I had to. I had to put it out of its misery. He'd strapped these antlers on it . . . on its head, wire . . . biting into its neck. I didn't want to, but . . . I did the Labor wrong. The deer's supposed to be *alive*. '*Tame the deer, don't hurt the body, tame the deer, don't hurt the body . . .* ' But I did. I *did* hurt it . . . But I couldn't leave it like that, suffering . . . "

I began keening back and forth, reciting nursery rhymes. Wendy stepped in to hold me, her clothes pelted by the shower. Past the plush white towels on my bathroom floor, sopping up water and blood.

"I'm so sorry. The hospital, the shot . . . the deer, everything . . . " I said, rocking back and forth in Wendy's arms.

"You did the right thing," Wendy said soothingly, back to me. "It's what I would have done too. Nobody could have saved it after that."

"I've never hunted, never killed anything. My dad did, he wanted me to . . . working out . . . then hunting. That's all he did. Hanging up those trophies: mounted heads, mounted medals . . . my medals . . . "

"Turn on the TV!" We heard Mizell running up the stairs to us. "They've got the sketch up."

Wendy helped me up and into my robe; she grabbed a still-dry towel as we went into the main bedroom, outside the bath. Mizell already had my little set turned on: It was that Dana Rossen reporter from this morning, now on the six o'clock evening news, showing the sketch of the man TJ had helped put together, the man who shoved the poem with the Second Labor at him.

"As we continue to follow the breaking story of the kidnapping of Elizabeth 'Skip' Holt, the daughter of Canaan professor Ethan Holt, this composite sketch has just been released by investigators. There is a reward, and the FBI is asking anyone with information . . ."

The landline phone rang downstairs. The line only *he* called on now. In my robe, I ran down to grab it, nodding at the cop stationed in the kitchen to start his trace equipment.

"I'm getting tired of that woman—Dana, is it?—having to be our go-between. We must meet. And soon. I am. Of course. *Disappointed*. About showing the sketch of my. Associate."

"*You* sadist. That deer . . . "

"Doe a *deer*. A female deer. A female *Skip*."

"WHAT DO YOU WANT FROM US?"

"From *you*. *For* you. To remember."

"Remember WHAT? I've had enough of this shit . . . "

A pause, a sort of sputter, as the kidnapper weighed what to say next, then snapped it out at me.

"*I* am the one who's had. 'Enough of this shit.' Which you will be cleaning out of the Augean stables. Very. Soon. Indeed. I see you've found. The next clue . . . "

"At least this way I can *read* it instead of having to listen to your *voice* . . . "

"My *voice*, I might remind you, is the only thing . . . "

" . . . your *voice* is like fingernails on a chalkboard . . . "

"I'll *show* you. *Fingernails.*"

The phone slammed down, on his end.

Mizell whipped off her headset. "Do you WANT your daughter to die? What the hell . . . "

"I'm sorry, I'm sorry . . . "

"Sorry doesn't count! Don't you get it? This is *real.*"

I sank onto the floor and looked at them, pleadingly. *Mea culpa, mea maxima maxima culpa.* Mizell, the cop, Wendy . . .

"He's making me *become* Hercules . . . don't you get it? The real Hercules. He kills animals, kills his wife, his children . . . he goes mad and loses it and . . . I've gone mad, just like Hercules."

CHAPTER THIRTY-SEVEN

The kidnapper was gasping for air, stabbing at the crook in his left arm with a fresh needle. Only stabbing at himself would take over his rage, the rage he wanted to inflict on everything in his wake. On that person. On the other end of the phone. And on himself and how far things had gone. He wanted to stab it all away. Make himself hurt so bad for what he'd done . . . but his body could barely feel anything anymore, as the disease took over more and more of it. He plunged the needle at his own useless thigh, wasting away in the wheelchair. He plunged the hypodermic through his pants, waiting for relief to come. But it didn't. He kept looking for a new patch of skin, as he yelled at Skip.

"He'll regret it, the way he talked to me . . . "

"Please, what . . . what happened, what did he say . . . "

He bucked in his wheelchair behind her, like the trapped deer of Ceryneia. "Tell me, tell me fast, like Scheherezade begging for her life, tell me something good about that man, tell me before I . . . "

"Please! What happened? What did he say? How can I . . . "

He gulped for air that wouldn't come, like the panic attacks Skip had had when she first woke up here, her chest so paralyzed she couldn't take in a breath. Giant hulking spasms, trying to get air. Get life.

"What, what? What can I do?" Skip said, straining at the duct tape that held her in place, terrified that she couldn't see behind her.

"Nobody can do anything. This! Cannot be. Undone," he screamed in return, now throwing the syringe across the room and picking up something else. Something that glinted, even in the dim light of the room.

"Undo me! I'll get help! Daddy'll help you!"

"HELP me? He's the one. Who DID this. To me."

His hand slammed a shining scalpel down behind her desk.

Where her hands were. *Into* her hands.

Silver, and blood, and fresh, hot, searing pain.

And then nothing.

CHAPTER THIRTY-EIGHT

The headlights of Mizell's unmarked police car cut a dim swath through a soupy November fog. We couldn't see much, but we could see a giant wooden thunderbolt, rigged with neon and flashing, almost like the kidnapper saying, "You are here."

And "here" was the Lambda Chi frat house. Wendy had figured it out back at my house; while I was wallowing in my misery, certain my actions had already killed Skip, Wendy was the only one who had actually done something, taking the blood-soaked poem I had gotten from the deer's antlers.

Number four is the boar
I'd like to hear it roar . . .
It's in the land of the Greek
You'll need to hide and seek
Your next clue will be under . . .
Where Zeus let loose his thunder.

"'Land of the Greek'—the poem . . . it's that row of frat houses over on Hennepin! The boar, the pig . . . they've got a pig, it's their mascot. The Lambda Chi's. I had to go out there last week to treat it . . . they call it the 'Zeus house.' They've got this thunderbolt in front . . . this cutout. With neon. That has to be what he means."

Wendy was right, and I knew it too. Knew them, at least. I had been a Lambda Chi when I was at Canaan, back when the frat was altogether different: made up of the BMOCs and scholars, the school leaders. Guys who wore khakis and V-neck sweaters. Over the years, the frat had devolved to party boys; it barely had a charter anymore. Now, they'd taken their fun and games—and their thunderbolt—off-campus, alongside a row of crumbling two-

188

and three-story houses, painted with garish fraternity and sorority colors, Greek letters camouflaged into the exteriors in some way.

Mizell cut the engine and parked across the street from the house, the homemade thunderbolt zig-zagging down off its roof. With the car windows down, we heard the sound of the car cooling off; metal pinging, mixing in with night sounds. And then . . . I wasn't even sure I heard it at first, but . . . something. A sound that *didn't* belong to the night, coming from the back of the Lambda Chi house. A low rumble, but no specific words that broke out into meaning.

It was just like the Arcadia ski lodge had been—the deer—a sound in the distance, luring me. And just like Arcadia—where Patti and I had gone—this group had a connection to me too. I had *been* one of them.

"It's like he's replaying my greatest hits. Scenes from my life. He *knows* me," I almost whispered to Mizell, inside her car. "Is that it? Why is he picking out these things? They're things I've done. Places I've been."

"Not just making you revisit them, but . . . it's more like he wants to *be* you. To have your life, starting with your daughter," she whispered back.

"*Fui quod es, eris quod sum,*" I repeated. When Mizell looked at me, I said, "That other paper TJ had. The one he'd kept from us. 'I once was what you are, you will be what I am.' Like he's making us switch places . . . turning me into him, while he turns into me. He's doing everything I used to do."

We got out of the car and crossed the street, trying to stay low to the ground.

Closer to the house, the sound got louder, more distinct. A lot of voices, not just one.

Soo-wee, soo-wee . . . com' ere, little piggy. Piggy piggy piggy . . .

From behind a spiked wooden fence in back of the house, I saw smoke, dark smoke, like that particular color a citronella candle gave off, inky and oily. I slowly nudged open the gate into the backyard, afraid its creak would give me away, but inside, they were too far gone to notice.

Nothing came charging at me, no wild animal lay dying, only . . .

Frat boys, drunk frat boys, animals in togas, performing some ritual around a bonfire. That's what I'd seen, and heard, and smelled, from across the street. The upperclassmen—I guess they were the older ones—were dressed in purple and red velvet, robes and sashes, olive leaves banded around their heads. The younger ones—pledges—were in silly togas made of cheap sheets. The older kids had made two rows, and their initiates were weaving down the middle, stumbling as the big guys pelted them with belts. One or two of the kids lurched away to throw up on the side.

Following them, I saw it: what I'd been brought here to . . . see? Confront? Kill?

Their pig mascot—the "boar"—the one Wendy must have treated, pawing against wire mesh in a long mud pen, wanting to get in on the action. It was decorated too—although not like the deer in the ski lodge. Just fake boar fangs, hanging around its neck.

Number four is the boar
I'd like to hear it roar
Or Skip will be no more.

The flames of their bonfire shot higher, and I wondered if they were going to roast the pig, if that was their big climax. Whether or not the pig was part of *their* ritual—no one was paying any attention to it, not yet—I knew it was supposed to be part of *mine*. I snuck inside its pen and the oinking got louder, going head to head with their chanting.

That got their attention.

The boys looked over to see something that was even more surreal than their own rites: me, slipping and sliding in the muck, trying to grab the ring of boar fangs off from around its neck. At first they must have thought I was one of their own, already so splattered with mud they couldn't make out who I was.

They cheered me on, whatever they thought I was doing. It didn't matter. It was all part of the fun, part of the ritual.

"Soo-wee, soo-wee . . . "

The sound of the pig got more desperate, as if it were already roasting on a spit. But alive.

I turned toward the bonfire, and they finally saw my face, cutting through the flames.

"*Professor Holt?*"

Their limbo dance stopped. So did their chanting, as they saw their professor, a respected member of the Canaan College community, sliding through mud and shit, holding on to this animal for dear life. Outtakes from *Animal House*, until they saw how desperate and deranged I was. Now there was nothing in the air except crackling fire and me—and a pig that was suddenly escaping. Dashing through the pen's open door. Squealing.

I couldn't let the pig get away—it's like the pig suddenly was Skip, my only link to her—and began chasing it, followed by thirty boys in wine-stained togas and one out-of-shape cop, her hand on her holster.

That's when I remembered the last part of the rhyme—the thing I should have started with.

> *Your next clue will be under . . .*
> *Where Zeus let loose his thunder.*

I ran to the front porch, and collapsed onto my back, to look up at what I hadn't seen before: that the tip of the thunderbolt touched right down onto the mailbox.

And underneath the mailbox, taped to the metal, was a folded piece of white paper.

I reached up and yanked; as soon as I grabbed it, I knew it wasn't just paper; it had weight, a weird squareness. There was something inside it, but my hands were so thick with mud and pig slobber that I couldn't get it open at first. I kept fumbling at it as three or four squares of something heavy fell out.

Photographs.

It was dark, the streetlights were flickering, the neon of the thunderbolt pulsing and buzzing. Mizell was running up on the porch, togas and boys were flying everywhere, and I was in overload, trying to grab up the photos and read at the same time.

Fingernails on the chalkboard? No, I've used my sword,
But at least I've left eight, for Skip's trip o'er the River of Hate.

Mizell, see-through plastic gloves on, snatched the paper from me and held it to find the perfect angle in the dark to read, because something else was there, glued below the fold of the page.

Little squares of black, with squiggles of white lettering.

I could see her eyes scanning back and forth, a line of type coming to the edge of the page and then getting zinged back to the beginning by the return.

"C'mon, let's go. We've got the next clue," she barked out, trying to pull me off the porch.

"What? What else does it say? What are those shiny things?"

"Let's get to the station where we can get some light . . . and get you cleaned up . . . "

"WHAT? What aren't you telling me?" I yanked the paper away from Mizell and felt them.

Hard. Squarish. Bloody. *Polished.*

Skip's fingernails. Two of them. The *A* and *H*, from where she had written "I HATE WENDY."

And one more thing. His PS, at the very bottom of the page:
HER FINGERS WILL BE NEXT.

CHAPTER THIRTY-NINE

Skip had been in the hospital once, after her mother died, with something the doctors couldn't figure out at first. Pain in her stomach. Excruciating pain, like a kidney stone or her appendix about to burst. The only time it went away was when she stretched out and sort of arched her back, like she was shifting the pain around and giving it more room to breathe. But they couldn't give her medicine because they needed her to *have* the pain to figure out what was causing it.

For three agonizing days—while tests were being run and fluids were being pumped into her body from IV bags, and doctors and nurses kept coming into her hospital room in the middle of the night so she couldn't sleep—she hurt too much to talk, so her father talked for her. He brought her goofy presents from the gift shop downstairs and held her hand and told her if she just listened to what he said, she wouldn't hurt anymore. He was going to give her a test when she was all better, so she had to pay attention to what he said.

And then he just started talking, nonstop, for three days. He told her anything and everything that came into his head. How much he had loved her mother, how they had fallen in love in college. He told her about his training years ago and what it had felt like being out on the track after his teammates had gone home at night and it was just him and Sig. How he'd listen to Sig map out their plans for the Olympics, the timelines they'd be on and the order of events and how to pace himself. And when her father's voice got too hoarse, Sig came to visit and took over the job, telling Skip about how he'd come up with the idea of making her dad put a hurdle in his living room so he could still keep practicing, jumping over that thing at least twenty-five times a day when he was away from the track. It had been agony then, but it seemed funny now, and Skip's dad and Sig started laughing, and she started laughing too, and that's when she knew she was going to be okay. Lying in that hospital bed, she wasn't thinking about her pain anymore, she was thinking about how much she loved her dad and Sig and what goofballs they were, for grownups.

Mesenteric adenitis, the doctors finally figured out, that's what Skip had. An inflammation of the lining around the stomach. Maybe it was caused by stress after her mother died; they didn't really know. Skip thought they were saying something about her adenoids, which she thought was something in her throat and not her stomach, but she even laughed about that.

She could laugh, because the pain was finally gone.

That's how much pain she felt now, the kind she'd had when she was first in the hospital, even with the shot her kidnapper had given her to put her asleep, before he hurt her hand, carving out those two fingernails.

Skip woke up—how many hours later, she didn't know—and the helper in the suit and the smudgy glasses was standing over her. She was still woozy from whatever drug the kidnapper had given her, so it took her a minute to focus.

He was looming over her, stroking her bandaged hand. Smiling so eagerly.

The smell of fresh spray paint was in the air. Up on the walls, two more of the murals had been crossed out with giant neon *X*s in yellow, almost like the same color from the spray paint can that had exploded on her face that time, when she'd stuck a screwdriver into the can. One of the murals had antlers nailed into it. Real ones, with the bristly part of the skull still attached, and the horns covered in gold glitter. And the other mural had a pig mask with a snout, thumbtacked into the middle of a forest scene. The pig face looked like it used to be a balloon or something, maybe a

Halloween mask, but somebody had stuck a pin in it and all the air had escaped, deflating it. All that was left now was hanging pink skin, with a snout. She'd seen a rerun once on *The Twilight Zone* about people with pig faces, their noses upturned and their cheeks all puffy, and it looked like one of them.

In her haze, she thought the man who was touching her looked like one of the Pig People. Puffy cheeks, nostrils, glasses. Hippocrates, the kidnapper had called him.

Hippocrates was a doctor. Doctors were supposed to help people.

"It hurts, I know. I'm sorry," he said, still running his fingers over Skip's left hand, where the two fingers that had held the *H* and *A* fingernails were wrapped up in the same gauze that had been wrapped around her eyes. Blood was turning the white gauze pink, so she could see where her two fingernails had been.

"*A* and *H*," she remembered her kidnapper saying, just as she was falling asleep from the shot he gave her.

She didn't know why he picked those two, and he wouldn't tell her.

At least she hadn't been awake when he did it.

Now her fingernails would just spell out "I TE WENDY."

"Hippocrates" was trying to comfort her, rubbing at the bandages on her hand, like he knew how much she hurt. Skip could use that. She could have him help her get away, while the other guy and the one in the wheelchair were gone. She had to talk through her pain to him, just keep talking and not stop, but she had to do it in a hurry, before the other two came back.

He'd told her he was sorry. Now she had to make him prove it.

"What's your name? Your real name?"

"Jeffrey."

"Are you really a doctor?"

"No. A CPA. A bean counter. This is . . . more exciting."

"But it's *wrong*. I need a *real* doctor. You've got to help me. Get me out of here and take me to the hospital. My hand hurts so much. Please. Untie me, and I'll take care of you. But we have to go. Now. Fast."

Skip made her voice go soft and high, like her mother used to do when Skip was sick. Skip thought how it was almost a maternal instinct, making your voice go high like that when you wanted to baby someone. The way you'd talk to an eager dog who was licking at your face. So that's what Skip had to do. Baby him. Jeffrey. She got as close to his face as she could, even though she was still tied up and it made her sick to look at him and his teeth, which she could tell he didn't floss.

"Get some scissors. Are there scissors in the other room? Go see. Hurry! You can cut the tape off my hands but keep the bandage on because I'm still bleeding . . . "

Jeffrey was trying to get her untied without the scissors, on one side of Skip's desk so he could keep looking toward the door, but his big clumsy hands were almost as useless as Skip's hands were, tied down.

"It hurts, I know," he said to her, as if he really did understand.

"Yes, it does. It hurts a lot," Skip said back to him, trying not to reveal how impatient she was. How desperate. "So we've gotta get away. I'll tell the police you helped me. You'll be a hero. They won't do anything to you. I promise."

"There's a reward from your father. I need the money. Can you get me the reward?"

"Of course I can! I promise! You just have to get me out of here . . . "

Skip was looking in his eyes—hard to see through the smudges on his thick glasses—trying to make a connection with him, even though he seemed so spaced out on some kind of drugs himself. She wasn't getting through to him fast enough.

"You don't wanna work for somebody who hurts people so bad, do you?"

"No, but . . . I know it hurts." It was as if that's all he was programmed to say.

"I know it does, I know, but you've already said that! Quit saying it! I don't wanna think about how much it hurts. I just wanna get away from here and you've got to help me!" Skip was screaming now, and crying. She couldn't ignore how much her hand hurt, no matter how much she talked.

It was her father's old trick, from when she was in the hospital, but it wasn't working anymore.

She saw the barest flicker in his eyes—maybe he did understand, after all—an actual physical flicker, like his eyes were registering something new, and . . .

A gunshot.

Jeffrey stopped.

The kidnapper was back in the doorway, with a gun. Now a smoking gun.

Jeffrey repeated the only words he seemed to know anymore. "It hurts."

"I know it does, I know." The kidnapper did a perfect imitation of Skip. She hadn't even heard him come back inside. She hadn't heard anything, except for the gunshot.

"Now it won't. *Hurt*, I mean. At least, not for him."

Blood soaked through the front of his shirt, and his dead body collapsed on top of Skip. She tried to scream, but no sound would come out, except the heaving of her lungs, trying to catch her breath under the weight of a dead man.

CHAPTER FORTY

"At least she's alive." That's what Wendy kept pushing me to focus on. "That's good."

"*Good?* A psycho's pulling out her fingernails and writing about the River Styx and you think there's anything goddamned *good* about it?"

"The River Styx?" Frick—or Frack—broke in, looking at the latest bounty from the kidnapper laid out on my kitchen table.

I pointed it out on the rhyme. "*'But at least I've left eight, for Skip's trip o'er the River of Hate.'* The River of Hate. Same as the River Styx. What separates the Earth from the Underworld . . . from being dead."

This wasn't happening.

My dining room table, crowded with food from neighbors, pushed aside to make room for four horrifying photos. Skip shot from different angles, but never so I could see her face. Just where she was tied up. Two fingernails, ripped from my baby's hand. The smell of burnt coffee from the kitchen. A setup of recording equipment from the police, tape recorders and head sets and switches on the marble top of the island in the kitchen, where Skip had her breakfast every morning. Where she'd left a plastic bag of groceries. Meatloaf ingredients, to say "I'm sorry." Two FBI guys in suits. In my fucking house.

That's what wasn't happening, except it was.

Eight fingernails left, out of ten. Two taken.

"See if we can find some detail in these photos . . . " Mizell started.

"What detail? Just look. She's tied up to a fucking desk. *That's* the detail. There's nothing else there. Oh my God. Oh my sweet Jesus . . . "

I saw the furtive looks between Mizell and Guillory, the cop with the recording equipment: *Get these away. Fast.*

Guillory started to take the photos away, along with the fingernails at the bottom of the latest rhyme, but I clamped my hand down on them.

"No." I scooped up everything on the table and held it to my chest.

Nobody moved.

"Uh . . . why don't you take one of my pain pills from the hospital?" Wendy offered. "It'll help you calm down."

I didn't want to be calm. I didn't want my senses dulled in any way; I needed to be on high alert to find Skip, and I didn't want anything she didn't have. If she didn't get pain pills, I didn't want them either. I wanted to feel her pain, and I did, looking at the four photographs of her tied up. A camera flash obliterating her face in every one of them, seeing her jerk away from its light.

She was sitting in an old-fashioned school desk, in the middle of what looked to be an empty room. One of the photos just showed her right leg, duct-taped to the side of the desk. Another showed her left leg, taped the same way. I could tell it was Skip because of her socks—blue on the left leg, red on the right—the same she'd worn the morning of our last run together. The third photo showed the back crook of her right elbow, still wearing the same long sleeve jersey she'd gone running in. She'd inked in a spider's web on both elbows; that's how I knew. And the final photo showed a spoon going in her mouth, with what looked like oatmeal in it. I could see the little scar on the upper right corner of her lip, from where she'd snagged herself with her school ID bracelet.

"Are you absolutely sure it's her?" Zaccaro from the FBI asked, but there was no doubt. Every one of the photos said "Skip," just like that painted outline he'd first made on her bedsheets. They couldn't be any other little girl, but the kidnapper was taunting me, by not showing her face. Not letting me see my baby.

Mizell smoothed out the newest poem on the dining room table and started reading, to try to get us all back on track. *"Hercules cleaned out the Augean stables . . . "*

I took over reading it aloud; this was mine.

By sweeping away shit with the water table.
But since I'm such a modern-day guy
I want you to go where the drugs they buy
Give it a twist, make it today
Instead of shit, sweep crack away.
For your lessons to learn,
Make those muscles burn . . . and I do mean burn . . .
To keep Skip alive, just do number five.

"Wait . . . what are those squiggles? Letters? What do they mean?" Wendy asked, out of the blue.

I'd been looking at the poem; Wendy had been looking at the fingernails glued to the bottom of the paper it was on. The one thing I couldn't look at anymore. The one thing I didn't want Wendy to look at.

That's the other way I knew this was my daughter. How many other teenage girls had written out "I HATE WENDY" on their fingers? I hadn't told Wendy because I hadn't wanted to hurt her, but I couldn't keep it from her now.

"She wrote something on her fingernails. The night of the party. After the party."

"What?"

"It doesn't matter. Just something stupid, to get back at me about that DVD. She didn't mean it, she was just mad because . . ."

"Tell me."

"Don't hate her. Please. It was just stupid teenage stuff . . . "

"What?"

"'I hate Wendy,'" I said, hating myself just as much for having to say it out loud.

Wendy let out a breath, then pursed her lips together. Shook her head, like it was her fault. "I shouldn't have come." This woman, still on pain pills from the hospital, still covered in stitches and plum-colored bruises . . .

She tried to turn her hurt into solving the riddle, instead of turning on Skip. "That's the, uh . . . *H*. And the *A*. From 'hate.' The first two letters."

"Wendy, she was mad, she was mad at me, not you . . . "

"It doesn't matter. Nothing matters but getting her back."

Michaelson broke in. "But why *those* two letters, out of all the ones he could have picked? *A.H.* That say anything to you?"

"Hitler. Adolph Hitler. That's what it says to me. Madmen. Both of them madmen."

"Something's changing here," Mizell said, moving the photos around, almost talking to herself. "Now there's . . . stuff. Props. That's a first. Not just a poem anymore. Like those antlers. And now these. So what does that mean? *'Fingernails on the chalkboard? No, I've used my sword . . .'*" Mizell turned to me, as if there was any doubt who she was talking to. "He's talking to you, directly to you, about what you yelled on the phone. 'Fingernails on the chalkboard.'"

"Don't you think I know that? Do you have to keep . . . "

She snapped around to Guillory. "When did that call come in? Let's figure out the timeline. We're missing something."

"Six, six thirty." Guillory flipped through his notes of the transcripts he'd been logging. "Here it is. Six twenty-six exactly. It was already dark by then."

"Okay. Six twenty-six. The call. You yell at him, that's what sets him off about the fingernails . . . "

Zaccaro figured out where Mizell was going before I did. "You figure out the clue . . . get over to that frat house on Hennepin . . . how long's that take?"

"I don't know . . . maybe . . . whole thing, hour and a half? Two hours?" Mizell told him. "But by the time we get there, the clue's already there, under the mailbox. We don't see anybody sneak up on the porch and put it there . . . so we must have just missed him."

Now she had me going. "You think it's somebody in the house? One of the frat guys?"

"I don't know, but the timing works out . . . it's convenient. He runs downstairs, sticks all this under the mailbox, gets ready for his toga party . . . you recognize any of them?"

"Yeah, but . . . it's a small campus," I answered. "You see everybody around . . ."

"But even if it's not one of the frat guys, it's somebody nearby. He got there in a heartbeat." Now it was Michaelson who was snapping out orders. "Let's get a squad out there, get a list of all the guys who live there. Drag 'em out of bed if you have to. We talk to all of them. We get a list of names, cross-reference it with anybody who's taken a class from you . . ."

I grabbed my jacket, ready to head out with them.

Mizell stopped me. "No. You're not coming this time. I don't want you around if things get dangerous."

"Like the rest of this *hasn't* been?"

"You've got another poem to figure out. What did he say? '*You had the body, I had the brains?*' Prove him wrong. Use your brains now. Let us be the body."

They all headed to the door, leaving me with copies of the photos and poem; they took the originals with them. And Wendy. She was going too.

"Wait. Stay. Rest."

"I need . . . I need to get home. I've got some more medicine there I'm supposed to take. I'm worn out. I need to sleep."

"You can sleep here."

"I just need to . . . get home. Sleep in my own bed."

There was something deflated in Wendy's eyes, even though she tried to hide it. I couldn't stop thinking about the fingernails; she couldn't either.

"Please. Don't blame her. It was just stupid . . . " I said, trying to convince her.

"I know." She started walking out, but stopped. "If I hadn't been here, at the party, you wouldn't have fought. If you hadn't fought, she wouldn't have been distracted. If she hadn't been distracted, nobody could have taken her. Same with animals. You can't get distracted. You have to be aware. All the time. I don't want to distract you anymore."

With that, they were gone. All of them. Wendy too. For the first time in what seemed like days, I was alone. No distractions, except for a riddle I couldn't solve, on the table in front of me.

For your lessons to learn,
Make those muscles burn . . . and I do mean burn . . .
To keep Skip alive, just do number five.

CHAPTER FORTY-ONE

How he loved poetry, things that rhymed, and things that . . . *shut up.*
It hurts, it hurts.
Of course it does, you idiot. I just shot you to death.

He was alone—except for that dead body—in the room, the school, where he had spent so much of his childhood. The only escape from the "housemates" who laughed and punched and pointed and whispered and . . .

He had thought he was dying then, but he knew that he really was, now. Becker muscular dystrophy, his disease was called. Well, *one* of them. The *first* one. It didn't show up right at birth, but it was *caused* by a birth accident. Being without oxygen for those few precious seconds, the umbilical cord wrapped around his neck strangling him, when he was coming out of the womb.

It caught up with him a few years later. Having to wear braces, then walk on canes, then crutches for even more support. Soon, the wheelchair would be the only way he could get around, not even enough strength left in his legs to walk upright, like something evolved. But that was just the part you could see on the outside.

Ashes, ashes, we all fall down!

He remembered the mnemonic his teacher Miss Moore had taught them, in this very same schoolhouse: "'Stalac*tites*' have to hang on *tight*, to keep from falling. 'Stalag*mites*' are *mighty*, strong enough to rise up from the ground." She'd looked at him then, a compliment she thought, to make her point. "Like you. You have to hang on *tight*, to keep from falling. You're a *stalactite*."

But now, the part you couldn't see. Well, except on x-rays. Motor neuron disease. Maybe due in part to his muscular dystrophy, the weakening of his body over time, maybe just . . . the luck of the draw. His muscles wasting away, his lungs going, going, gone . . .

There wasn't much time left; all the doctors had told him. The clock wasn't just ticking away on Skip, it was ticking away on him.

What had he done? This little girl he had watched grow up, from afar, always from afar. Watching her and her father, all those family occasions. Why not just send anonymous gifts at Christmas, instead of . . . take her? Think of the money he would have saved, every dollar he'd put into this place, every lock on every door, every amp of electricity, dragging in equipment and setting up this control panel where he could call without being found, where he could watch, without being seen. Where he could hack into all the Facebook passwords he would ever need. With all the extra eyes he had, he barely needed Ethan to post his . . . *activities* on Facebook, but it just added to the fun. He liked the idea of there being a permanent record, something to help Ethan . . . remember.

That had always been their problem: *remembering*.

He remembered too much, and Ethan didn't remember anything at all.

Well, he *would* remember, soon enough.

To finish the job, the kidnapper had to get rid of dead weight, as he and "Iolaus" would soon do in their van, as they buried *Jeffrey's* dead body in one of the graves they'd already dug.

One less passenger to worry about, as they made room for the new one, who was next on their list.

Skip was about to get a new playmate, something he had never had.

CHAPTER FORTY-TWO

Why these four photos, along with the rhyme?

Nothing the kidnapper had done so far had been random; there had to be some reason he'd taken these *particular* photos. I kept looking at them for any detail we'd missed, but there was nothing, no context. No windows, no walls, no door, nothing in the background. Just that desk. A bit of floor. And Skip. And not even all of her, just bits and pieces.

Skip's mother had once photographed me like that, during college. The scholar/jock, and the crazy artist. Patti, the student yearbook photographer. She was always sitting up in the football bleachers, snapping photos. Not ones that told a story, but ones that suggested what was *between* the lines. Photos of the goalpost *after* a game, when the torn paper scrim the team ran through was still floating around in bits and pieces. An unsnapped chin guard or a piece of helmet where the mascot painting was flaking off. The giant stadium lights, where some of the light bulbs had burned out.

The other school photographers caught me in all my glory, racing across the finish line, but Patti shot me from the back, when I was just a blur walking away from the field house with a gym bag slung over my shoulder. She did some motion-capture thing where you could see the bag in mid-flight, leaving a streak of neon in the dark. But she'd never photographed me so you could see my face.

One night, as I was about to start one of my late runs through the college cemetery, she came up to me and said she wanted to do a series on me, in the art building, away from the track, away from my comfort zone.

She didn't ask me, she told me. I liked that about her. Everybody else was always asking. I was the BMOC. The star. The Olympic hopeful. They asked.

Not Patti.

That first night, she photographed me in the darkroom, with just the red developing light on, the door opened just a wedge, so a light from the hall came through and seemed to bisect me down the middle. A person, split in two. It seemed right somehow: Was I the gym stud, or the classics scholar? Could I be both? That's what I was trying to figure out, and somehow, Patti seemed to know that, without me saying a word.

The second night, she said *I want to take a picture of your feet*, and I took off my shoes and socks for her. She got a shot where my big toenail on my right foot was all blackened, and half torn off. Blisters, my skin rubbed raw.

The third night she said *I want to take a picture of your shoulder, where you had that surgery.*

How did you know about that?

I just do.

I took off my shirt for her.

The fourth night she said *I want to shoot you naked, but you can cover your junk. If you want to. But you don't have to.*

That's when we both took off our clothes.

She showed all those photos—me in bits and pieces—in her senior art show. My foot, my chin, my shoulder, with the surgery scar. The flame tattoo on one of my ankles.

Never my face, just . . .

Shit.

Is *that* why the kidnapper had taken these photos of Skip? Because they were *supposed* to remind me of the ones that Patti had taken, all those years ago? Just fragments, not the whole thing? Not her face? He must have *been* there, at her show. How else would he know? Like mother, like daughter. It was the same thing he'd done with the ski lodge and the frat house. Places I knew. Places I'd been.

Patti didn't hold her senior show in the gallery on campus that everyone else always used. She wanted the environment to be as fractured as the photographs themselves, so she picked an old riding stable that was no longer in use, a few miles off campus. Like one of those back mews in an English alleyway.

That old stable, now smack-dab in the middle of the drug dealing area in town, if it hadn't been torn down years ago. *That's* where I was supposed to sweep out the Augean stables, where photographs of me, broken into bits and pieces, had once hung on a wall. *Deconstructed,* Patti had called it. It was the perfect word for what he was trying to do to me now: *Deconstruct* me. Tear me apart.

I looked at the latest puzzle again.

I want you to go where the drugs they buy
Give it a twist, make it today
Instead of shit, sweep crack away.
For your lessons to learn,
Make those muscles burn . . . and I do mean burn . . .
To keep Skip alive, just do number five.

That was the Labor: go to that old building, and then set it on fire. Whether or not anyone was in it.

CHAPTER FORTY-THREE

The police station felt different in the middle of the night. All you could smell was congealing cheese and garlic, from the pizzas that had been delivered. All you could hear was the hum from the fluorescent lights; the cops quiet, huddled, intense, and almost whispering as they did their work. Aretha Mizell had told them there was no money for overtime, but they didn't care. They wanted to find Skip.

Now, something else was different. It was the first time Detective Aretha Mizell had ever taken her own daughter to the station, but it couldn't be helped. She hadn't been expecting to work this late—2 A.M., she'd never been there at 2 A.M., except when she'd been working Janice's kidnapping—and she couldn't get a babysitter. She couldn't leave LaTrice at home by herself; she was just eleven years old. Mizell had shielded LaTrice's eyes when they walked in, past the crime scene board that was right there at the entrance, and she'd made up a pallet in her office for LaTrice to sleep on, but still, she wondered if she was doing wrong. This was no place for a child. But looking at those four new photos of Skip—*parts* of Skip, her arms and legs and knees and elbows, tied to a desk—taped up on the dry-erase board, Mizell didn't think she'd ever let LaTrice out of her sight again. For a millisecond, she thought, this was the safest place in the world for her.

Mizell and the FBI had spent the last three or four hours at the Lambda Chi house, interviewing the guys in the frat. Some of them were still in their togas. She didn't know which smelled worse: the vomit and booze and smoke on them from the bonfire that was still smoldering outdoors, or the house itself, that looked like it hadn't been cleaned since she was in college. But they were game. They'd never been interviewed by the police about a kidnapping before. About being too loud, too late at night, yes; a kidnapping, no.

About torn-out fingernails found on their porch? No.

A professor going crazy in their own backyard? That would be another no.

But after all that, they'd come up with zip. None of them had done anything worse than parade a pig through the streets.

One of Mizell's guys was playing and replaying a reel-to-reel recorder that had all the kidnapper's phone calls on it, and these words from him kept spiking on a speaker in the room, from his pissing match with Ethan: *"I am the one who's had 'enough of this shit,' which you will be cleaning out of the Augean stables, very soon indeed."*

"Enough of this shit."

Rewind. *"Enough of this shit."*

If the shit don't fit, Mizell thought, a throwback to another crime, one she'd only watched on TV. This one she was living, and none of it fit. Mad rhymes, no DNA hits, no fingerprints; they'd run everything and come up blank. A mechanical genius, who could thwart every trace they tried. But still—why? With everything she'd said to Holt about revenge and somebody he had kept waiting, they were still coming up blank on that one too. Some nutjob just making Ethan chase his tail—but what was the end game? Twelve Labors down, and then what? Was he really going to let Skip go free? Even if he did, what would she be like after all she'd gone through?

She had to go look in on LaTrice again, sleeping in her office, just to count her blessings.

Only LaTrice was gone.

CHAPTER FORTY-FOUR

To keep Skip alive, just do number five.

It was the mantra playing over and over in my head, as I drove through this *other* neighborhood that every college town had, besides "Greek Row." Mt. Gresh's very own version of the Augean stables, where people bought drugs. Long ago, it had been the "historic" area of town: old riding stables for the moneyed crowd; a small river even, the Hoosatonic, separating it from the woods and mountains. Those double barn doors from the old stables were still here, but now they were covered with peeling paint and bolted from the inside to keep police away, home to squatters and dealers. The cobblestone streets were still here too, but the only cars that drove over them, this late at night, didn't pause to pay attention to the historic details. They didn't pay attention to anything except the quality of the drugs, and they weren't too picky about that. Furtive handshakes, slipping baggies of pot and Adderall, meth and coke, from one palm to another; suspicious glances, especially at a scared white man like me, slinking down in the driver's seat and cruising along at two in the morning.

There could only be one reason I was here.

No, there was another reason, even if I still couldn't believe I was actually going ahead with it.

Fire.

A goddamn building on fire. A crack den. It all made sense. Demented sense. How else was I supposed to interpret the latest poem? Occam's razor. *Lex parsimoniae.* The law of parsimony, economy, succinctness. The simplest solution.

Burn it down. The derelict building I had once been in, where Patti had had her art show. Yet another page ripped from the playbook of my life, by someone who seemed to have been following it for years. I remembered borrowing Sig's van to drive out here, to help Patti unload her work. Her photographs of me. We'd gone in through a side door in some alley, and I'd helped her hang the show. It was a success. We'd stayed in the place by ourselves after it, getting drunk on the cheap rot-gut wine she'd served, along with little peanut butter and banana finger sandwiches. We'd fed each other and mapped out our future together, sitting under the portrait of my flame tattoo, etched into my ankle.

How she was going to become a famous photographer.

How I was going to the Olympics.

How we were going to get married and have kids.

How we'd been followed, and someone was staring in at us.

It just came back to me now. We'd been alone in the room after the show—two of the photographs had sold, seventy-five bucks each, a fortune to us then—and someone was looking in at us through the half-moon window that was part of the carriage door. Patti saw it before I did, and screamed. I turned to the window—in that second, I saw a fractured face, just like the ones in the photos hanging on the walls. A quarter of forehead and brow and eye, and then it was gone.

"Maybe it was just another art lover," I joked to Patti, trying to calm her down, going to the door and making sure it was locked on the inside. "You want people to see your stuff."

I'd completely forgotten about it, until now. Had he been following me since then? *Waiting* for something from me?

I thought I remembered that the gallery space had been blue—slate blue, maybe, that sort of New England historic color?—but now there was no color on any of the buildings. They were all the same weather-beaten gray, at least in the dark. On one side of the street, a lot strewn with rubble; on the other side, an alleyway. That looked familiar. I slowed down to twenty miles per hour and . . .

There. I'd almost driven past it, until I saw the street numbers ascending. Seven, nine . . . back up, five. Number 5 River Run, with a rusted horse medallion knocker sticking out in front of the door.

A horse. A river. Crack. The right address. Number five. My past. Somewhere I'd been with Patti. Check check check check check. It was all there. I'd come to the right place.

One last look at my phone: should I call Mizell? Her name was there, spelled out in LED and attached to a number; she'd borrowed the phone to add it in herself.

No.

I had a job to do, and I had twenty-eight hours left to do it.

And we'd already traded places. I was just like him now. Insane.

CHAPTER FORTY-FIVE

LaTrice's blanket was still there—the shape of her body practically outlined in it, knees drawn up to her chest, the way she liked to sleep—but she wasn't.

Aretha Mizell wasn't going to panic. Nothing was wrong. The blanket was even still warm, from her body heat. She'd just woken up and had to go to the bathroom. Who didn't? Aretha had to get up and go three times in the middle of the night. Like mother, like daughter.

Mizell was just being paranoid, working on a case like this. Maybe she should have said it was a conflict of interest, too close to home; that she couldn't do another child abduction after everything she'd gone through with her niece Janice, but then they'd start taking cases away from her. They'd say she was weak and hormonal and not as strong as them, just because she was a woman. They'd think she was soft and leave her off the big gets. She wasn't going to let that happen.

She took a deep breath and forced herself to walk nice and slow to the bathroom. No big deal. Everybody had to go. The *men* on the force had to go. That's where LaTrice was.

Only she wasn't.

It wasn't a big room; Aretha barely had to say her baby's name for there to be a sort of echo, bouncing back at her from the pink tiles. Honestly. A woman's bathroom in a police station, and they put in pink tiles? There were two stalls, and that girl was gonna get a whopping if she was hiding in one of those, standing up on top of the commode with the door closed, just to fake out her momma. Ain't nobody got time for that, a joke in the middle of an investigation.

"LaTrice Elaine Mizell, you are gonna pay holy hell if I find you in there . . ."

But she didn't. Neither stall.

Well, there were plenty of other places her baby could be. She was always playing practical jokes on her mother, and this was just another one of them. Not even a joke. A police station was a fascinating place. Lots of places to wander off to and look at, when no one was around to say you couldn't. The evidence room had fun stuff in it, although it was locked up this late. (Thank God, because it had guns in it too. Aretha had taught her daughter about guns, not to play with them. She'd even gone to her school and given speeches about it.) Or the snack room. That's where Aretha would go, if she woke up here in the middle of the night. Make a beeline for those vending machines with potato chips and cookies and soda. Those little orange crackers with peanut butter? Those were Aretha's own personal Waterloo. She couldn't remember if LaTrice had her little purse with her, but maybe she'd sweet-talked one of the squad guys into giving her some change.

But she wasn't in there either. The vending machine room, or the evidence room.

LaTrice wasn't in any of those places.

Mizell was running out of places to look.

Maybe the interrogation room. A little girl would like that, with a one-way mirror she could look into. She'd be running back and forth, outside the room looking in, where she could see everything, then inside the room looking out, where she couldn't see anything. LaTrice would get such a kick out of that. Or inside, fiddling with all the gizmos they had in there. The filming equipment. If Mizell went in there and found out that LaTrice had filled up those things with nonsense . . .

But she wasn't there either. The room was locked. Dark. Mizell caught a glimpse of herself in the one-way mirror. It wasn't good, what she saw staring back at her.

Okay, now she was panicking.

Why did you bring that child here with you tonight, here, of all places, with so much evil out in the world? So much evil staring you in the face?

"What's wrong, chief?" one of her guys called out.

"We've got a problem. Stop whatever you're doing." She called it out to all their tables; that's what they called them, their working units. Tables. One for robbery, one for vice, one for domestics, one for kidnapping.

They'd never had to use that one very much. Except for Janice. And Skip.

She couldn't go through it with another little girl.

Not her own.

CHAPTER FORTY-SIX

The narrow hallway was littered with crack vials and condoms, and there was a smell in the air. Not just acrid, stinging pot, but *presence*. Sweat, which never washed off. Desperation, for a high. A hothouse of smells, trapped inside for who knows how long. I could almost imagine that I heard rolling papers, crinkling and burning, turning to ash. Outside, cars cruised by, heavy bass blasting from their mega-speakers, making the rickety walls of the place seem to vibrate.

I'd never been in a crack den before, but this seemed to fit the bill.

I'd never burned down anything either, but that was next on the agenda.

I had the cigarette lighter I always carried with me, the one that my father had thrown at me, right after he burned his own ankles with it, instead of mine. My only inheritance.

"Gold," he'd said. "The only color that matters." He'd held the lighter in front of my face for just a second before he turned it on his own ankles. Through gritted teeth, he hissed out that gold was the only color I should ever see, from then on.

Ironic, considering it was one of the last colors *they* had seen, my parents. They'd died in a fire. Both of them, in our burning house, after my father had fallen asleep smoking in bed.

The sins of the fathers. And now, I was following in his footsteps—up a set of tumble-down stairs to the second floor—about to start a fire of my own.

Debris was everywhere; it would be so easy. I just had to rub the tip of my rough-hewn thumb against that tiny metal cylinder on the lighter, and the place would go up in a flash, every man for himself; if you're too strung-out to *get* out then you deserved to die. . . .

No. I couldn't do that. I wouldn't. Skip's captor couldn't push me to that.

Yes. He could.

I was running down a hallway, banging on doors, yelling, nobody yelling back, nobody threatening me, all good signs, coast clear, no light except the flash and butane from my father's lighter . . .

And then, a door, open, at the end of the hall.

Like all those other open doors I'd seen over the past days.

I walked through it, a small room, no windows inside, like the eaves under an attic . . .

. . . and that's when I felt the hands behind me.

Pushing me.

And then slamming the door behind me. Locked from the outside. No give, except for flakes of rust coming off the doorknob in my hand.

From outside, I heard footsteps running down the stairs I'd just used, and then another door slamming shut, the one I used to come in from off the street.

"Hey! I'm in here! HEY!"

Pitch dark. Down on the floor. I tried to find my cigarette lighter so I could see, but it was gone. Flown from my hands when I was pushed inside. My cell phone too. I heard the clack it made when it hit the ground. The floors were slatted, so it could have fallen through.

I reached for the doorknob again—but it was hot to the touch. And getting hotter, almost glowing orange. Smoke was beginning to waft in, from under the door. And a stronger smell with it, something that overpowered my puny little butane.

Gasoline.

I'd gotten the poem all wrong: it was burn the place down, but with me in it.

CHAPTER FORTY-SEVEN

How many prayers had Skip said? Had the hours she'd spent in this place been one long prayer? Afraid to go to sleep, her mind too frazzled to think, to even form complete thoughts, but every thought was to God. And her father. Father God, God the Father . . .

Save me, save me, help me, please God, please Daddy . . .

She wouldn't let her kidnapper hear her; she wouldn't even let him see her lips move, but she kept it going, a chant in her head. *Please God, please Daddy, tell me what to do, I'll hear you, I'll hear you in my head* . . .

But it wasn't working. Now the only thing she heard was the van returning outside. She knew what one sounded like, from helping out with the drama department: the extra heavy sound that the two back doors made when they were being opened. And then the sound of his crutches and . . . him coming inside. He was making more noise than usual, as if, now that he knew that Skip knew about the crutches, he didn't care what he sounded like anymore, or that she could track his comings and goings.

"Surprise!" he called out, from the hallway. "Are you decent? We've got company!"

Skip could hear more commotion in the hall; the other guy, the big one, the only one who was left, carrying in something. His footsteps even heavier and slower outside the hall than they normally were.

"Thank God for my helpers. Well, helper. So many errands we've been running. Dropping things off. Like Hippocrates' body. Picking things up. Pushing things *in* . . . lighting things *up*. Since we're down a helper, I decided to get some extra company for you. So we could be a. Threesome. Again."

"Who? Who else is here?"

"All good things to those who wait. And I am one. Who has. Waited. Now, you will too."

CHAPTER FORTY-EIGHT

I was not going to burn to death in a crack den.

In just seconds, the fire had jumped from just a smell—a crackle—to what seemed like a conflagration. Like the Olympic torch my year. Cathy Freeman had run into the stadium with it, dipped it into that bizarre, UFO-looking Olympic cauldron, and in all of five or six seconds . . . a giant ring of fire, for the whole world to see. An explosion, kicking off the games.

More smoke was coming in from underneath the door; it was getting harder to breathe, as the smoke rose up. But in such a small room, there wasn't anywhere for it to go. I couldn't get out the door—I heard flames there, falling beams; there wasn't a window—so I had to get out through one of the walls.

I began feeling around with my palms.

Peeling wallpaper on all four sides of me; I could detect strips of something underneath it, layered on top of each other. Maybe this had once been a make-do bedroom, for a stable boy. I knocked on it; it sounded hollow, so at least I knew there wasn't anything solid underneath the wallpaper. Maybe it adjoined another room.

A room with a window I could jump out of.

I scooted around on my back and laid flat on the floor so I could brace myself and kick into the wall with my legs, using every bit of muscle I had. Thank God I'd kept up with my running; I still had power in my thighs.

But now, the smoke had nowhere to go. It had finished rising and was now filling the room, as low down to the floor as I was. Every panic-fueled breath I took brought more of it into my lungs. There was no time to do anything except keep kicking, and it worked: the wall was so paper-thin, I was pushing through a lattice work of wooden strips and crumbling lath. Dry-as-bone plaster, that would soon be eaten up by the fire. Broken edges of lumber and rusty nails ripped into my legs with every thrust, but my adrenaline had almost anesthetized me. I barely felt anything, even as I scooted closer to the disintegrating wall, up to my thighs now with dry wood and rot disintegrating around my body.

One more push, two, then three—I thought of Patti pushing Skip out, the doctor urging her on, *Push, push, push*—so I did it for her. For both of them. Patti and Skip. Feeling like I didn't have any more in me left to give, but the baby still hadn't been born.

It was dig in, or die. For both of us. Me *and* Skip.

"Aaahhhhh . . . ahh!" There, with a grunted-out scream.

One last push, and the opening was big enough for me to climb through, a miraculous *whoosh* of cool air on the other side.

There was a window. It was open.

That's when I remembered the *second* thing I knew about fire: not just that it rises, but that it abhors a vacuum. It would do *anything* it could, to fill it up. And it already had.

The room I was in now was worse than the one I had just escaped: licks of fire were whipping up the walls and cascading across the ceiling. All of it beginning to grow into one big mass of *fireball* that wanted to fly out of that lone window.

Just like I did.

Beams from the ceiling were crashing into the room, fire was raining down on me. Wood, ceiling, lath, wallpaper, even the *air* seemed *to be* on fire.

I ran to the window and straddled myself over the ledge, hanging on by my fingertips.

Then the fire burned the ledge away, and me with it.

I was in free fall—*airborne*—down two stories: no air-filled mattress to land on this time, just gravel and glass and needles.

What little breath I still had was knocked out of me; my right ankle, now tattooed with *real* flame, was slammed against the ground . . . but I was alive.

In agony, but alive and grabbing air, rolling on the ground to put out the fire that had traveled through the air with me, a ridgeback of flame shooting off my spine.

In the distance now, sirens and the heavy honking that went with them. Flashing red lights, against the huge spiral of black smoke I'd just flown out of.

He wouldn't need a Facebook photo now, with that as evidence.

His crime, and now mine I thought, as I crawled to my car to drive to Wendy, for her to patch me up. And for us to patch things up.

CHAPTER FORTY-NINE

"Abandon All Hope, Ye Who Enter Here."

It was the homemade sign that TJ had posted months ago outside the door to his tiny study carrel in the library, back when he thought it was funny. Back when he was trying to be despairing and ironic—*look how hard my life is! lol*—like the "cool kids." Back before any of this had become all too real. A familiar line borrowed from Dante's *Inferno,* part of *The Divine Comedy*— actually, the original LOL—the welcome sign to Hell. Now that TJ had actually lived there for a few days, he wondered if he could ever get out, or if he would be dragging the scent of sulfur and smoke with him for the rest of his life.

Now, with the library closed and everyone else gone home for the night, TJ ripped the sign down and replaced it with something that told a more accurate story, ready and waiting for the next geek who would inherit the tiny room: the wanted poster of the man with ginger hair and glasses who gave TJ the poem that he had deliberately kept from Ethan and the police. The Identi-Kit artist had done a good job, but TJ thought she hadn't gone far enough. The poster should have had a flip side, with a drawing of TJ on the back.

"Wanted Dead or Alive: TJ Markson: Accomplice."

It would be the only time he'd ever be "wanted."

He was going to be kicked out of school, after what he'd done. Maybe they wouldn't kick him out, but they'd certainly take away his scholarship so it was pretty much the same thing. He couldn't stay at Canaan without the money. Without the money, he couldn't afford his apartment, but that didn't matter because he wouldn't need to be in Mt. Gresh anymore. He wouldn't have classes to go to. Without going to classes, he wouldn't graduate and without graduating, he wouldn't be able to get a job, certainly not a teaching job, which is all he'd ever wanted. At least once he actually got to Canaan. And without a job, he wouldn't be able to pay back the student loans he'd already used up, even *before* they took away his scholarship. And without . . .

He was fucked, no matter how he looked at it, and he'd been looking at it every way possible since they let him leave the police station.

"What about me?" TJ had said, the last thing he'd ever said to Ethan. And there wasn't even an answer; that's how pitiful TJ had become. They hadn't arrested him for anything, they hadn't kept him at the police station or really even interrogated him, they'd just . . . left him there, while they went to work out the next Labor. TJ had been forgotten, standing there like an idiot while the rest of the station went back to work.

Why had he even done it? That's the only question that was in TJ's head anymore—well, after *"What the fuck do I do for the rest of my life?"* It's not like four years of Greek and Latin were a big calling card on a resume, a job application for flipping burgers. He'd come to Canaan with revenge in his heart; he was going to get back at the great Ethan "Hercules" Holt after what he'd caused his father to do. Kill himself. That deserved payback, didn't it? TJ's father hadn't left a note telling his son to go after Ethan, but TJ was sure that's what he would have wanted. TJ had always been fascinated by the past, and classics is what he would have studied anywhere, so he didn't have to fake anything to get into Ethan's classes.

But when TJ got to Canaan he found out that he was better at studying than getting revenge. (Even when Rodger with a *d* had dumped him, he couldn't get revenge. He just figured he deserved it, for being a bad boyfriend.) The classics were all about it—getting revenge, declaring enemies, going to war—but TJ couldn't actually pull it off in real life. He didn't want to get back at Ethan, he wanted to learn from him. TJ didn't see evil in him; he didn't see a man who went after people. He just saw a good teacher. A good father. A good man, who'd lost his wife. And Skip . . . she was a good daughter. Always hanging around school. Already so grown up, because she'd been around adults so much of her life. Because she'd grown up like TJ had, an only child.

So why—after years of being dormant—did TJ's stupid idea of "getting revenge" finally jolt into high gear after such a terrible thing had happened? A man TJ admired—at the lowest possible place he could be . . . and *this* is what TJ does?

He sits on a stupid line of Latin for a few hours?

How much more of a loser could he be?

He couldn't do anything right. He couldn't finish anything.

Well, now he would.

Maybe they'd miss him in death; it was the only time TJ had really missed his own father. His father had loved the football field, so that's where he'd done it; TJ loved the library, so that's where he'd do it too, both of them swinging from the end of a rope. He had all the materials he'd need here at hand: he could use the rope from that mailing tube sculpture thing that hung from the ceiling, all the way down through the open part of the stairwell. TJ didn't want Mrs. Castle, the head librarian, to be the one who found him, but since she was the one who always opened up the library in the morning, it would probably fall to her.

Fall to her? No, that was his job.

At least he could write her a note, apologizing in advance. Explaining everything. His father had one, a suicide note, explaining what Ethan had done to him. Like father, like son.

And that's when TJ remembered—he *wasn't* finished. Not yet.

TJ had said it to Ethan at the gym, when everything began going to hell. "You tell me what happened at the Olympics, and I'll tell you what I know."

TJ had kept his side of the bargain. Ethan hadn't.

Now he was about to.

Scire et taceo.
To know and keep silent.
Ethan wouldn't stay silent anymore.
Then TJ could come back and kill himself.

CHAPTER FIFTY

Four in the morning, and Wendy's door was wide open. She liked living out on the edge of town, in the middle of nowhere, but not so much that she didn't lock the door at night.

"Wendy? Wen?" I didn't care if I woke her up, running in. "Wendy?"

Oh Jesus. Oh Jesus . . .

Even in the middle of the night, this was the wrong kind of stillness, the same thing I'd felt when somebody broke into our house. There was a different DNA. You could almost smell it. The scent of fear left over. I knew something was wrong, even before I saw the bedroom.

The sheets were tousled, a chair was overturned, and there was blood. A lot of it. Probably from where Wendy's wounds from the lion had started bleeding again and some new ones had been started. And there was the same kind of outline on Wendy's bed, in spray paint, that had been on Skip's. This time, the shape of a grownup. Wendy's shape. With a note pinned in the middle:

"You've got a strong one here. She was harder to take."

And on another sheet of paper, the start of another long, insane, rambling poem. The longest one yet. Epic. I'd barely started reading it when a cell phone rang. Survivor's "Eye of the Tiger."

"Yeah, I know. I'm a goon," Wendy had said, the first time I'd heard it play as her ringtone.

Now, "Risin' up, back on the street," words from the song, came at me from somewhere under the sheets. I dug through and snatched up Wendy's phone.

On the other end was that voice I could now recognize anywhere.

"Smile! You're on candid camera!"

"You sick fuck! What the hell have you done with . . . "

"Labor Number Nine. Stealing the leather belt of the Amazon Queen. Your girlfriend just happened to be *in it* at the time. That belt she always wears at the zoo. I know I've jumped ahead in the lineup, but it was just too good to Skip. '*Too good to Skip*,' get it?"

"Please . . . "

"*Please, please*, it's all you ever say," the voice mocked me. "If you only knew. How many times *I've* said it. . . . "

"I'll do anything."

"Yes. You will. The next four Labors. All combined."

"What do you WANT?" I screamed back at him. "You don't want me dead, you could've killed me already . . . so take me, take me instead. I'm begging you. Who are you?"

"If you don't know. If you can't *remember*. On your own. Then it's no good."

"Know what?"

"ME. Who I am."

"Give me a fucking clue . . . "

"I've given you. Six of them. Already. And here's one more. Just ask yourself: what did Hercules. *Do?*"

CHAPTER FIFTY-ONE

Wendy's eyes flickered open in the dark, just coming to, and the first thing she saw was Skip's hands. Her fingers. Her fingernails.

"I TE WENDY" they read, the fingers between the *I* and the *T* taken up by gauze on the fingertips.

Even in pain, Skip tucked her fingernails down, under her palms, so Wendy wouldn't see, but the damage was done. Those tiny white letters, painted onto the black polish, the relief of white against black in this room.

"I'm so sorry. I didn't mean it. I was just mad . . . " Skip stammered out.

"Oh my God, Skip, what did he do to you? We saw the letters, the *H* . . . the *A* . . . oh my God, are you okay?" Wendy moved to grab Skip's hand, but she couldn't. Her own hands were tied up the same as Skip's, in front of her.

"It's okay. It doesn't hurt anymore," Skip whispered. "He keeps giving me shots."

"He gave me one too I think."

Skip could see Wendy trying to make her tongue work in tandem with her brain.

"He'll give you some water. It's okay. It's not poisoned. I thought it was at first, but it wasn't."

Skip had been moved from the desk in the middle of the room and was now on the floor, leaning up against the wall, next to Wendy. It felt good to touch against someone again, even though it felt sticky. Wendy still had blood on her, from where he must have attacked her. And she was still bleeding.

"Where are we?" Wendy asked. A light spilled into the room from the command post, and Wendy could just begin to make out what Skip had lived with for days now.

Madness, turned into murals of the Labors of Hercules. Some of them had a neon *X* from spray paint slashed through them, as if they'd been completed, or the artist had decided he didn't like his work anymore.

"We're okay until he finishes them all. I think," Skip said. "He says . . . he says he knows Daddy. He says . . . " Skip dropped even further into a whisper, afraid he would hear, and she wouldn't let him hear her fear. " . . . he's on crutches . . . sometimes a wheelchair, but he's scary. I'm so glad you're here. I'm so scared."

"I know, I know." Wendy kept swallowing, trying to wake herself. Her eyes went over the murals she could see—Skip could feel her body move next to her, just the tiniest little bit, taking it all in. "Your dad's going to save us, I know he is. He's got this all figured out , , , these Labors . . . and he's doing them. You can't believe how smart he is, how strong, how much he misses you. He's doing them, one by one, he's going to do all of them." Then Wendy paused, as if the Labors really were sinking in, the ones left to be done, and she saw the enormity of it all. "We just have to wait and . . . we can get through this . . . we'll take you to the hospital, we'll get your fingers fixed . . . "

Now Skip tried to make it better for Wendy, so she wouldn't be so scared. "Some of the girls at school wear press-on nails. They're not so bad. You can decorate them with different colors and stuff." Skip didn't know if she should tell Wendy everything, but she did anyway. "He's already killed somebody. His helper. This guy who was trying to help me, and he shot him. He fell on top of me."

"Oh my God, Skip . . . "

They heard him moving into the room, and his voice. "Ah, 'girl talk!' That's what I like. To hear! Up and at 'em!"

He moved in front of them, and what Skip saw was maybe scarier than seeing what he really looked like.

His face. He was wearing some sort of light ski mask sort of thing; only his eyes, mouth, and nose were visible, through slits in the material.

"Forgive me. For not having my. *Face* on yet."

"Isn't that hot?" Skip said, then hated herself for even caring how he felt.

"Hot is the. *Least* of my problems."

Skip would have thought that would be enough to recognize him, the shape of his head, if he'd known her like he said, but with all the other connecting stuff gone—cheeks and skin and a forehead and a chin—it still didn't add up to anything. He still wasn't anybody.

Wendy pushed against the wall, trying to shield Skip from whatever was coming next. He leaned on his crutches and reached toward one of the murals, of Hercules stealing the belt off the Amazon queen.

"Pardon my reach while I. Check you off. Labor Number Nine. AKA Dr. Borden."

As Wendy and Skip cowered together, he nailed Wendy's leather belt she wore at the zoo into the mural. It fell down onto the top of Skip's head, as the sound that had become so familiar to her started again. The cap coming off the spray paint can. A ball, rattling inside. A whiff, sprayed into the air, as he made a fresh *X* through the mural.

"This is the true. Nectar of the gods. All I had, when I was little, to take myself . . . *away*. One huff and . . . Valhalla."

As much as Wendy wanted to look in Skip's eyes and let her know that everything was going to be fine—she couldn't. She could only look on in terror and not have a single thought of what to do next, because she was more terrified than she had ever been in her life.

"Of course, if you're keeping count, Skip—and I'm sure that's *all* you've been doing—you'll realize I've. Jumped ahead a few Labors. He'll have to backtrack. Do the ones I jumped over. But then we'll have a. Party! Doesn't that sound fun? He had one, a birthday. Didn't he? I was there. Watching. Across the street."

"You were there?"

"I hadn't been. *Invited*. Of course."

Skip moved closer to Wendy, their bodies pressed so closely together they were like conjoined twins.

"But even at a distance . . . it made me. Jealous. Everyone forgot *my* birthday. So I'll just have to. Make do with *you two*. As my presents! But what will we do for cake?"

Skip took the lead. She could do this. She could show Wendy what to do.

"I could make you one. German chocolate. I made one for Daddy, and I could make you one too. It's his favorite, even though he doesn't like coconut just by itself. Do you . . . do you have a favorite? I could make a different kind for you, whatever you like most . . . "

"Jelly bean."

"What?" Skip tried to keep her voice even, to not let him know how strange it sounded.

"Jelly bean. My favorite. White icing, studded with jelly beans. One of the nurses. Made it for me. Not a whole one. Just a little . . . what are those called? Just a few bites . . . "

"A cupcake?"

"A *cupcake*! I wasn't even worthy. Of a whole cake, just . . . a *cup*. But my Mamarie made it for me. My favorite . . . teacher? Nurse? My earliest . . . *helper*. A party for two. Mamarie and me. Yes, we'll have. Jelly bean cake. When this is all . . . over."

His voice began to wind down, and he slowly moved on to the bas-relief of the Sixth Labor, the Stymphalian Birds. So tired it seemed as of he could barely lift his arms, he taped an old photo, torn out of a magazine, to it: of a birthday cake, in faded Technicolor. He blew at the imaginary cake, but he started choking, barely able to get a lungful of air to speak.

"I'll huff. And I'll puff. And I'll. Die. We all will."

CHAPTER FIFTY-TWO

Mizell hated herself, but she couldn't help it. She was glad it was Wendy who was gone, instead of her own daughter. LaTrice had just been in the back seat of the car the whole time, curled up and sleeping there. She said she couldn't sleep with all the talking in the station. Those pictures. It all scared her.

"I'll scare you . . . for giving me a heart attack. Why didn't you tell me you were going out there? I've told you . . . " Mizell grabbed her shoulders, about to shake her, when she started shaking herself. And crying. So relieved that she hadn't been taken. That she was just sleeping.

She'd fallen to the tarmac out in the police parking lot and cried and prayed, scaring LaTrice even more.

And now, this other woman had been taken, and Mizell wanted to cry again.

Not just because it was a horrible thing, but because it wasn't her little girl.

◆ ◆ ◆

"You know what to do," Mizell said to her forensics team in Wendy's bedroom, and they started doing it. I flashed back to days ago, the nightmare starting all over again, déjà vu, except with a different victim. Fingerprint powder came out and went on the bedposts and doorknobs; Wendy's twisted sheets were picked up and dropped into giant evidence bags.

And they swabbed up blood and put it in plastic vials.

"She's already lost so much blood on account of me, at the zoo, and now she just gets home and . . . " I couldn't finish saying it. Or thinking it.

"Hopefully she hurt him," Mizell said. "If there's blood other than hers mixed in with this, we can start running it through the system. We might get a hit."

"There wasn't any blood with Skip. Not when he took her. Well, her fingernails. There was blood on her fingernails. When he sent them back," that other FBI guy said. Zaccaro. Walking dead.

"He's ratcheting up," Michaelson said to Mizell. "At least with the fingernails, he'd been provoked . . . "

Didn't they realize I could hear them, sitting right there in a chair, dazed, as Mizell and the two FBI guys worked through Wendy's bedroom, dressed in white paper HAZMAT suits and booties and looking for a hidden camera.

"That's what he said, when I first picked up her phone. 'Smile. You're on candid camera.'"

"We've got a team over at your house, looking to see if there are any hidden cameras there, like this one." Zaccaro pulled what looked like a tiny little bulb from the crown molding at the ceiling, in Wendy's bedroom. "You have any workmen in your house over the last few weeks?"

"A cable guy. They offered us a free upgrade," I said, still in a daze. "Skip wanted it. More channels."

"That could have been him, planting cameras instead. It's like he always knows where you are. We're going back in, double-checking all the sites you've been to . . . the science lab, the ski lift . . . if there are cameras, there could be fingerprints . . . "

"My fault, it's all my fault. Wendy was mad at me, and distracted. She says you can't get distracted around animals, but she was, and he was . . . he was here. Waiting. He's taking everybody I love. And he's trying to kill me now, with the fire . . . "

"I think he knew you could get out. I think he just did that—to distract you. Tie you up, while he was here, doing this. Make sure you didn't show up," Mizell said.

"It's like the Olympics. He keeps getting me to the point of exhaustion, like I can't go on, like I want to be dead, and then . . . one more thing you've got to do. It's somebody who *knows* what that feels like . . . it's like I'm redoing the whole fucking thing, all twelve events at Sydney, for an audience of one."

"I think we should get you to the ER, get you checked out," Mizell said, looking at me. "Your ankle. Your burns. Make sure you didn't get a concussion."

"No hospital. I don't have time."

Twenty-four hours. I had twenty-four hours. That's all. And I knew where he wanted me to go next. I'd figured it out, the minute I saw part of the latest poem he had left for me on Wendy's bed.

They guard the nests at the old petting zoo . . .
A fun place to go . . .
Before the horses became glue.

CHAPTER FIFTY-THREE

Skip had been so careful to just whisper, to not draw attention. To stay . . . under the radar. No more. She raised her voice, to the man in the next room. She could feel him in there, just waiting. Looking. "Please, get Wendy some help. She won't stop bleeding where her arm's hurt so bad. She won't wake up. You've got to help her . . . she'll bleed to death . . . "

He wheeled himself into the room in his chair, evidently too tired to stand anymore, and still wearing his mask. Skip watched his hands grip the wheels, pushing himself along; his hands seemed more fragile now, like it was almost too hard to even gain any momentum on a flat floor. "I've often wondered. How that would feel. Bleeding out. It's not sudden . . . you're mostly asleep . . . it doesn't hurt. You just. Slip away. That's how. *I'd* like to go."

Ignoring Skip, almost lost in his own world, he wheeled himself to the murals on the wall and began adding in more elements.

A bird's wing, crawling with lice.

A toy plastic horse, white with black markings. A tiny strip of leather for reins and a metal bit in the mouth, to complete the picture. He hammered it with a long nail into the eighth mural and barely seemed to notice when the long nail smashed the hollow body of the horse to pieces.

"You've gotta let us outta here," Skip said, risking everything. "If something happens to you . . . it looks like you're . . . that you don't feel well. We'd be stuck . . . nobody knows where we are . . . we'll starve . . . please . . . "

He started gliding back to the other room. But just before he went over the threshold, he suddenly reached up and whipped off the mask he'd been wearing.

"Here, wrap up her hand with this." He flung the mask over his shoulder to Skip. "I won't be needing it much longer."

To Skip, that could only mean one thing, as she whispered in a panic to Wendy, trying to shake her. "He's going to kill us. He's getting ready to show us his face. He doesn't care if we see him anymore. You've gotta wake up. He's just got three Labors left. We've gotta get out." Skip joggled her body against Wendy, both of them still tied up down on the floor, but Wendy didn't move.

"Please, wake up," Skip pleaded to her. "I can't do this alone."

Wendy moaned, maybe trying to say something, but it was just . . . breath, caught in her throat. It wasn't words, or at least anything Skip could understand. She had to get Wendy to wake up. Skip thought maybe if she just started talking, Wendy would hear, even if her eyes weren't open. She'd hear how serious things were. Maybe some of her pain would even go away, if Skip just started talking and didn't stop, like her father did to her that time in the hospital.

She said the first thing that came into her head, anything but think about where they were now. "They let me take drama at the college, but that's just because Daddy teaches there. They say I'm their mascot."

Skip was so scared she didn't know what to say next, but she had to keep talking. To take her *own* pain away. As she talked, she tried to twist into position to wrap the man's face mask around Wendy's bleeding hand. Wendy moaned—it must have hurt— but she still wouldn't wake up.

"One of the teachers does improv, but I'm not so crazy about that. Making things up, as you go along, although I guess that's what I'm doing now. The other teacher, the one I like more, he says, 'Add an *e* to it and you've got *improve. Improvements*, not *improvisations*. Why risk anything to chance?' Please, wake up . . ."

Skip's hands were still taped at the wrist, but her fingers were free to move, so she could just reach to Wendy's bleeding hand and get the cloth mask clamped down on top of it. It started soaking up blood. Wendy groaned and shifted.

"The pain'll go away. Just listen. I'm gonna keep talking. Mr. Jasperson—he's the one I like the most—he does plays with words. Old plays. He's old too. He's always doing sad plays, and this one he put me in was the saddest. It's about all these dead people who come back to life. *Spoon River Anthology*. That's the name of the town, and the cemetery. Spoon River. All these people just wander around their tombstones, talking about how they died and who they were in real life and what they missed the most. They weren't really in heaven or hell, they were just sort of floating around because they didn't want to leave Earth. We did it outside, at the Canaan cemetery. 'Site-specific,' Mr. Jasperson called it. He set up lights on the graves and hung them from the trees, and we just stood by our tombstones and did our poems. There weren't any chairs, so people could just walk around and go listen to whoever they wanted to. It wasn't in any order, so it didn't matter. There's a little girl who's dead in it, and I played her. I used this makeup that Mama had left behind and painted my face all white with it, because I thought that's what a dead person would look like. I got some of her mascara and put that under my eyes too, to make me look like I was really tired, like I couldn't sleep anymore. I bet that's what I look like now, like I'm almost dead but not quite. Like I'm just sort of floating because I'm too afraid to go to sleep . . . "

Skip had made herself cry by telling that story, but she couldn't move her hands up to her face to wipe away her tears. She couldn't stop putting pressure on Wendy's hand.

"The fog was out at this one performance, and it really did look like we were ghosts, walking around in limbo. Daddy said, 'You look like a raccoon,' but what he really meant was, 'You look dead. You look like Mama probably looks like in her coffin' . . . Do you think she still looks like she did when she was alive? It would be great to see her. That part of being dead won't be so bad. At least I'll get to see her again."

Skip didn't know what else to say. She had run out of words. She tilted her head over onto Wendy's shoulder, but she wouldn't close her eyes. She had to keep talking to Wendy.

She had to keep talking for herself.

"Who do you wanna see when you're dead?"

CHAPTER FIFTY-FOUR

The petting zoo. It was another page ripped from my life story, being written by someone who seemed to know it as well as I did. A tour of my life, from someone who'd been on the outside, looking in.

"We made it there just once with Skip, before Patti died," I said to Mizell, in the passenger's seat beside me as we drove to the old children's zoo, slicing the morning fog, the sun barely up. I clutched the steering wheel and pushed the gas, twisting my right wrist up to keep rechecking my watch, every ten seconds.

Six A.M. Just over twenty hours left to go.

"Think about it. It's the only place the new rhyme could mean." I ticked them off for Mizell. "The old stable where Patti had her art show. Arcadia, where we'd gone skiing. The same frat I'd been a part of in college. And now this kiddie farm my parents had taken me to. That I'd taken Patti to. And Skip."

"Could it be somebody who's pissed off that you're dating again? Somebody from Patti's family?" Mizell had raised it once, but I'd dismissed it. Now I wasn't so sure.

"Her family . . . we got along great. They told me at the funeral . . . they wanted the best for me. And Skip. I don't know."

But now . . . a fucking *petting* zoo, grimly perfect for Wendy, a woman who loved animals.

Grimly perfect for how it intersected with so many parts of my life. When Patti first got pregnant with Skip, before we even knew if it was a boy or girl, we went to it, about an hour away from Mt. Gresh. I wanted it to be a tradition for us: I remembered going to the same place when I was a kid, for some birthday. My fourth, fifth maybe? I was little; we'd just moved to Massachusetts, one of the many moves my parents were always making, and I didn't have any new friends yet. There was no one to invite to a birthday party, so my parents took me there, saying all the animals could be my friends instead. It became a yearly thing for us until I got too embarrassed—too old—to be at a "kiddie zoo."

I told Patti I wanted the same for our child. Tradition. Things you could count on. But we'd gotten to take Skip there just once before it closed. Now, I was going to be the one to reopen it.

Well, *he* was, if I was right.

Mizell read the new rhyme aloud, her French tips clacking in time on the dashboard. Reminding me of something I could never forget.

Skip's fingernails.

Hercules got rid of the Stymphalian Birds,
Whose beaks could kill, just like my words.
They guard the nests at the old petting zoo . . .
A fun place to go . . .
Before the horses became glue.
Birds, a bull, mares, and cattle . . .
Do them all, or hear the death rattle.

"He's throwing them all in at once. Four Labors, all out here," I said, counting them off on my fingers while my hand was still on the steering wheel. "The Stymphalian Birds, the Cretan Bull, the Mares of Diomedes, the Cattle of Geryon. Six through ten, minus taking Wendy. That was nine. The Belt of Hippolyta. The Belt of Wendy."

An insane inventory, in what must have sounded like a foreign language.

Mizell put her hand over mine. "You can do it. We can do it. We have to."

I coasted through the open gate in a split-log fence; the old billboard advertising the place leaning on poles that were barely upright now, the paint falling off it in giant, jagged strips. Whatever colors had once coated the place—and there had been a lot, if I remembered right; bright primary colors to grab the kids' attention—were long gone. We parked next to a lake, the sound of our car doors opening enough to frighten all the geese away. They lifted off the lake as one, breaking through the fog. The flap of their wings, the honking . . .

Mizell and I went silent. This was a place where you didn't talk, you didn't want to disturb. So peaceful. So perfect in its isolation, and desolation. So primed for us, just . . . waiting.

"I'll be right behind you," Mizell whispered. "I have my gun."

So do I, I thought, but didn't tell her. It was tucked in the back of my pants, covered over by my jacket. She didn't need to know that.

"I don't want you getting trapped like last time."

It wouldn't be by fire again, I knew that much. He'd already tried that. And the flood had been what the real Hercules had done, rerouting the river.

So what other way did he have planned, to end my world?

As we walked toward the main house, every sound was magnified: our footsteps over the dead grass, coated with the tiniest bit of hoarfrost that crunched; every little wave and rustle in the few leaves that were left on trees. A weather-beaten sign hung over a corral where there used to be a little rodeo; the sign dangled by a few links of rusty chain that creaked in the wind. Next to that, a barn, where the animals used to wait their turn in the ring. Sniffing deep, I could smell its history: empty stables that had never given up the smell of manure; milk gone sour and dried out in rusty metal cans, from cows that had last been milked years ago.

Hadn't my parents taken me inside there, to put my hand on a teat and give it a squeeze, until I squealed and ran back to them?

Something squishy, the smell of hay on the floor, a farmer who laughed at me and joked with my parents . . . two hands on the teat, the farmer's over mine? Cow flesh, my flesh, other flesh.

That's where the petting zoo had been. Inside, children on horses, petting lambs, playing with goats. Shetland ponies, with tangled manes of hair so thick you could hold that instead of reins.

The memory faded away, as Mizell and I kept walking up toward the main house.

Up on the porch, flies had batted themselves to death in the wire mesh of the front door screen, trying to get inside. Broken window glass littered the porch; rags that had once been lacy curtains whipped back and forth. I heard something—more than just the wind?—and turned around to look back out at the farm. The creak of that wheel and pulley, hanging high on one side of the barn? Or him, watching me?

Inside the old house, the shadow of what used to be the owners' home. The couple who ran the place, who had turned their living room into a gift shop. A stray chair with no seat; a table, tilted over and collapsed on three legs. Outlines where family portraits had once been, now just dark squares of peeling wallpaper. An empty display case, which used to house items for sale. Divinity and fudge. Rock candy. Taffy. Belts beaded with fake Indian mosaics.

I remember that too—I'd begged my mother for one. It started unstitching the minute I wore it the first time, all those cheap little plastic beads falling off, scattering everywhere.

In a corner of the room, windblown into a pile like dead leaves, were little photos with jagged edges, the kind that used to shoot out of an instamatic, their colors now dulled to an underwater green. I rifled through them, wondering if I'd find one of myself there.

A color . . . colors coming to me, real colors, not what time has reduced them to.

Blue . . . and black . . . white . . . the cowboy shirt I used to wear when I was a kid? My pride and joy. Silver snap buttons, white fringe on the cuffs.

*I can almost remember wearing it here, and my mother telling
me to smile, just as a camera flashes. Mother's putting me on top of
a little swaybacked horse; I settle in the saddle, but something else is
there too. It crowds me, and the horse bows lower, as more weight gets
added behind me . . .*

Upstairs, now, a sound. The house still settling, after all these
years? Wind?

No, something more . . . alive. Cooing. Pigeons? Wings
flapping, then settling down. Waiting for me.

"I think that's where you're supposed to go next. It fits," Mizell
said, nodding upwards, then starting to read again, the poem now
a treasure map that she was in charge of.

*To survive number six,
You'll have to take your licks.
At the top of the stairs
Start saying your prayers.*

I went up the stairs in front of Mizell; an attic door was open,
waiting for me.

At first, all I could see were the shapes: trunks and toys, junk, a
family's life, now left to the elements. A draft of air, a hole in the
roof, a slick of bird droppings glossing the floor, calcified white
and green, hardened and crusted and feathers, feathers everywhere
. . . molting, and . . .

Alive. Everywhere. *Now.*

Starlings. Attacking me, hysterical at my intrusion, invading
their haven.

Man-eating birds. The Sixth Labor.

My arms swung up in a crisscross over my face as they swarmed
me with their beaks and talons. I knocked into a trunk and fell
down, trying to wave them away, more of the poem ping-ponging

in my head, even louder than the cacophony from the birds and the screams from Mizell, bringing up the rear.

If you want the birds to rid . . .
Just do what Hercules did.

But what the hell did Hercules *do*? I couldn't remember.

I couldn't remember anything—except to try to stay alive. And then it hit me. Hercules scared the birds away with a loud metal rattle; any similar sound would drive them away. I grabbed the pistol from the back of my belt and started shooting. Blindly. Anywhere. Everywhere.

"What the hell . . . " Mizell was as shocked by me pulling out a pistol as she was by the birds she was trying to beat away.

I screamed, to add to the noise. I screamed at *him*, who was making me do all this.

"GO AWAY! GO AWAY! GO. THE FUCK. AWAY!"

With each outburst, more of the birds flew out of the hole in the ceiling.

I kept shooting. All I wanted was them gone. Off me. Off Mizell. That sharp sound of bullets discharging was deafening in this tiny room, filling it gunpowder and burning smells, bird shit and bird flesh.

And it was working.

With each shot I took, more of them flew away, out of the hole in the ceiling. A final tornado of feathers, a funnel cloud of sleek black getting sucked back up, just as I reached the end of my bullets, my hand still vibrating from the kick of the pistol.

Silence. Shock.

And then they were gone. Just like that. A few of them still perched around the jagged rim of the hole at the roof, peering down, practically cooing, waiting to see what *man* did next.

As carefully as I could, I began walking out of the room, motioning Mizell out before me.

Slow. Steady.

I was afraid that the smallest movement would set those few birds off again.

We both were finally out the door, so I slammed it behind me. Those birds couldn't get us anymore.

And that's when I came face to face with the next Labor: yet another piece of paper, tacked to the front side of the door, which had been open when we went in. That's why we'd missed it before.

But *he* hadn't missed anything. A paper trail, literally—leaving his breadcrumbs for us.

Before you cry uncle, your work's not done.
Head to the stable, and make it three for one.
The Cretan Bull has horns in Labor number seven,
Bring them down, or your girls go to heaven.

I yanked it down and started reading it out loud, as Mizell and I flew down the steps and out the house, stumbling toward the barn.

"Where the hell did you get that gun?" she was screaming as I ran across the lawn, slipping and sliding in the morning dew; that, or the gore on my shoes from the abattoir in the attic.

"It worked, didn't it?" I yelled back, ahead of her.

I could almost remember running in the same direction with my mother all those years ago, after I'd bought my little mosaic belt inside with my allowance; pulling her by the hand and saying, "Hurry, it's starting, come on," as a tinny loudspeaker, hissing with reverb, announced that the rodeo was about to begin. Cowboys yelling and roping, hooves digging into the dirt, kicking up clods of earth into the stands . . . clowns scrambling to protect riders who'd been bucked off. Children laughing and clapping and screaming . . .

The memory vanished as we got to the stable, for a different kind of rodeo.

A stampede of animals, rushing out of the barn.

The Cretan Bull. The Mares of Diomedes. The Cattle of Geryon.

Three Labors—seven, eight, and ten—all careening together for a perfect storm of animal flesh. No telling how many tons of it, crashing through the corral fence, bearing down.

On me.

Hercules—the *real* Hercules—was supposed to capture them in the Labors, but short of shooting them all, that wasn't going to happen. This was madness in motion, a Tower of Babel of whinnies and moos and roars, hooves and horns, flying manes and choking, blinding dust.

Horses pawing and snorting phlegm, bucking and raising high. Nostrils, gums, teeth, and metal bits.

Mad cows, crazed, as if they had been kept in waiting in there, for all those years. Starved.

A single bull with horns, pawing and snorting with all the fight it had stored up.

It roared past me, scraping off layers of my skin and clothes, heading straight for Mizell.

It was her or me, and there was no time to think. I'd gotten her in this mess, and I was going to get her out.

I did my best long jump—arcing through the air, almost faster than the bull—and my legs hit Mizell first, knocking her flat into an open metal chute. I tucked myself in after her, on top of her, and the livestock continued barreling past, a mad dash divided down the middle by our chute, their slobber and skin grazing the open metal and us.

The animal kingdom kept plowing through that rickety corral fence, the dried lumber cracking like brittle bones against the force of them. And they kept thundering away into the distance, finally free, the storm of dust they kicked up almost making them disappear into the horizon. For a minute, neither one of us moved.

I didn't know if we were as splintered as those fence rails.

I pulled myself up, then pulled Mizell up after me from the face plant I'd knocked her into.

"If you wanted to get on top of me, all you had to do was take me out for a drink," Mizell said. And then she cried. "You saved me."

"Better check for broken bones before you say that," I said, and then hugged her.

Dry, arid wind and dust swirled around us as we kept holding on for dear life, afraid to let go. Afraid to leave that thin metal chute that had saved our lives.

A breeze whistled over the farm, almost taking it back to how things had been when we first got there. Everything untouched, natural, almost purified. And then . . .

. . . like the flap of a piece of paper, rustling and flapping with the hollow, scraping sound of something bone dry that had been left out in this field forever. I don't think Mizell heard it; she was still in shock, but I did.

It was coming from a tall wooden utility pole, on top of which was mounted a loudspeaker. The kind that used to announce the names of rodeo riders and cowboys.

Something was nailed to the pole.

In that morning air, a chill ran through me.

I was already a broken man, just what the madman wanted; all four Labors he'd sent us out here to do were over—my body pelted, skin broken, legs barely working anymore—but he still wasn't done with me. Not yet.

Oh my God no, no . . . please God no . . .

I released my hold on Mizell and staggered away from her, practically crawling.

"Where the hell are you going? I still need . . . " she began.

. . . and then she saw it too. Twenty, thirty feet away, a package, brand new and dazzling white, and tied with twine. It hadn't been here forever; it just got here. For us. For me.

I got to the utility pole and pulled the package off where it was being held there, nailed to the pole like a bull's-eye.

I felt it. Something spongy inside, that gave when I pushed against it.

Mizell came toward me and mashed into it too, trying to feel what shape was inside.

"I can't . . . you have to . . . what if it's a finger . . . fingers . . . he said 'her fingers will be next' . . . oh my GodohmyGod . . . " I'd been so strong, but I couldn't be strong anymore.

Mizell began untying the twine and pulled the outer covering of white paper away, to reveal what was inside. She looked before I did, then looked at me, confusion on her face.

A shirt. A child's shirt.

My shirt. My faded little blue and black cowboy shirt with silver snap buttons, which I had worn here so many years ago.

And scrawled in large letters, facing me when I lifted the folded-up shirt off the paper:

If only you'd answered your fan mail.

CHAPTER FIFTY-FIVE

After all his planning, it didn't seem fair that it would all be over, one way or another, in mere hours. But there were many things to do before then, miles to go before he slept.

Messages to be delivered.

Contact to be made.

Labors to be . . . completed.

He flipped a switch on a movie projector to make sure it was working, and a conical beam of light hit a wall in the principal's office, away from the girls, searching for just the right playing surface. Ah, his favorite sensations. Old school. The scratchy print of leader film, Xs and slashes and what looked like strands of hair, embedded on the film . . .

The burning smell of a light bulb, bringing the plastic to life . . .

The hiss of celluloid, crinkling and threading through an old-fashioned reel-to-reel projector . . .

And the sound of Hercules, the fake one, the movie one, in agony.

It had been the only good thing they ever did at the home, show them movies.

His favorite had been *Hercules Unchained*, but they got the title all wrong. Steve Reeves was *completely* chained, trying to bring down the colossal columns on either side of him. That's when all the boys would cheer, as they projected the movie on one of the walls. All the bumps of paint, layered and layered on top of each other through the years, would show through on Steve's face, making him look like he had pimples.

Just like all his cellmates. *Class*mates.

Of all of them, he was the only one who'd been smart enough—who'd been *good* enough—to be allowed out, to go to a real school, even if it was just a few rooms. And now, he'd recreated it much as he remembered it, with some crucial improvements, especially in the principal's office.

Yes, there was still the heavy wood desk, the wire baskets, even the heavy, looming portrait in the gilt frame of the man who had been the principal. How that portrait had escaped the looters over the years, he didn't know; surely the frame was worth something, even though pigeons had taken to roosting on top of it and, well . . . relieving themselves. It looked like he was crying, old man Somerset, the founder of The Somerset School, tears of bird shit running down his cheeks.

Guano? Was that it? No, that was for *bats*. Cave-dwelling bats, but he was sure they must have made a home here too. Hanging upside down. At least they hadn't done *that* to him when he was a student here.

How many hours had he spent there, sitting on that burnished bench outside the principal's office—happy to be there, on that gleaming, golden wood—preparing to beg to stay here overnight and not be taken back to that *other* home, where one half of a bunk bed was waiting for him. How he could make do here, put his little lopsided head down on top of his desk and take an eight-hour nap through the night, using a towel for a pillow. In the morning, he could go in the bathroom and splash cold water on his face and be good to go. He could even help the teachers get ready for the day . . .

Just please, please, don't make me go back there.

But *no, no,* they never listened to him.

Now they would.

CHAPTER FIFTY-SIX

Mizell was at the wheel this time, on her cell talking to Frick and Frack while driving us to Sig's house. She and I had reversed positions and now I was riding shotgun, trying to figure out where that old cowboy shirt had come from. I hadn't seen it in a million years, not since kindergarten or first grade, maybe. I remember wearing it for a school picture, smiling at the camera, a big gap between my front teeth; I probably still had the picture thrown in a junk box at home. The buttons done up all the way to the collar. But after that . . . who knows?

Well, *he* did.

The shirt had gone in the rag bin, I suppose. Or my mother gave it away to Goodwill or something, like she was always doing. But wherever it had gone, it hadn't existed for me anymore.

Until now. The thing I took out of that macabre package *was* mine, from over thirty years ago; the fringe on the cuffs had even gotten worn off by the time I quit wearing it. No—not worn off, *bitten* off. *Chewed* off. That's what I used to do. Put it up to my mouth, even while I was wearing it, to gnaw on it; the hard metal of the silver snaps against my teeth . . .

I held it up to my nose and smelled it. It was fresh, like it had just been laundered; no yellowed underarm stains or the residue of deodorant, it was long before puberty, long before I started sweating. I was trying to smell my childhood on it, wonder where it had gone, but nothing . . .

And then something.

Something that wasn't me.

Initials in magic marker, on the label inside the collar. BCH. What the hell was BCH? *Who* the hell?

And fan mail? 'If only you'd answered your fan mail.' What the hell did *that* mean?

Sig had taken care of all that, or the PR firm we hired had. There was an impossible number of fan letters coming in, requests for an autographed photo. Part of the Wheaties money had paid for that, so I could go on with my life. Now it was coming back to bite me in the butt.

Mizell pulled up in front of Sig's house, one of the little cottages the school owned on a street that was right off the track field. You'd think he'd want to live somewhere else, have time off, but his boys on the field *were* his life. He loved being able to roll out of bed and pretty much be at work, and Canaan was good to him, letting him coach until he was ready to call it quits, not the other way around. Sometimes I thought he'd spent the nearly twenty years since I was a student there looking for his next Olympic star. He'd never found one, not even a close contender.

And the house was always unlocked. Whenever I warned him about it—yeah, little sleepy town, nothing bad ever happens here—he always came back at me with, "Let 'em take whatever they want. Me, the TV. There's not much else." And he was right. Just piles and piles of junk. But to Sig, it wasn't just junk, but *history*. Newspapers, trophies, plaques, barbells, brochures about new sports equipment, scrapbooks full of clippings of the boys he'd trained. And a room with a view: he could always look out his front window, across the street to the track, and see his guys running there.

Now, Sig had just seen his greatest guy come in—his big star, his biggest success—wounded and limping, covered by dirt and dust, holding a little boy's cowboy shirt that was thirty years old. With a question about fan mail and what it had to do with his daughter and girlfriend being kidnapped.

There was a lot to talk about.

"Jesus Christ on a crutch, you look like you've just redone your entire Olympic program, with a partner," Sig said to me and Mizell. "We gotta get you two fixed up."

Before I could tell him what I was there for, he went digging through his medicine cabinet for Band-Aids and butterfly sutures. Mizell and I had started cleaning ourselves up at his kitchen sink when Sig's front door came banging open.

It was TJ, who must have been following us, looking almost worse than we did. Tortured, but in a different way. And he didn't waste any time getting to the point, even if it was in another man's house.

"We had a bargain, remember? I tell you what happened, you tell me. I told. You didn't. We're not finished."

"Oh please. Not you again," I shot right back at him. "Get the fuck outta here before she gets you for breaking and entering."

Mizell jumped in. "Markson, Casey, whatever your name is, right now is *not* a good time . . . "

"There's *never* a good time to find your father's body hanging by a noose."

That's when Sig came back into the room. "I know all about you. What you did. You are *not* welcome here."

Sig started pushing TJ out the door. Pathetic, and scary, this once powerful old man, his bony arms now covered with liver spots, pushing against this kid who was just as bony. But there was something desperate about it. Something Sig wanted to make disappear.

TJ was pushing back just as hard. His eyes weren't just crazy anymore; they were in agony. I could see it through the smudges on his glasses, the rat's nest hair hanging over his forehead. "Just give me this one last thing, then we're done. I'm begging you."

I'd said the very same thing to the kidnapper. Your life, reduced to one thing, one phrase, one plea.

I'm begging you.

TJ stood his ground, still huffing from his set-to with Sig. "Did you turn in my dad? Tell them to test him? That's what his suicide note said. He blamed you. Just tell me, once and for all, and then I'll go. Forever. Just like he did."

"This isn't the time," I said. "Or the place. My daughter is missing. Wendy's missing. Because of you . . . "

"My father's *dead* because of you. So just say it. Tell me the truth."

"TJ, please . . . " Now everyone was looking at me, waiting to see what I'd do. Maybe I'd known what I had to confess from the second I'd found that very first note, pinned in the silhouette of my baby girl. Maybe I'd known it ever since the second I did it, thirteen years ago.

"He's right. Your dad was right. I was the one who did it. I was the one who called him in."

My entire lily-white history, changed in seconds, with just a few words.

It was the hardest thing I'd ever had to tell anybody, as hard as telling Skip her mother was dead. And for now, it was the only thing in the room. Skip, Wendy, their tortures were all on hold, in the shock of silence.

I kept going. "They needed a fall guy, and I gave them one. Your dad. They just needed one example. One face. There was a rumor going around, that they were going to do random tests . . . "

I saw thirteen years ago like it was now: one phone call. That's all it took. That was the night the real Hercules was born, the minute I hung up that phone. Mark Casey got randomized to pee in a cup, and I walked away with thirty pieces of silver.

A gold medal.

"He killed himself because of you." TJ spat it out at me. "You were the traitor. The Ninth Circle of Hell. That's where you belong."

"Nobody belongs in hell. I'm there now, and I know," I answered TJ back. This was my fight now. "But he was the traitor, because he cheated to win. He fucked with the honor code. The Olympics. You build yourself up with hard work. Not with drugs. You stay as pure as they were in ancient Greece."

Mizell finally spoke up, putting two and two together. "That's why he attacked you on the tape. At the games. He knew you were the one who did it."

"No, there was somebody else." I turned toward Sig. It all made sense now. That's why he'd been trying to push TJ out of his house. That was the secret he was trying to make disappear. My secret. "You knew, the whole time. Didn't you? That it was me . . . the traitor."

Sig opened the front door so he could look out at the track, hundreds of yards away. He'd die happy, if that was the last sight he ever saw. His team. His boys. What he said told me everything I needed to know. "I wanted to win as much as you did."

I needed eyes to look into, eyes to say this to, so I looked at TJ. The person who needed to hear it the most. The person who'd been waiting years to hear it. I needed to give this kid back something, so he could go on living. So I could too. "*What's the worst thing you ever did?*' Isn't that what you asked me that night at Cousin Charlie's? The worst thing I ever did? I'll tell you. It wasn't just that I wanted your father gone because he was doping . . . I *needed* him gone. He could have beat me *without* the drugs. He was that good . . . he would have won without them. That's my truth. And his. He knew it. That's what I've gotta live with. That it should have been him up there. Not me. *That's* why I quit the Olympics. I didn't deserve to be there."

I nodded toward Sig. "Ask him."

"Could my father have won . . . instead of . . . *Hercules?*"

Sig gave him his truth—and mine—with a single word. "Yes."

I didn't have any more secrets. I didn't have any more *life.* "I deserve this, what's happening. This is what the kidnapping is about. Somehow. In some way I don't understand yet . . . I fucked with the code. You do wrong, you're punished. I did wrong to somebody, and now I'm being punished. *That's* what the classics are all about."

When Mizell's cell phone rang—mine was lost to that fire at the crack den—it was almost a relief. Even if it was the kidnapper. Especially if it was him. He was my fate, for whatever reason.

Mizell put it on speakerphone, so we could all hear.

"At least you saved your girls from *buying* the farm . . . when you were down *on* the farm."

"Please. Who are you? Just tell me."

"Do I have to spell everything out for you? Just like the fingernails . . . spell it out . . . "

"Spell out *what?*" I yelled back at him. "*AH* is all they spelled out. Or *HA*. Like you think this is all one big fucking joke."

"Language. You sound like you were raised in a . . . fucking *orphanage.*" He spit the word out. "If you'd just answered your fan mail . . . "

"What the hell are you talking about?"

"I was your. Biggest fan. I sent you fan mail. Fan mail, from some flounder. And oh, how I floundered."

He slammed down the phone, and the connection between us, our umbilical cord, was cut.

And then, as if he'd just remembered something, Sig started moving. "Jesus Christ on a crutch . . . orphanage . . . your *fan mail* . . . "

Sig went to his roll-top desk and began rummaging through a bulging scrapbook of Olympic clippings. "You got all sorts of crazy stuff back then," he said, flipping from page to page, gray paper almost turning to dust in his fingers. In those pages, I saw my younger self fly by, a victor making wild crazy grins for the camera. "I didn't show it to you, because I didn't want you to lose your focus."

At the very back of the scrapbook, stuffed in between the last page and the hard binding, were a handful of letters, opened, but then stuffed back in their envelopes. All with the same return address.

"The Bruckner Children's Home, Pittsfield, Mass. What—you mean that old orphanage?" I said, pulling the pages of run-on writing from an envelope, an envelope Mizell grabbed from me, then held up next to the cowboy shirt I'd gotten.

"Wait . . . look at this." Mizell held the envelope's return address up against the inside collar of the shirt, with the Magic Marker writing. "BCH. Those initials. They're the same initials. BCH. Bruckner Children's Home. *That's* where the shirt is from. That's where we've gotta go now . . . "

And then I saw it. Four lines, four lines of terror, from the same person who'd been plotting and planning ever since then. Buried at the very bottom of the final page of one of his insane fan letters to me. Clearly an adult; no child could be this evil.

They sent me away, so you could go play,
They left me alone, so you'd be on your own . . .
They'll feel my gloom, when they meet their doom . . .
But since you're greater, I'm saving you for later.

CHAPTER FIFTY-SEVEN

Mizell didn't use her siren driving to The Bruckner Home, some thirty minutes away, but still, we couldn't have raced there any faster.

"There" was where we turned into another place I vaguely remembered from childhood. My mother taking our little Sunday school class there, to see where our tithe was going. It all looked so normal, after the fire and brimstone stuff we'd been scared with in church.

"If you're not good, if you don't work hard and win for your father, you'll end up there."

Clean and orderly, at least the parts they showed us. One little girl from the home was leading our group, and I asked her—in all innocence—"But where are all the orphans? They said we'd get to see orphans."

That was the last time she'd ever taken me there, horrified by me; maybe it was the last time she ever went. I never knew. We moved again, right after that.

I didn't like going there then.

And I didn't like going there now.

Something bad was there, or had been.

At the turn-off, the sign leading to the home was big, with a curlicue cutout on top, like some antebellum mansion. A few of the painted letters on it were peeling; it could have used a fresh coat of paint, but it wasn't foreboding. It wasn't something out of Dickens—as I had expected years ago. A curving driveway led up to the main building; it looked like stucco or some sort of concrete. An old English manor house, its exterior meant to survive the harsh winter. Windows were decorated with kid stuff, on display as much for the outside as the inside. Music posters and WWF wrestling. Hand-drawn signs and cutouts.

Now, it looked so . . . normal. A dorm, for kids. This place that I hadn't thought of in years, until Sig had dug out those old letters. The "fan mail" I should have answered.

I'd brought them with me, for . . . I don't know. Good luck? Evidence? To prove we weren't crazy?

To prove someone in here *had* been crazy?

Mizell parked, and I got out from the passenger side door, hobbling toward the front entrance on a cane I'd borrowed from Sig. Every step hurt because of my twisted ankle; running at the petting zoo had just made it worse. Instead of walking up the four curving marble steps to the front porch, I took the wheelchair ramp, covered in black-ribbed rubber; it was easier to manage.

The door set off a tinkling bell; inside, the lobby looked like a nice European hotel. After the war. The kind of place you'd expect to have a little bell on the front counter, to ring the harried wife and proprietress with, and a guest book.

"Hello?" Mizell called out, already pulling out her badge. "Anybody home?" Her voice echoed off the marble of the entrance hall. The floors, polished to a high gloss. The smell of janitor stuff, left behind.

"I'll be right with you," someone called from inside.

A woman in her sixties came out from the back office, behind the front desk. She was a multi-tasker; as she moved, she was still looking back, to some helper in the room she had just left. "If you call the computer guy, then we can . . . "

Her skin was powdery, jowly and soft, like biscuit dough before you pop it in the oven. Black hair, with some gray coming through—two weeks away from her hairdresser's appointment. She was wearing slacks and a nice top; not a uniform, not a nurse uniform.

Then she stopped short, as she turned around and saw me over the counter.

Advancing slowly, carefully, on my cane. It gave me a strange, crab-like lope, leaning to one side, favoring the leg that was good.

"Oh sweet Jesus . . . " she said, her hand flying to her heart, her face turning whiter than it already was. "Just one cane now! You're doing so well!"

I looked at her, uncomprehending. So did Mizell.

"Now don't go getting all bashful on me, just because you're grown up! It's your Mamarie. Your Mama. Your Marie. Your Ma-ma-rie. Don't tell me you've forgotten?"

"*Who?*"

Now it was her turn to step back, as afraid as I was beginning to feel. "I'm sorry, I . . . who are you?"

"Ethan Holt. Who . . . who did you think I was?"

"*Aaron* Holt."

"What are you talking about? Who? No, it's Ethan," I said. Almost in horror. Dread.

"I'm sorry, hon," the sweet old lady said to me. "I knew this day was going to come. Aaron Holt. *He's* the one who was here. Your twin brother."

My cane clattered to the floor, the only sound in the room, echoing against the marble.

CHAPTER FIFTY-EIGHT

Skip must have finally fallen asleep because she was having a wonderful dream, where her father came to save her. He was actually in the room, and he was looking right into her eyes. She smiled, and he smiled back at her.

And then he didn't.

His face collapsed. The mouth *tried* to lift into a smile, his cheeks struggled to hold up the corners of his lips, but something was off. Lopsided. So much like her father, but . . . not.

Everything she'd dreamed and prayed for, for days now, but . . . not.

She wasn't dreaming. She couldn't feel her body in a dream, and she felt every inch of it now. Trussed up on a rotten wood floor, her back pushed into the pebbly wall that had been painted over a million times. The only comfort she felt was at her left side, Wendy there, just beginning to wake up too. Both waking up from the same nightmare, because of who was looking back at them.

Skip's father, but . . . not.

It was a version of him that was smushed: pudgier, slack, a choppy haircut, the pale skin of someone who never saw the sun, but his eyes were the same. Just attached to a different body, one that was twisted and malformed and sitting in a wheelchair.

"Who are you!" Skip didn't care if she cried anymore. She didn't care if she screamed. All her schemes and tricks had gone out of her head the minute she saw this man pretending to be her father.

"Iphicles. The twin brother Hercules forgot. But you can call me . . . Uncle Aaron. This little . . . "—with difficulty, he raised his arms to display the handiwork that was all around him, all twelve murals of the Labors of Hercules—"*gesture* . . . is to help him remember."

"You're trying to . . . to fool us or something. He doesn't have a twin. He's an only child."

"No. He *became*. An only child."

He wheeled his chair next to one of the magazine clippings of her father, and posed, face to face. Skip almost couldn't tell them apart. He pulled at his face to show it wasn't a mask, but it almost looked like one, shipped from the factory before it was finished.

"The mirror doesn't lie. It cracks, perhaps, when it sees this sad sight, but it doesn't lie. Oh, I didn't believe it either, not at first. But I did the research. At the orphanage. The *home*. Everything in my files. Names, addresses, cashed *checks*. The paper trail, to prove how my parents had given me away, at age three. After I got out, I talked to doctors. I read case studies. And it is possible. At that age, just three years, you can forget. And Ethan did. They came to visit . . . and then he forgot to come back."

"Ethan doesn't have a twin . . . I would've known . . . " Wendy sputtered.

"Skip can fill you in. I've already told her the story. I just left out one crucial detail: that umbilical cord that was wrapped around my neck? Turning me into . . . this? That was *his*. His cord, cutting off my air. My brain. My legs. Choking the life out of me."

"That's . . . that's just . . . how you were born then. He didn't have anything to do with it. He was just a baby!" Skip couldn't stop. "No. NO. He would've said. You can't forget something like that."

"Forget? Yes. Forgive? No. I was the . . . *runt* of the litter. Taken away. *Given* away. And soon, *forgotten*. My parents—*his* parents— told everyone I had died. And then I did, because they stopped coming. They stopped bringing him. Ethan. Because who likes to be reminded that a child is . . . less than perfect. Less than . . . Olympic material?"

"This is . . . insane. This can't be," Skip gasped.

"Really, for the daughter of a classics professor . . . let me set you straight. Once upon a time, the great god Zeus had sex. With a mortal, Alcmena. One of his many affairs. He was a very bad boy. Alcmena had twins, but only *one* of them was from Zeus. The other was from her . . . *earthly* husband. That would be me. The one who *wasn't* . . . of the Gods."

"His parents! They're the ones that gave you away. Just tell him. Tell Daddy what you told us, he'll . . . he'll make everything okay."

"This . . . cannot be. *Made. Okay*," Aaron screamed at her. It had come back. The stop and start.

But Skip's words came even faster and louder. The words of the teenager that Aaron Holt had never gotten to be, the words he never dared to say, to anyone in power.

"FUCK YOU."

His hands came flying to her face, almost knocking it off with its force. She buried her face In Wendy's neck, to try to escape.

"Most people. In your situation. Would know. *Not*. To talk. Like that."

"I'm not most people. I'm your niece," she said, finally crying in front of him.

CHAPTER FIFTY-NINE

So many lives, crammed into so many file cabinets. An entire history of a person and the most heartbreaking moments of their young lives, scribbled on eight-and-a-half-by-eleven-inch forms, stuck inside manila folders, which in turn were stuck inside upright coffins of gunmetal gray. That's what "Mamarie" was thumbing through now, to get the one she wanted to show us. Her fingernails were clipped short, so she flew through them quickly, every one of them a face, a person to her, not just a file.

Flying fingernails.

My daughter's fingernails.

A.H.

Aaron Holt.

My twin.

I put my head down between my legs to keep from throwing up.

"Your brother used to do that too. All the time. He got sick at the push of a button. I'd get him a Coca-Cola and let him stay in here and help me file, just to get away from . . . " She didn't finish the thought. "Well, things are pretty good now, but I can't promise they always were. Not when I started here."

In a corner of the room, Mizell was on her phone, filling her team in on the news. She was cupping her hand over the phone to shield what she was saying, but I could see it in her eyes. She couldn't believe it either.

"I still can't believe it . . . I had . . . I *have* a twin brother? Who was *here*? It's not possible. I'd know. I'd remember. I couldn't just . . . forget my own flesh and blood. It's a mistake, it's gotta be . . . "

"Children don't remember much of anything before three years old, and that's when Aaron came here. That's when his parents . . .

well, *your* parents . . . I guess that's when they finally gave up. They just couldn't cope with his condition."

"Or didn't want to." I suddenly saw it, why my father had pushed me so hard. I had to be perfect, physically perfect. I was living for two, except I'd never known it.

"You wouldn't believe the grownups I've met who didn't know they had a brother or sister who was given away. It's not your fault," Mamarie said, trying to make me feel better. "You were too little. There's no way you could remember . . . "

"But I should have . . . somebody I shared the womb with?"

"They brought you here a few times to visit. Well, your mother did. Your father almost never came. It's in the visitors' logs, you can check if you want to, but . . . so many kids over the years, some get adopted, some don't, but I remember him like my very own. All he needed was some love, and I tried to give it to him, but I think a child knows who's a parent and who isn't. I tried to make up for it, though . . . "

A paper cut. "Shoot." She sucked at the blood as she put the file out on the table in front of me. "Here we go."

Inside, a life. *His* life.

Forms and copies of cashed checks and report cards and medical forms. Pictures of Aaron, growing up. I could almost visualize myself next to him in every picture, the two-for-one that twins should have, except he didn't. I'd been left out of the picture.

He'd been left out of the picture.

"Oh my God. Look," I said to Mizell, pointing to one of them.

He was smiling at the camera, so proud, wearing the very same cowboy shirt I had. The one he'd left for me, as the last clue at the kiddie farm.

"She must have brought him one too, your mother," Mizell said.

And then, a change coming over him.

We were identical and then, we weren't.

Instead of seeing him grow up like me, the photos showed him getting weaker and weaker. One of his eyes, drooping. His chin, falling. His head, tilting. His legs, giving up.

"We moved a lot when I was little. I guess that's why. My parents cut any ties with anyone who knew. So I wouldn't find out. So *nobody* would find out."

"And then, after they died, there were no other relatives . . . " Mamarie continued.

I completed her thought. " . . . who even knew he was here."

"Nobody ever adopted him, so we just let him stay here. He helped us out. We all loved him. He was here into his twenties. The caretaker, helping all the other little kids . . . he was so good."

"But where is he now?" Mizell asked. "That's what we've got to find out. Fast."

"There's something else I want to show you," Mamarie said, getting up. "It might help. Or at least help you understand."

She was wrong. Nothing could make me understand this.

"Call it that . . . *connection* that twins have. I knew he was my twin, my blood, my *other*, the first time I saw his picture. Mamarie showed it to me, all the way back in high school, when I was still at the home. When I was a . . . *client* there. We looked alike, but it was more than that. It was like . . . I saw him, and knew . . . I've found my *real* home."

As long as he was talking, he was breathing, and so were they.

"Of course, no one believed he could be my twin, my other half, because we looked so . . . different. The same, but . . . not."

His words were going somewhere beyond them, to a mirror in his head. To his memory. It seemed to make him happy; his voice was even and smooth again. Or maybe it was just the new shot he gave himself, in front of them. He waited a moment for it to take effect, then began anew.

"So I had to prove it. Unlike this place, which I selected for its privacy, the one thing I *didn't* have at the home was privacy. A dorm, bunk beds. Shared with so many other . . . lost boys. I learned to snap open my eyes in an instant if I heard someone moving near me in the dark; I learned to keep weapons under my pillow. The one thing I didn't learn to hide—and you might call this my tragic flaw: my pride; it goeth before a fall, and how many times I *fell*—were the photos of my brother, that Mamarie gave to me. There was no denying him, *us*, our kinship; even to the boys who said *no* and *you can't* and *you're a liar* and *it's not true*. They only had to look at the pictures to see it *was* true. We were identical, except for . . . our styles of walking."

He gripped the side of the chair, to steady himself, and went on.

"One night, one of the boys stole one of the photos of him I kept inside my locker. They started passing it, making fun of a boy who had a *pin-up*. They made me hobble around to get it back, slipping and sliding on my crutches. But when I finally did get it, I tore it into pieces . . . so they couldn't make fun anymore."

He stopped; he was back there, at the home, a teenager, just like Skip was now.

"I tore it into pieces . . . to make the other boy *eat* it. And when he balked, I started hitting him in the head with my crutch. The other boys cheered. The sound of applause . . . just like my brother was getting, on the track field. My tormentor's face was bloody on the concrete floor, he was crying, and . . . and Iphicles was born."

"Mamarie" was taking us down the main hallway, to the thing she wanted to show us. I looked at every picture on the wall, every tile on the floor, trying to force a memory of visiting here with my mother. Being shown off to the kids. Showing them how to play sports, how to toss a football, when most of them could barely get around.

All I could remember was them *looking* at me: *You get to go home. You have a home.*

"We didn't even have a school here then, or classrooms," Mamarie said, playing tour guide. "They had to be bussed somewhere else. When Aaron was here, he was the only one smart enough to go . . . science, machines, poetry, art . . . he could do everything. When he aged out and it was time for him to leave, he didn't have anywhere to go, so we kept him on here as a handyman. He could fix everything. Machines, computers. You name it."

Mizell was on her cell as we walked, checking in with the FBI guys, but I got the sense that she was also trying to give me my privacy. To let everything soak in, to see if any memory came back. It was something I could only do by myself.

She clicked off her phone and shook her head at me. "They can't find anything. No records, no social, no last known address, no anything. He's completely off the grid . . . "

"But his Facebook?"

"Anybody can make up an account, and we've gotta move heaven and earth to subpoena their records."

At the end of the hall, Mamarie took us into an art room. Bright, alive with color. Grade school kids, some in wheelchairs, working on Play-Doh art projects with a hip young teacher. I smiled at her, but the minute she turned away, I broke. In every little face around the tables—mouths in concentration, hands gluey with tempera—I could see my brother.

I saw myself, what could have been. "This is . . . I don't know if I can do this."

Mamarie squeezed my hand. "You can. This is a gift, what these children can teach us. Just remember that. *They're* the gift."

She walked us through the kids and their little tables and little chairs, past the effusive art teacher, and took us to a smaller side room, a sort of walk-in closet.

"This is what I wanted you to see."

◆◆◆

In his darkened control room, Aaron punched on his bank of monitors, and several screens lit up. One of them was filled with people. An entire stadium of them, as a video of Ethan at the Olympics came up.

Family movies, of the family Aaron never had.

Ethan, his little brother by all of five minutes, preparing for the pole vault at Sydney.

An entire stadium, breathing with his brother, who was not breathing at all, but frozen in anticipation.

Aaron's lungs were bounding out of his chest, pushing against his rib cage, watching him. He couldn't get his breath. Then, or now. It was always the same. His brother was always somewhere unreachable.

If he is Hercules, the strong, then I'm Iphicles, the weak. The twin brother to Hercules.

He punched up all the other monitors, and the room was now filled with his brother, in every language of the world. Ethan "Hercules" Holt, at the Tower of Babel, as every country saw him. Chants and cheers coming from the Olympic stands, the play-by-play narration from a sportscaster.

The pictures and sound took over the room, and they took over Iphicles.

They became one, sight and sound, then and now, brother and brother.

In that moment, Iphicles *became* his brother.

Hercules and Iphicles. Ethan and Aaron. One and the same.

If one could do it, they *both* could do it. That's what twins did. That's what twins are.

We're the same, just look at us!

Iphicles grabbed his metal crutch that was leaning against a wall and used it to torque his body out of his chair. Ready. Prepared.

His crutch aloft, just as his brother positioned his running pole in front of him, for perfect balance.

On those screens, Ethan started running, gathering wind, the pole an eighteen-foot extension of his arms. Faster and faster he went, the pole bouncing in sync with every step, already vibrating at the miracle that was about to happen.

He was about to fly.

He was about to conquer man's greatest dream.

If Ethan can do it, I can do it. Become a bird. We came from the same egg, didn't we? Eggs turn into birds. Birds have wings. Birds can fly.

I can leave my crippled body behind, and soar.

Aaron got in position, his crutch aloft, ready for liftoff, trying to conjure a muscle memory he never had.

He looked at Ethan for courage, waiting for his little brother to tell him what to do.

Let's go, my twin. It's time. You'll finally be free.

On screen, all the screens, Ethan went arcing into the air.

He flew.

Aaron, completely lost to the moment, lost to the dream of a happy family and a brother and a body that worked, tried to do the same. He planted his crutch solidly against the floor, using the strength of his upper body to catapult himself out of his wheelchair . . .

. . . their eyes met, just as they once did in the womb, just as they did when they were forced to say goodbye to each other at just three years old . . . a few visits after that at the home . . . after Mamarie told him he had a twin brother.

A soon-to-be-famous brother.

Fly, brother, fly, join me in midair, oh, what fun we'll have . . .

Aaron closed his eyes to the dream, his eyelids trembling, a vision of perfection, of ecstasy, of weightless euphoria on his face . . .

I can do it.

I can change all this.

I can be forgiven . . .

I can . . .

At the very moment Ethan "Hercules" Holt went sailing over the bar, to the cheers of the crowd . . .

. . . his brother, *this* brother, collapsed in a heap on the floor.

Iphicles. A mass of dough and flesh, of hardened stick bones and atrophied muscle that could no longer do what his mind commanded.

Except hurt.

Himself, and everyone around him.

◆ ◆ ◆

"This is it," Mamarie said, sidestepping shelves of art supplies and displays, pegs full of little coats and scarves.

"What?" I said, crowded into the tiny closet with Mizell.

Mamarie pulled on a dangling chain that turned on a bare light bulb. "This."

"Oh my God."

I crouched down in the tiny room, but the power of what I saw knocked me back on my haunches, just like when I'd found that very first note on Skip's bed.

On the very back wall was a faded mural of Hercules and his Eleventh Labor—stealing the golden apples of the Hesperides.

This was where the Labors had begun, a million years ago.

It looked like some outsider artist had done it, primitive and childlike. Bold primary colors and heavy outlines, with a three-dimensional bas-relief of apples, spray-painted gold, hanging from a tree. I reached toward one; it was a real apple or had been, once upon a time, even though it had long since caved in on itself, shrunken to the core.

In the lower right corner, a signature. The beginning of the end, left over from all those years ago.

Aaron "Iphicles" Holt.

"Who the hell is Iphicles?" Mizell blurted out.

I reached toward the mural, tracing the strokes of my twin brother's handwriting. "The twin brother of Hercules. Twins, but with different fathers. Iphicles is on the human side. Hercules is a product of the gods."

"Am I just a dumb cop, or does everybody know that?"

I was lost to the past. My past. His. Ours. Theirs. Hercules and Iphicles.

"In mythology, two snakes come into the babies' room. The weaker twin, Iphicles, screams his head off. But Hercules picks up the snakes like toys and wrings their necks . . . and that's . . . that's pretty much the end of the story. At least the only story anybody knows. After that, Iphicles just disappears. He's just . . . gone, like he wasn't a good enough character. Like they got tired of him."

One brother becomes a part of mythology, a name for the ages; the other becomes a mere footnote. Just because he was afraid of snakes.

"Let's give you some time in here." Mamarie took Mizell out, sensing how lost to the thrall of the room I was.

My brother, my *twin*, had made this. *Before.*

"I'm sorry, I'm so sorry . . . "

I couldn't say it enough. Whatever else he had done, I couldn't say it enough, to make up for this.

What my parents had done to him, by putting him in here.

What I had done, by forgetting. Maybe that was the worst sin of all.

That was how I had broken the code.

I put my own palm over his tiny little handprint; I dwarfed it, as he must have always thought I did. This must have been where

Skip got her artistic talent; it wasn't from me. She got it from her uncle . . .

. . . the uncle, who had been a part of me, and then hadn't.

The uncle who was now holding Skip and Wendy hostage.

The uncle who had said he would kill them in just four hours.

I plucked one of the golden apples off the mural and slipped it into my jacket pocket, seeing my watch as my wrist went by.

I reached up to pull on the tiny chain that controlled the lightbulb in the closet and . . .

There. Wait. A lightbulb moment, at the lightbulb.

At home once, on a break from college. I'm snooping around. Reaching up in a closet in my parents' bedroom, for something up on a shelf. A single light bulb you turned on with a chain. That metallic click, the light bulb, swinging around . . .

I reach up onto a shelf, behind a stack of sheets and towels. Behind them, an upright metal safety box.

I pull it down, and open it; it's not locked, how valuable could the things inside be?

Inside, two pairs of bronzed baby shoes, one set normal, the other twisted and bent over, but both sets perfectly frozen as they'd been, shoelaces askew.

I don't hear my mother come in behind me. She doesn't say anything, just yanks everything out of my hands.

"What the hell are you doing?"

"Are these my baby shoes? Both pairs? The crooked ones too?"

"Of course they are. That's why we got you into those gymnastic classes. To correct your feet. Don't you remember?"

No, I didn't.

No, I do.

When my parents died in that house fire, my mother was found trying to crawl out of the room, her charred body wrapped around the crooked pair of shoes.

Protecting them.

Now I remember.

I crawled out of the closet to Mizell. From the look of things, she'd filled Mamarie in on what was going on. There were tears in her eyes. Shock.

"It can't be. He wouldn't . . . "

"We don't know for sure . . . " Mizell started in, trying to make it better.

"Yes, we do. It's him." It was the first time I'd said it. Now I knew, for sure.

"If you were him," I asked Mamarie, tears forming in my eyes too, at what I knew I had to do, "where would you go?"

"I'd go to the place I loved the most. For him, that was the Somerset School . . . where he could get away from here. If it's him, *this* is the place that made it happen."

CHAPTER SIXTY

The classroom looks better now. The walls are painted and decorated; not with murals from the mind of a madman, but with the stuff of a real grade school education: relief maps of Switzerland, growth charts and posters showing the different parts of the human eyeball, stencils of the letters of the alphabet in cursive. There's a stanchion holding an American flag, and a square wooden box above the blackboard, a "squawk box" from which their principal speaks. Miss Moore's big wooden desk isn't yet battle-scarred or carved up with initials, but is still freshly varnished; a gleaming gold beacon at the front of the classroom. There's even an apple on one corner, which young Aaron Holt has brought in that morning.

He's stolen it from the cafeteria at the home, but Miss Moore doesn't have to know that.

In the middle of her desk is his latest, greatest creation, a paper-mache volcano mounted on a square of wood, for the science fair. The volcano's surface is contoured with crags and ridges and screaming villagers made out of Play-Doh. Inside the volcano, baking soda and vinegar are ready to be set off, with an electrical cap battery charge. Tiny orange twinkle lights will flash on at exactly the same moment, in tandem with the "lava" flowing over.

Aaron teeters on his crutches for just a moment, and his hands shake. He's nervous that he didn't have a chance to test it out first, because once he did that, he'd have to start all over, and they'd barely given him enough materials for one good explosion. He'd had to sweet talk the cook at the school for what he got.

Two copper wires carefully blend into the lava and snake off the edge of the wooden mount. He just has to touch them to the battery cap—negative and positive, coming together—to set off an explosion.

It's time.

The whole class joins in with their teacher, counting down to the moment of destruction:

"Five, four, three, two, one!"

He touches the battery cap with a strand of wire and gets a little shock. That sets him off balance, but he doesn't think anybody notices. They just think he's excited, like they are.

The charge takes, and a sort of hissing whisper starts, as the chemicals mix together inside the cheesecloth and chicken wire and old shredded newspaper. Deep down inside the crater, the bubbling starts, then thickens, filling up the inside tube—a paper towel tube in disguise. The goo gathers volume and speed, and it's more than Aaron could have hoped for.

A sulfurous flow of lava erupts over the tip-top edge and pours down the serrated wall of the volcano, and the kids in the room cheer.

Boom.

Miss Moore seems just as surprised as Aaron that he's actually pulled it off. Before she remembers that she's not supposed to show favoritism, she throws her arms around him and gives him a squeeze.

That throws him off balance, but he doesn't mind.

"You did it! You made an explosion! You made a volcano! You're our winner for the science fair!"

◆ ◆ ◆

Aaron could still hear his teacher, still remember his happiest time, even though the only sound in that same room now was Skip crying, softly, just like the baking powder and vinegar as they began to bubble up and gather steam.

He could feel the same thing happening in his body now; something inside, his blood and nerves, bubbling up, gathering steam; tremors, the explosions in his muscles like little bombs going off inside the volcano, hitting against the inside of his skin, causing his arms and legs to jump on their own. Each tic was a cell dying off, and exploding. A supernova. The cells going necrotic, one by one. How he used to love that word: *necrotic*. Necrosis. A college word, even though he'd never been. But now . . .

It was a word that told him he didn't have much time left.

He wheeled into the main classroom. "Have we packed our bags, ladies? It's time to go. Haste makes waste." As he spoke, he maneuvered himself over to the mural that contained the twelfth and final Labor.

Skip nudged closer to Wendy on the floor; even though they were tied up, they were able to hold hands, and that gave Skip courage. Wendy's bleeding had stopped, but even in the dark of the room, Skip could tell how pale she was. Her eyes were open, but just barely. Skip kept having to knock into Wendy, to have her keep them open.

And as weak as Wendy was, she still pleaded with him. "Please, let Skip go. She's just a little girl, she didn't hurt you. I'll stay here, do whatever . . . "

"Oh, we're long past . . . *whatever.* 'Whatever' says there's no plan, no thought. And all I have is . . . *thought.* No, we'll all stay *together*, to see if your father remains the hero."

"But what if he can't?" Skip asked.

"Then all his other . . . *labors* . . . will have been in vain. Love's . . . labors . . . lost," he said, punctuating each word as he stabbed in a new picture to the final mural.

All his other photos had been of Ethan, but this was of some other people. They looked familiar to Skip, but she couldn't place them, not at first. A handsome man and a pretty woman, dressed up. In front of a small aluminum-sided house. Skip had seen that too, but she couldn't remember where; if it was in person, or just in a photograph.

"I was still on my feet then, on crutches . . . and quite the mechanical genius. I could move a few wires, cross them . . . I was the expert on crossed wires, I was born with them."

Then Skip remembered. It was her grandparents. Their home.

"It was after the Olympics, and a celebration was called for. V for Victory! For Victims! Your father was with them, his parents— *our* parents—showing off his medal. Letting them wear it, taking pictures of them with it. I was hidden in the trees—how many times have I done *that*?—taking pictures of *them* taking pictures . . .

"Then they all got in the car and drove away. Coming to see me, maybe! Finally picking me back up, after all those years. Their car got smaller and smaller, until it completely disappeared, and I could go into their house and do my . . . handiwork."

Only now did he look at Skip and Wendy, as if he'd forgotten he was reciting the story to anyone but himself.

"Didn't your father ever tell you what happened to your grandparents? 'Grandma and Grandpa?'"

"They died. When I was little. A baby."

"Not just *died*. Died *together*. In their house. In flames. *Boom*."

He didn't have much power left in his voice, after talking so long, but still, Skip and Wendy jumped, as he stabbed one last photo into the mural.

A photo of that house, on fire, in the middle of the night.

"Maybe the smoke killed them first. Who knows? I hope not. I hope they . . . hurt. Just like me."

"Oh my God. You killed them? Your own parents?"

" '*You killed them?*' I had to. They killed me, after all . . . or they might as well have. Giving me away to that . . . *place*. And your father. He's not going to die, although he might wish he had. We're going to trade places. Let his . . . *wheels* do the walking, from now on."

CHAPTER SIXTY-ONE

We almost missed it, the turn off onto a hidden side road, from the map that Mamarie had drawn for us, her careful printing more like a grade school teacher's than the hurried, frantic scribble of a nurse. The Bruckner Home. The Somerset School. The names sounded so good on paper.

So did Aaron Holt. Iphicles, even. Names of stature. From the Bible. Mythology.

And then I remembered what he had done. What he was *still* doing.

"He said it to me, and I completely missed it. I begged for a clue, and he told me: 'What did Hercules do?' The Labors . . . that's what Hercules did. He did *labors*. Going into labor. Having us . . . two of us . . . he gave me the only clue I needed and I completely missed it . . . "

"But how could you even think that, if you grew up thinking you were an only child?" Mizell said. "That's like . . . I don't know what it's like but it's ridiculous. Sherlock Holmes couldn't have figured that out."

Mizell cut her headlights and slowed the car to a crawl. Up ahead, a sort of Norman Rockwell building gone to seed, its windows boarded up. No light. No sign of life.

"But look at those electrical lines," she pointed out, parking away in some trees. "An abandoned building, full of juice? Something's going on in there."

"Then what are we waiting for?" I opened my door, as she pulled me back.

"We wait for backup. I've called it in but . . . "

"Not with my family in there."

Skip, Wendy. *Him*. My family.

Nothing was keeping me in that car.

I jerked away from her and jumped out of the car, crouching down low to cat-and-mouse my way through the trees to get closer, all the way up to the back porch.

Through the barest crack where the back door didn't fill out its frame, I could peek inside. Pitch dark, but with an eerie sort of glow at the end of a long hallway. I put my ear against the opening and slowed down my breathing, the same way I'd learned to do years ago, to calm myself before a race, and I heard . . . something. Low and garbled, but noise. People. Voices.

I put my hand on the doorknob . . .

. . . and somebody put their hand on me, slapping a palm against my mouth and holding it tight. My heartrate went from resting to heart attack in five seconds flat.

"Are you crazy?" It was Mizell. "What if . . . "

"What if nothing. I'm going inside."

"Then so am I."

She moved in front of me, her hand on the doorknob. It turned. Open. Waiting for us. We'd come to the right place, like all the others before. She shined a flashlight low to the floor, and we began creeping in.

A long foreboding hallway was in front of us, with display cases broken out, glass littering the floor. Lockers hung open, every wall a fantasia of color and graffiti. Impossible to imagine that this was the place where my brother had grown up, where he had once been his happiest; this place where I could have been, if we'd just switched places at birth. Now that I'd seen Aaron's pictures in his file at Bruckner, I could imagine him here, even in the dark. That sensitive little boy with huge eyes and dark circles under them, forced to drag his feet along or walk on canes and crutches. Always having to be on the lookout. Always ready.

Now we'd switched places. Now I was the one on the lookout.

Mizell and I hugged the walls as closely as we could, edging our way along them, past the animal droppings, the spider webs, the bird shit that slicked everything. I could hear them, night animals. Outside and in.

And something else, at the end of the hall. That low jumble of sound I'd heard earlier.

People sounds.

People smells. Shit and urine.

And now, something moving in the room. Something flickering.

Mizell pointed her pistol out in front of her and pivoted around the doorjamb.

Then stopped. Gasping.

"What?" It was the first sound I'd made in minutes, what felt like the first breath I'd taken in hours. I swung around too, no precaution, no safety net, into the room and . . .

. . . I saw myself. Looking back at me. On the walls, cut-out pictures of me from years ago, on slick magazine stock. Black-and-white newspaper photos. And film too, taking over our bodies like we were the projection screens.

Lights, camera, action . . . everywhere.

Cones of light in our faces, bodies moving over our bodies; the room was alive.

All those images, filling the room like air, blinding us—but I finally got used to the light and saw where it was coming from. Two old-fashioned film projectors, set up on a desk in the middle of the room, each aimed at different walls. Four metal reels, moving in sync, the celluloid rasping and squeaking as it moved from one spool to the next.

"What the hell is this?" Mizell still whispered, like she'd lost the ability to speak.

On one wall, an old Hercules movie from the '60s was being projected. Flexes and grunts. Greased-up he-men, in loincloths.

On the other wall, me. In Sydney, at the Olympics. In short shorts and a sleeveless shirt, flying over the pole vault bar like a half-man, half-bird.

But it was all mixed together, the projectors positioned so they crisscrossed each other. Me, in a Hercules movie; those greased-up actors, in Sydney.

Madness.

Mizell was scrunching around on the floor, trying to find cords and outlets and plugs, to turn them off. But the film ran out before she could: strips of celluloid whipping against the metal reels and then finally unspooling onto the floor. A tsunami of brown and gray plastic, now falling off and tangling around our feet, like snakes. Blinding white-hot light still shooting out of the projectors, warming the room and . . .

"Shit. There's more." I saw it first.

Only now did we see what the darkness had hidden, what those projected images playing on the walls had obscured: the Labors of Hercules, like a sick exhibit in a sideshow. Aaron's version of them, displayed up on the walls in twelve separate panels. Grown-up versions of what he'd first made back at the Bruckner Home, each one telling a story drawn from the past few days. Antlers from a deer, hammered into the wall. Shards of broken pottery. An unbroken peeling from a golden apple, still wet and fresh and dangling like entrails, like he'd just carved the apple and left it waiting for us before he departed. Like he'd known we would make the pilgrimage to the Bruckner Home first, all the clues leading us there, before they'd lead us here.

Twelve macabre chapters, all but the last one crossed over with giant neon Xs, declaring that he'd been here.

So had Skip. So had Wendy.

They were right there in front of me, in the final, unmarked panel.

Two separate photos of them, snapped in a moment of terror, as if he'd captured them mid-scream, the flash of the bulb blinding them. Each one tossed over the shoulder of some mammoth man, like sacks of potatoes.

Mizell angled the light from one of the projectors, so we could see every detail.

The full mural, into which their photos had been pinned.

Underneath them was the drawing of a sort of dragon with three heads, covered in real snakeskin, the see-through, scaly kind that a snake sheds and leaves behind, ragged and torn with the effort of transformation.

"The final Labor. Cerberus. The three-headed monster. He guards the entrance to the dead, by keeping out the living."

Pinned to the top of the two outermost necks, like heads, were the photos of Skip and Wendy.

And on top of the middle neck, twisting and reaching up the highest, was a photo of me. *And* Aaron, age three or so, dressed up in our matching cowboy shirts and sitting on top of a sagging pony at the kiddie zoo.

I was beaming; he was grabbing onto my waist for dear life, his mouth open and screaming into the camera.

Mizell reached out. "But why isn't this one all crossed out like the others?"

"Because he's not done yet. *I'm* not done. There's one more Labor left to do. You get help. I'll head here."

I pointed to a place on the bottom of the panel, where a signature would normally have gone. In what must have been the very last thing he added, eked out in the last few dribbles of spray paint, was a final map for me.

A real map, of the Canaan College cemetery, spray-painted with two shaky rectangles in DayGlo orange.

Two graves.

And two final words, A to Z, nothing else left to say.

Womb.

Tomb.

CHAPTER SIXTY-TWO

The massive iron gate that guarded the Canaan cemetery was locked this late at night.

A tall, grillwork fence circled all the way around the perimeter, but it couldn't keep me out. It never had. In college, when I ran through here late at night, scaling that fence was just another part of my workout; there to keep out vandals and college kids on a dare, but not me. Now though, everything was different. I finally understood the fence's true purpose: separating us from them. The living from the dead.

I barely knew which one I was anymore.

Every movement I made inside the gates set off a swirl of fog that seemed to reshape itself into monsters and gargoyles. Faces in the air, or on grave markers? I couldn't tell. They seemed to leap out at me, guarding the way.

And now, a voice, just as wispy and impermanent as the fog.

"Just a few more. Steps."

The voice I'd heard on the telephone.

My monster.

My brother. Luring me to the mausoleum at the top of the hill. Exactly the place that he'd marked on the map.

The words seemed to come from everywhere, and I could only call back in kind, looking everywhere. Searching. Lost. Half-dead. And panting so much I sounded like him.

"I did. My part. I did. The Labors."

"Did you . . . get the golden apple? A mocking laugh. "Did you . . . find my. Lair?"

There, at the top of the crest, eternal flames on torches shot out on either side of the mausoleum's heavy marble door; the fire was so overwhelming it was all I could see at first.

Before I saw the person behind the flame.

Behind these last three days.

Behind these last thirty-six years.

Aaron. Iphicles. *Him,* in front of the mausoleum, in his wheelchair throne.

"My God."

Nothing Mamarie had said could have prepared me for the reality of this.

We were together, face to face, for the first time since childhood. We were the same. Like looking in a mirror, but one that was broken, the silver plating behind the glass worn off.

Even he seemed dumbstruck.

"We meet. Not for the first. Time. But certainly. The last. Pardon me for. Sitting already." His voice, his lips moving in front of me. No phone between us anymore, no words on paper, to get in the way. Just graves of the dead. "They took me away. Before I could. Even say your name. Ethan."

"I didn't know, I swear . . . how could I? I was too little. I didn't . . . oh my sweet Jesus in heaven . . . "

"What's so. *Sweet* about him? *I* knew. I never forgot. How could *you*? You were my brother and you. *Left* me."

"I didn't know! Nobody told me!"

"They shouldn't have to. *Tell* you! Three years and . . . *here today. Gone tomorrow.* I tried to . . . reach out. So many times. Here, and . . . there."

"Why didn't you just step out and . . . "

"Stepping isn't my . . . *forte,* as you may have. Noticed. I tried to . . . get your attention. In college. The Olympics. My *fan* letter. Letters. From the home. Rebuffed. When you were. Married. When it was . . . snowing. When you were . . . happy . . . "

My house, five years ago. Dusk. Magic hour.

A snowball fight. Bodies, laughing and falling in soft snow mounds.

A wonderful smell, winter and fire smoke and evergreens in the yard.

"How I wanted to . . . *join in* . . . the fun. You tossed the keys to your. Lovely wife, and she . . . caught them . . . "

An arc of silver, through the air. A jangle, like a wind chime.

Those keys, her death sentence. Patti detoured from her car and got in mine.

"That small twist of fate: 'Take mine. The chains are on.' The *mishap* . . . was intended . . . for you. My way of saying, '*Forget* something?'"

Patti, in *my* car.

"One snip of a brake belt, and. A bang. Not a whimper. That I regret. Truly. She hadn't. Hurt me. It took a little more. *Ingenuity.* To take our parents. *Boom.*"

The house on fire, killing them.

The car, skidding on ice, killing my wife.

I lunged at him, the moment it all came together in my head.

"I will. Fucking. KILL you."

I was just feet away from him when the door to the mausoleum flew open, as if on cue. A muscled behemoth was practically pulled out, barely able to restrain three snarling pit bulls on leashes.

Cerberus, the watchdog of Hell.

"Of course, the *real* Cerberus has three heads and snakes all over its back, so I've had to . . . *improvise.*"

Iphicles—I couldn't think of him as Aaron; this man wasn't my brother—wheeled himself to a small wooden box on the ground, almost a miniature coffin. He opened the lid; inside was a mass of writhing snakes, a jumble of guts come to life.

"Hercules and Iphicles. Together again. With snakes. Remember? I cried at them. You snuffed them out. Held them in your hands. Played. With them."

He put the box on the ground, ready to be tipped over.

"But that . . . that's a story out of mythology," I pleaded with him. "That's not real."

"It *is* real. It's our story. Lights, please."

The muscle man grabbed one of the smoking torches from the mausoleum and came down the steps, light in one hand, the snarling dogs of hell in the other. He held the flame over Iphicles' head, almost like an umbrella, and . . .

I could see. I could finally see everything.

At the edge of his wheelchair, a grave. Six feet deep, four or so feet across. A mound of dirt to the side, where it had been dug.

A brand new grave, with Skip and Wendy tossed down in a heap on the bottom, their eyes closed, arms and legs bound.

His final mural, come to life. Or death. It was so dark, I couldn't tell if they were breathing.

"Are they . . . are they . . . "

"Spit it out. *Sleeping* . . . for now. But I'm sure the snakes will. *Wake* them up. Or the dogs. The choice is. Yours."

"Let them go. I'm the one you hate."

"Hate hardly begins to convey the . . . *range* of my feelings. Of course, there's another. *Option*." He pulled out a gun, from where he was sitting. "My pronunciation may be a little. Rusty. Latin wasn't. *Required*. At the home. But . . . *Fui quod es, eris quod sum*."

I stared at him. "'I once was what you are, you will be what I am.' The note your guy gave to TJ."

"Sums things up pretty. Nicely. Don't you think? A swap. *I* live. You get the. Chair. *This* chair. *My* chair. My *wheel*chair."

"What are you talking about?"

"I shoot you. In the spine. Not to kill. Just to. Paralyze."

"You're insane."

He looked down at my family, asleep in that grave. *Waiting* for me. "Finally—he notices." Then back to me. "Your legs. For their lives. So you can. *Truly*. Walk a mile in my shoes. *Tradsies*."

"And then what? We're both in wheelchairs?"

"Just *you*. I'm soon to . . . depart. I've got nothing. To lose. This disease you cursed me with. Left the door open for so many. Other. Infections. A perfect storm. Of *shit*. In my body. Killing me."

A million words in my head, but none of them were coming out of my mouth. I fell to my knees—on his level now, looking straight into his eyes—and started crawling toward him. I was the prodigal brother, begging forgiveness for a sin I hadn't even known I had committed. A sin of omission.

A prodigal brother with a plan.

The dogs strained, the closer I got.

The snakes whipped up, hearing those low-throated growls.

"I would have saved you, I swear. I still can." Part of what I was saying felt real. Part of it wasn't a ploy. Part of it was every ounce of grief I'd ever felt.

"You left me! You forgot me! You should have. *Remembered*." Every word he said, choking in the night air. Every word he forced himself to say, using up the last words he had on earth. "You came to the home. Mother brought you. Did you ever think. To ask yourself. Why? And why I was there. In the first place? Your umbilical cord. My neck. *Voilà*."

"You're right. I should have known. I should have . . . remembered. Us. In the womb. Together. It's my fault, so take me. Just don't hurt them. I'm begging. My legs, for their lives. Just let me do it my way. Let me brace myself for it. Let me look at my girls one last time."

Every word I spoke, getting closer and closer to him.

I stood up and put my hands full out to my side, in surrender.

"Let me be close to you, so it's a sure shot," I said, hoping I was right with my plan. "A righteous shot. You've earned the right. Don't miss. Don't kill me. Just . . . take my legs."

His mouth open in shock at what I was doing—at what I was *letting* him do—I was now just a few feet away from him.

"No. Don't look in my eyes. I don't wanna see it coming. I don't wanna see you pull the trigger."

I slowly faced away from him, my back a perfect target.

Him—a perfect target.

I kicked *backward* with all my might. My right leg felling him like a sledgehammer, knocking him out of his chair with all the might of the strongest man in the world.

He went flying, and so did I.

◆ ◆ ◆

Every decathlete says the 1500-meter run, the very last event of all ten, is the hardest. That the decathlon is "nine Mickey Mouse events and then the 1500." Maybe because it comes at the very end. Maybe because you're running faster and harder than you've ever run in your life, three and three-quarters laps around a track 400 meters long. Maybe because it's the one last thing left between winning—and losing. A Wheaties box and—*who?*

Now, it was the one thing left between life—and death. Skip's. Wendy's. Mine.

I was running the 1500 again, thirteen years after the last time, with a gimp leg and a pack of feral pit bulls on my tail, and I had to win.

Or else.

Arms pumping, feet flying like pistons, muscle memory took over.

Instead of being chased by three mad dogs, it was the seven other men I raced against in 2000. All of us in a row, evenly spaced, but the minute the gun sounded, we edged toward the innermost track, closest to the heart of the circle.

But here, in this cemetery, it was like I was running the last lap *first,* already at my breaking point before I even started. No more time to pace yourself, no feeling out the pack, just a needle-sharp, stomach-churning hunger to *master* the pack.

I conjured up every bad thing that had ever happened to me to push me on; I turned them *all* into a monster that was nipping at my heels, just inches from taking me down.

I forced those tattoos of flames on my ankles to come to life.

I forced myself to remember my father holding that cigarette lighter so close to my skin, close enough to singe off the hair on my legs before he turned it on himself.

I forced myself to remember what he did to my brother.

I forced myself to remember what he did to *me*, turning me into a machine that had to win.

The barking, mad dogs of Cerberus were almost on me. So close, I could feel the rabid saliva flying out of their black-speckled mouths and onto the back of my legs. Whippet-thin tree branches flogged my face, as I ran past the graves I always saw on my daily runs.

That's when it came to me what I had to do.

The excavation pit, where I'd landed just a few days ago, on my run through the cemetery. On my way home to a daughter who had already been taken. I'd made my silly bargain with God just before I jumped: if I landed on the other side, then everything would be okay with Skip when I got home. Our tiff would be forgotten.

Then God had failed me. I hadn't made it. Skip was gone.

Now, I made that bargain again, praying with everything I had: God, if only I can jump over this pit—then everything will be okay with Skip.

It had to be.

I had to be. Good enough to fly through the air, and land on the other side.

I was almost there, every last muscle at the breaking point, my hurt ankle almost melting in pain . . .

I screamed one last time, in agony, adrenaline pushing me into overdrive . . .

I flew . . .

. . . over the pit, my legs peddling for momentum, through thin air . . .

And landed, hard. On the *other* side.

A miracle. I cleared it.

The yapping dogs of hell didn't.

They leapt—twelve legs pawing at nothing but air—and disappeared into the fog that covered the pit. I slammed to a stop as I heard three yelping thuds . . .

Whimpering, trapped . . .

I didn't have to do anything to get their master to stop and lean over the edge; his dogs did that themselves. Moving his torch around in the darkness to try to see them—or me—I snuck around behind him and pushed.

Just like he had done to me in the crack den.

"Shit. It's you."

It was the last thing he said on this earth, before he landed in the pit with the dogs.

Now the three-headed dog of Cerberus had something to feast on. And it was hungry.

◆ ◆ ◆

In the distance, the snarls died away. The screams.

Now, just smacking, and the sound of my footsteps on dead leaves, coming back to my brother. Stop, then start, on my guard; what he must have sounded like dragging himself around.

"Who is it! Who's there! Answer me!"

I stepped out from the fog. He was still where I had left him, spilled out on the patch of bare ground, next to the turned-up earth from where the grave had been dug.

"How did you . . . "

"It's just us now. Your helper . . . the dogs got him."

I had the upper hand now. I was standing. He was still lying on the ground.

But he had a *better* upper hand, with a gun in it. And he was pointing it down in the grave, at Wendy and Skip.

"Don't come any closer. I'll kill them!" he snarled at me. "The measurements are . . . regulation. I've watched so many funerals . . . your wife's, our parents . . . that I've got them. Just right."

I was at the edge of that grave now; down inside, Skip and Wendy were covered with dirt. Roots and rocks cropped out of the sides; the smell of fresh loam rose up, suffocating. Wendy's eyes were still closed, but Skip's eyes were looking straight at me, the only light in the dark. Tape covered her mouth, but I could still hear everything she thought.

Save me. Help me.

My daughter, my baby, who had never even been to a funeral, not even her own mother's.

I would rip out *his* fingernails.

I would throw *him* into the bottom of a grave, once I got Skip and Wendy out.

I couldn't grieve someone who had done this. I couldn't save him. I couldn't love him. I couldn't forgive him.

Iphicles was as close as he could get to the grave, the gun in his hands, that box of snakes on the ground, to the side of him. Writhing. The same thing that Skip was doing, six feet below me.

"Here, please. Give me the gun, it's not too late . . . " I fell to my knees and reached across the grave to him. "Let them go, and we'll . . . "

"NO! Get away! I know what you're doing!"

He pointed the gun at me, just as beams of flashlights cut through the fog—so unexpected we both jerked—and then blood was on his face.

A tiny red dot, on his forehead.

Then another.

And another.

It was Mizell and a team of sharpshooters, finally arriving, their infrared scopes drawing beads on him.

Their red dots grew larger, as they got closer.

His eyes became just as enflamed. Red. On fire. "They can't kill me. I'm already dead. Years ago. Waiting for *you*."

His battle cry, as he plunged his arm into the snakes.

He made some kind of sound—his mouth was open—but it wasn't a scream. The snakes were eating up whatever sound was coming from him, biting into his flesh. His legs were moving like they hadn't in years, kicking and bucking.

He was trying to extend his arms up triumphantly, like the images on the broken pottery of antiquity. Hercules and Iphicles. One baby, grinning and holding up snakes. The other baby, terrified and crying in a corner.

"See. See. I can do it now. I can make the myth, *Real*, I'm strong. I'm. Better. I'm worthy. Of . . . keeping."

He tried one last push upward—holding up the snakes, or throwing them off, I would never know; maybe Mizell and her team thought he was trying to poison me with the snakes—and that's when they shot him. His body convulsed, like he was being bitten by the snakes all over again.

"NO!" I think that was me, but for once, we sounded the same.

Those red dots, now bleeding. His chest. His arms. His legs.

Mizell and her guys raced in, their circle of red dots closing around us.

"Holt, get away from him . . . " she growled at me.

"Don't leave. Not again . . . " my brother exhaled.

He was talking just to me now, not them. Just us. I barely even needed to hear the words anymore. We were speaking in the silent, secret language of twins. The language of the first time. And the last. I knelt down to him, and looked in his eyes. I saw terror. His hair was so spare, so wet and sweaty; slicked down against his head, like a newborn's. I could feel the heat pouring off his head, even in this cold night air. I tried to see the one part of him that wasn't sick, that had once been my twin.

"I'm. Sorry." Every word he said to me a supreme effort. "Skip . . . sorry."

Behind me, rushing around. Mizell on her walkie. Calls to an ambulance. Someone in the grave, pulling out Skip and Wendy. Now they were pulling at me too—I felt hands on my midsection—but I couldn't leave him alone again. The one thing I had ever wanted—him, dead—and them, back, safe. But I couldn't let him just die by himself. He must have been so terrified for most of his life and . . . no. I couldn't leave. Not yet.

"Aaron"—I whispered his name, the name I never got to say, or even to know . . .

But then, another name broke in. The only word I'd wanted to hear, for the last three days. "Daddy?" Skip's voice.

And now, Wendy too. Awake. Alive. "Ethan, we're safe. Just leave. I'm begging."

They started pulling me away, but he moved, trying to crawl after us. Using his hands like claws to pull himself along. Looking up with his eyes, the only part of his body that still seemed to work.

"I'm begging. Too. Stay."

I tried to blink away my tears, but they filmed across my eyes, blurring everything. And in the prism they made, it was as if I saw three of him. Three heads, swirling around.

He was the thing I had to kill. He was Cerberus, the monster with three heads. This was the true final Labor.

He tried to say something, but no words came out of his mouth. Just blood.

But he knew. He knew. I could see it in his eyes. Twins know. It's what he wanted.

For me to finish the Labors. For me to put him out of his misery, that had brought him to this point.

I took Mizell's pistol from her, just like I had up at the ski lodge with that deer that was past the point of saving.

"Holt, are you crazy?" Mizell barked. "What are you doing . . ."

"The final Labor. Killing Cerberus. I've got to finish what I started. It's what he wants."

Tears still blinding my eyes, I put my finger on that cold metal of her gun, pointed it at him, and he smiled.

And then I remembered. For the first time, I remembered him. Aaron, in the womb, smiling at me. Perfect. Happy. Floating. Ready. The two of us hugging on to each other for dear life, before we had to leave the womb. It had all been so perfect up until then.

I smiled back at him, the last image he would ever see on this earth—*it's your turn to fly now, my brother*—and squeezed the trigger.

And then I kept squeezing it, his body jerking and exploding, until all the bullets were used up.

CHAPTER SIXTY-THREE

The college told me to take all the time I needed—they could get somebody else to teach my classes, not TJ though, he was taking time off too—but I like being there. It's what I do. I pass on the past. I actually think I'm a better teacher now. I understand the classics more deeply. All that passion, all that love and hate.

All that revenge. I finally get it.

His, and mine.

Some days, after class, I help Sig out on the field, and that feels good too, to live in my body again, instead of just my head. I've done that for too long. We work up a good sweat, and then talk strategy in the locker room over the shower stalls, our heads full of shampoo. With his cane, Sig steps out and onto a towel on the cold tile floor, dusts between his toes with Gold Bond powder, then goes to the mirror and slaps on the cheap cologne he's worn for the past umpteen years. He wriggles into the colored bikini underwear he's taken to wearing in old age. (Oh Lord, is that going to happen to me too?) He pulls the waistband forward and whooshes a spray of Gold Bond in there, too, then lets the underwear snap back into place.

I still do my runs with Skip every morning, weather permitting, even after everything that's happened. At the end of them, when I veer off to campus and she goes on her way to school, she always makes a big point of asking, "You okay? You sure?" The very thing I should be asking her, that she won't allow. The thing everyone said to us after Patti died, and there was no answer. Then Skip always turns back to look at me one last time, before she disappears from sight completely.

She thinks I don't see her, but I do.

Skip. My daughter. My life. Same thing.

I've asked her if she wants to move to a different house, to get away from everything, but she says her mother is still there, and she doesn't want to leave her behind. I feel the same way. I repainted Skip's bedroom so you can't see the fingerprint powder anymore, although I think I'll always know what's under all those layers of fresh paint. And it's not pink! My baby's not a pink girl anymore. Sage green. She said she wanted it to look like a color you could actually find in nature. Up on her ceiling, I've painted the constellations in DayGlo paint that you can only see at night, so she can focus on something when she can't sleep. I guess that makes it "Night-glo."

When *I* can't sleep—which is often—I hear Skip go up to the attic, after lights out. She says she's working on something new, but she won't let me see it yet. So she's still doing her little sculptures, I guess, and being in her plays. At first, I tried to keep her from those; I thought that make-believe and drama weren't good for her anymore. I wanted her to do kid things for a while. Read Harry Potter. She argued with me about that, so I knew she was starting to come back to her old self.

Dad, you're so out of it, she'd say. *Do you know how many people die in Harry Potter? And besides, they're doing "Legally Blonde" at school. Nobody dies in that. And I'd get to wear a wig. And fake fingernails. Please . . .*

My eyes got a little watery when she said that, and she came over and gave me a hug. Kissed me on top of my old head. My hair is whiter now than it was just a few months ago, definitely more salt than pepper. I gave in about the play, and she's in rehearsals now. She got the lead. My tall, beautiful string bean with freckles and braces, and now, a blond wig, singing and dancing, after . . .

I can't go there, not yet.

Aretha is going to the play with me and Wendy; she said she's going to wear a brand new blond wig too, in honor of the occasion. "I paid for it, I guess that makes it legal!" I've finally broken down and started calling her "Aretha," although it still feels strange, like whenever I say it she'll break into song. "Respect" or "Chain of Fools." She still calls me "Holt"—usually followed by "Are you crazy?" I like that. It feels like my new name. "Holt-are-you-crazy."

Sometimes "Aretha" comes running with me at night, to shed some pounds she says, but I think it's to look after me, same as Skip. She can keep an eye on me that way, without me knowing it. When she sees tears in my eyes, she can pretend it's just the wind, or a speck of something caught there.

Mostly, though, I run by myself. I still even run through the cemetery, the way I used to do back in my college days. I still leave my goofy presents on top of the tombstones, to remind those spirits that I was there, that somebody still remembers them. A torn shoelace or a stick of gum, whatever I have at hand.

I do it at strangers' graves, and I do it at my brother's.

Aaron's grave is a ways off from all the others, tucked away in the same corner where we ended up that night. In the same grave, even, that he dug for Skip and Wendy. When the school asked me what they could they do to help, it was the first thing I thought of.

It's bizarre, I know. Sick even. To have him there, in the very same place, as a reminder of the worst night of my life. You'd think I'd want his body as far away as possible from my town, my job, my daughter, my life.

You'd think I'd want his body burned, turned to ash and dust, something I could get rid of.

But I still need him there, nearby. In that very grave, the same one he'd dug for Skip and Wendy, and maybe even me. Most people would think it was crazy; Aretha would, for sure. That's why I never let her come running through the cemetery with me.

Holt-are-you-crazy . . .

Yes-I-am.

But this is what I need right now.

I don't completely understand it, but this is my penance, for forgetting him.

For not *feeling* him there, in my blood.

I did it once, and I can't let that happen again.

It seems as if there's always a light dusting of snow up in that particular corner of the cemetery, higher than the rest of the school property. Looking down, the perfect vantage point. Fir trees surround it, so the sun never really gets a chance to come through. All these months later, a few pieces of yellow police tape still flutter around, from where they were anchored around the trees for the crime scene investigation, and I've never taken them down. I don't know if that's my job or the police's, but I've come to like the whipping sound they make, when the wind blows. Now, it's just like another sound of nature to me. The place would seem empty without it.

After Patti died, I'd go to her grave and talk to her, about how to go on. How life could possibly continue.

Patti, at least, answered back; she must have, telling me how to raise our daughter by myself, to become a beautiful and brave young woman, because that is certainly what Skip is turning out to be.

Aaron, though, never says a word, as I keep asking him the same question: Why?

Why everything?

Why did he do it, to me, to Skip and Wendy, when he could have just reached out and . . .

But no. There is only silence, except for that plastic yellow police tape whipping in the wind. So I just keep talking and hoping, someday, for answers. Like I talked to Skip in the hospital when she was in such agony. I just open my mouth and keep talking, and somehow, I keep finding things to say.

Thirty-six years' worth of things, to fill him in on.

I sit cross-legged in front of his stone marker—my *zane*, copied from the ancient Greek athletes, a testament to my crime—and talk to him. I tell him about the past he missed, the past we could have shared, and the future we could have shared too, if only things had been different. And somehow it helps to take away the pain. Not completely though; I don't think that will ever happen.

For that to happen, I am still waiting.

It's what he had to do for so much of his life—*wait*—and now it's my turn, as I pull myself up from that cross-legged position and start running back to the school and home.

To Wendy, to Aretha and Sig, to my life. To Skip.

She's promised to finally have that meatloaf waiting on the table.

Acknowledgments

Thank you to my agent Jennifer Lyons (the one and only) and Ben LeRoy and Ashley Myers at Tyrus for bringing *Dig Two Graves* into the world. Also, many thanks to friends and editors who have helped me with readings and notes along the way: Laura Zaccaro, Jay Michaelson, Marlene Adelstein, Leslie Wells, Amy Schiffman, Jody Hotchkiss, Will Schwalbe, and Jim Mulkin (for the Latin translation of "up shit creek"!) Thanks to Anthony Nunziata and Will Nunziata for their friendship and for letting me borrow part of their twin story (actually, I just took it, but whatevs . . .); to Don Birge, Jay Russell, VJ Carbone, and Michael Trusnovec for weekend fun; and to Marjorie Hass and Carol Daeley for helping me feel safe and welcomed on a college campus once again. Finally, to Jess Goldstein and Tim Powers, my inhale and exhale. *I love you more.*

Author photo by George Paul

KIM POWERS is the author of the novel *Capote in Kansas: A Ghost Story* as well as the critically acclaimed memoir *The History of Swimming*, a Barnes & Noble "Discover" Book and Lambda Literary Award finalist. He is currently the senior writer for ABC's *20/20*, and has won an Emmy, a Peabody, and the Edward R. Murrow Award for Overall Excellence during his time at ABC News and *Good Morning America*. A native Texan, he received an MFA from the Yale School of Drama, and also wrote the screenplay for the indie-favorite film *Finding North*. He lives in New York City and Asbury Park, NJ, and may be reached at kimpowersbooks.com.